THE

ALTAR

BOY

THE
ALTAR
BOY

A DARK TALE
OF COMEDY, SORROW &
THE CATHOLIC CHURCH
IN THE 1960s

PHIL STEPHENS

To Roger, I hope you enjoy my first novel.

Phil Stephens

First Edition

ISBN:

978-0-9978745-0-1

DEDICATION

This book is dedicated to all struggling single mothers in the world. May you always find true peace and happiness.

INVOCATION

And now, you priests, this warning is for you. If you do not listen, and if you do not resolve to honor my name, says the Lord Almighty, I will send a curse on you, and I will curse your blessings. Yes, I have already cursed them, because you have not resolved to honor me.

Because of you I will rebuke your descendants; I will smear on your faces the dung from your festival sacrifices, and you will be carried off with it. And you will know that I have sent you this warning so that my covenant with Levi may continue, says the Lord Almighty. My covenant was with him, a covenant of life and peace, and I gave them to him; this called for reverence and he revered me and stood in awe of my name. True instruction was in his mouth and nothing false was found on his lips. He walked with me in peace and uprightness, and turned many from sin.

For the lips of a priest ought to preserve knowledge, because he is the messenger of the Lord Almighty and people seek instruction from his mouth. But you have turned from the way and by your teaching have caused many to stumble; you have violated the covenant with Levi, says the Lord Almighty. So I have caused you to be despised and humiliated before all the people, because you have not followed my ways but have shown partiality in matters of the law.

—Book of Malachi, Chapter 2:1-9

CONTENTS

Chapter I: The Dark Road Back

I SAT AT the stoplight pondering the phone call from my older brother Mike. He doesn't call an emergency meeting at Darby's on a Tuesday afternoon without just cause.

Mike hinted that dad might be coming back *here* to live. Not long ago our older brother Lanny had spoken of dad definitely coming back. Mike and I made it clear to Lanny and dad that he should stay put in Nevada. It wasn't that we didn't want to see him at all. We wanted to keep the peace that our family had enjoyed for the past couple of decades.

Still sitting at the light, I was hypnotized by a bad daydream. All the old demons were returning. It was 20 years ago. 1967. I'd just gotten home from school. In the driveway sat dad's familiar green pick-up. He hadn't been home in well over a year. Mom would be home soon and they would meet. It was one of the worst days of my life.

✝

Mercifully, a car horn blared, catapulting me back to reality.

I strolled into Darby's and gazed with usual pleasure at the familiar surroundings. It was early evening, only about 5, and it wouldn't be crowded on a Tuesday. The open bar stool pulled me toward it like a neodymium magnet. Dave the bartender greeted me.

"Hey Carl, it's been a while."

"You mean since a couple of weeks ago, right?"

"Well, that's a while for you, man." Dave poured my customary cold Coors Light on draft. I was a staunch draft beer man. I liked the smoother taste of cold, unpasteurized beer out of the barrel.

1

"What brings you here tonight and so early?"

"My brother's meeting me for a beer. He said it was kind of important and I'd need a couple dozen just to listen to what he had to say. Quite frankly, I'm frightened." I was kind of kidding but kind of wasn't.

"Wow, a dozen is a lot. I'll save him the stool next to you," Dave said.

"Thank you, sir."

"How's that beer?"

"COLD!" I smiled. I was always amazed at how extra cold the beer was at Darby's.

✝

Staring into the large mirror behind the bar I began wondering when the hell Mike was going to arrive. I was pretty anxious.

Mike was six years older than me, taller, and with the same blonde hair and blue eyes. I was closest to Mike. The two of us had experienced most of the family chaos of the 1960s. We went on hunting trips with our dad, out-of-state visits to his job-site projects, and train trips to New England to see our aunt's family. Mike was personable, liked to drink beer, was a hit with the ladies, and a great golfer. He and I had gone through the most during the family chaos of the '60s and he also had a massive amount of mental baggage about our family. I'd watched him get more and more hostile toward our mother back then. He resented her for letting a certain someone intrude into our family, an intrusion that split up our parents for good. I hated him for that but kept it to myself. However, I loved him just the same.

✝

Darby's was an intricate part of the renovation of the Bridgeport downtown area in the '80s. Just a few years earlier it was a vacant restaurant in the run-down, vacant train station. Now it was one of the most popular local nightspots. What made it unique was its '50s-type décor and the fact that it played music from the '50s and '60s. It wasn't a big place, about the size of a large studio apartment. Just the right size. It had a dance floor, the beer was cold, and the food and service were great. Darby's changed the Bridgeport nightclub scene dramatically. It was the right bar in the right place at the right time. People walked into the bar area and instantly felt cool. They felt like the baby boomers who'd finally come of age. Their generation ran the show. Now they had a right to sit down, have a drink, and listen to the music they wanted to hear. It was a beautiful time to be 30 years old.

The floor was green, retro-style tile and the ceiling was made of album covers of that era. You looked up and saw some of the albums you still had at home. The bartenders were friendly smartasses in a cool sort of way. Some would say the '80s were a smartass time.

An older man sat at the far end of the bar, looking around and drinking Pabst Blue Ribbon beer. He seemed out of place from the regular yuppie crowd. He was a great prop. Everyone called him Popeye because of his perpetual goofy expression. No one ever bothered him, and he bothered no one. He was great for a few good laughs.

The only thing I didn't like about the place was the huge mirror behind the bar. When I sat at the bar I unfortunately had to watch myself drinking, which was uncomfortable at times. Sometimes I felt it wasn't me staring back.

Mike and I found it a wonderful place to bird-dog the scores of inebriated ladies who were always present. Some nights we wound up with chateaubriand for two and other nights pig in a blanket. Most nights we wound up with nothing, but we loved the thrill of the hunt.

Mike was taking longer than usual to get here and I was getting anxious. A woman I'd met here before sat a few seats away drinking a Margarita. I remembered her because she had some sort of foreign accent, which got my attention in a sexy way. Last time she'd looked a bit chunky. It looked like she'd thinned out. I struck up a conversation with her.

I said to her, "Hi, my name is Carl. I think I've talked to you here before. Maybe a few months ago. What was your name again?"

"My name is Gwen," she said in broken English.

"Oh, that's right."

"And I think you're Carl. Right?"

"Yes, that's right. You have a good memory, Gwen. Hey, you've slimmed down. You look great."

"Well, thank you," Gwen said, smiling.

"What's your secret?"

"No meat."

"No meat?"

"No meat!"

"Oh, you're a vegetarian?"

"No, I'm a Catholic."

WOW! How much has she had? Something got lost in that translation!

I gazed toward the mirror again. I got the feeling it wanted to tell me something.

Suddenly, a tap on the shoulder. It was my brother.

"Hey, man, didn't you see me walk in? What were you thinking about?"

"Oh, sorry. I was just thinking about when Catherine first told me about this place."

Dave welcomed him. "Hey, Mike, and how are you doing today?"

"Fine, Dave, just wonderful. Can you give me a Miller Lite?" I detected a hint of anxiety in Mike's tone.

"On the way. Umm, are you guys on autopilot tonight?" asked Dave.

"I'm afraid so," Mike said. I stared over at him. *Oh no.*

Mike's expression said he knew something he was dying to tell someone. Something he knew would cause anxiety and piss off all concerned. He knew it, and I knew it. I knew all of Mike's facial expressions and how to interpret them.

Mike reached into his coat pocket for a cigarette and, grinning, lit it. By that time his beer was in front of him. He, too, began staring into the mirror. I sat in silence as I waited for the conversation to start.

"Well, do we need a couple more beers before we talk?" I asked.

"A couple thousand!" Mike said.

I took a gulp of beer and lit another cigarette.

"That's a lot, but okay, lay it on me."

"Lanny called me today," Mike began. "Remember when dad was here a couple of years ago? Remember what the three of us talked about at Mickey's? Remember we told dad it would be a bad idea for him to move back here? Remember he basically agreed with us?"

"Uuhhh...yeah. This isn't what I think it is, is it? Wait. Shit. I don't want to know. Dammit. Oh crap, lay it on me." I was getting suspicious and sick to my stomach.

"I don't know how to say this ..." Mike hesitated.

"Okay, what is it?"

"Lanny and dad talked about dad coming back here to live. I think he's going to do it."

"Here? In Bridgeport? You've got to be kidding! Are you fucking serious?"

"You heard me right. But not here. Down in Brimstown where some of his family is from. There would be a little distance, thank God," said Mike.

"How in the hell did this come about? We agreed this would be a bad idea. What in God's name happened?" I rolled my eyes as I took another gulp of beer.

What in the holy hell is he thinking?

Lanny was our older brother, 13 years older than me and a retired police officer. He was good looking, had a great sense of humor, and was a full-blown ladies' man. He, too, saw what happened early on in our family. But he suppressed it. He'd discuss it only after several drinks. Some things he told and some he didn't.

Lanny had worked with dad in his irrigation business. Dad was proud of him and wanted someday to pass the business to his sons. But one day while Lanny was working with dad on a project outside the Bridgeport police headquarters, he saw the Chief of Police walk out the door in full uniform. Lanny was mesmerized. The encounter changed him. Less than two years later, he enrolled in the Bridgeport Police Academy and became a full-fledged police officer. Dad was heartbroken. This was one of the first incidents that later made him leave Iowa. It was ironic that Lanny, of all people, was now giving us a heads-up that dad was returning home.

"This doesn't make any damn sense! He knows what kind of shit's gonna happen." I was almost shouting. Dave quickly plopped two more beers in front of us.

"Lanny's been talking with dad about this a lot," Mike said.

"Can we talk to dad? Can we talk to Lanny? We need a full court press here to get dad to stop!"

"I don't think there's anything we can do. Dad's house in Henderson is already on the market."

I lit a cigarette. We sat and stared into the mirror. We were mentally exhausted.

"I thought it was a done deal. Dad knew it was a bad idea to come back. It'll upset everything. We'd be able to keep it a secret for only so long before mom, Catherine, and Father Jacobson find out. Then guess what? We'll be the bad guys. We'll be the ones behind it all. Now that Lanny's retired, hell, he's talking about moving down to Key Largo where he'll be out of the line of fire! God only knows how long this has been in the works behind our backs. Can we talk to dad? Can we talk to Lanny? Can Lanny talk to dad?" I ranted again.

"I think this is a lot farther along than we realize. Lanny said dad's house is already on the market in Henderson."

"Shit, I don't believe it! Well then…he's coming. After 20 long years he's coming back here to live. Pandora's Box is not only going to open, but Pandora's bullshit will get all over the floor and eventually on our faces. There won't be enough toilet paper on the planet to clean it up."

"I'm pleading insanity. I know nothing about anything and this conversation never happened," Mike said.

I lit another cigarette and nodded in agreement. We both knew what the other was thinking. We sat and stared into the mirror. The conversation had taxed us both.

This negative development was going to change the politically delicate family equilibrium that had mercifully governed it for years. When my dad finally left for good in 1967, essentially driven out of my life by a Catholic priest, a Father Jacobson, it confused and crushed me. As a result, I really didn't know my dad, whose name was Dean. This severely damaged my subconscious for years and negatively impacted my educational abilities, social life and marriages for the rest of my life.

Looking back then, I knew the break-up of my parents' marriage and my family was inevitable. Things couldn't go on the way they were. With all the fighting,

7

screaming, crying, and tension between my mother and father it was too much and would be best if one of the two left the stage. My father was the obvious choice as he wasn't strong enough to withstand what he was up against.

Now, this is where it gets mystifying. I never figured out which came first: the chicken or the egg. Was my mother, Madeline, driven to Father Jacobson because of dad's general disinterest and increasing coldness and hostility toward her? Or was dad's growing coldness toward her a result of Father Jacobson's more frequent intrusions into our family? I did know one thing. The intrusion and chaos became more intense after my younger sister Catherine was born.

My dad was a simple, working-class man who enjoyed golf, sports, independence, running his own business, and the opposite sex. He had human weaknesses just like the next person. He didn't come from a strong, tight-knit family like mom's. There was absolutely no support for anything of the magnitude he faced. My mother, on the other hand, was raised in a large, strong, and tight-knit Catholic family, solidly under the spell of the Holy Mother Church. Her family was an open door to that influence and to people such as charismatic priests. They saw all education, decisions, potential friends, potential wives, potential husbands, boyfriends, girlfriends, politics, schooling, socializing, drinking, eating, and just about everything else through the prism of the Catholic Church.

†

It all came down to a Catholic priest — a Father Jacobson — and the pitched battle between him and my dad for the souls of our family. Father Jacobson was not the normal, run-of-the-mill Catholic priest. He didn't come close. He had been the superintendent of two high-profile Catholic high schools in the area. Not a tall man, he had a hearty laugh, good wit, and a love for Scotch whiskey. I rarely saw him without a fat cigar sticking out of his mouth. To this day the smell of cigar smoke reminds me of Father Jacobson. A friend and counselor to the rich and famous, he was politically well connected with Bridgeport politics and was the chaplain of the city's police department. He was also one of the most narcissistic human beings I have ever known.

I stared into my beer trying to read the hop leaves. I tried to remember the last time I'd seen dad. It was in 1967, back at the Leabor Road house.

Some drunk brushed past me and bumped the cigarette out of my hand, jolting me out of my little daydream. Sparks and ash flew all over my jeans. *Shit!* Then Mike's voice. . .

"I know what's going to happen. We won't be able to keep this quiet and it won't stay quiet on its own. There are too many big mouths in this family."

"Oh, I know," I nodded.

Mike continued, "You know what really pisses me off? If Lanny moves to Key West, like he's been talking about, that leaves us here to deal with the nuclear fallout with mom, Catherine and Father Jacobson. This won't be over till we're all dead." He was extremely serious. It would have been funny under other circumstances.

"I know."

Just then they played Gene Chandler's "Duke of Earl." That perked me up. "Hey, remember this one?"

"God, I haven't heard that in years. I think I had the 45 when I was a kid," Mike said.

"Just who *was* The Duke of Earl, anyway?" I asked. Mike looked a little perplexed like he hadn't really thought about it.

"I dunno. I guess it's whoever you want it to be."

"Well, after a few beers *you* could be the Duke of Earl, the Pied Piper or Mr. Tambourine Man, for that matter. At least you wouldn't be Carl Sanders and have to go through the shit parade coming down the road."

"Yeah, well, that is indeed true. Yes, it certainly is, isn't it?"

Mike and I sat and stared in silence, looking around, looking at each other, smiling, and then looking into the mirror behind the bar. We wondered how it all came to this. How did it all get so convoluted? How did it all get just so sad?

There would be nothing more to say, analyze, or speculate at this point. That part of our conversation wound down as we were mentally exhausted. The beer count was piling up as well but we never counted. Beer tallies and bar bills scared us both. We were always so surprised whenever a bartender or waitress handed us the final tab.

"I gotta take a piss," Mike said.

"Well, that's the most constructive comment I've heard since we got here," I laughed.

As Mike left, "Puff the Magic Dragon," the popular 1960s song by Peter, Paul and Mary, started playing on the jukebox. I lit yet another cigarette. *I can't believe it's 1987 already. Did I really live through that chaos in the 1960s?*

I hypnotically stared into the mirror once again. This time, though, I distinctly saw the ghostly reflection of my family's past coming toward me like an ominous specter through the glassy mist. It held out its long arm and gently pulled me in.

CHAPTER 2: JOHNNY ANGEL

I WASN'T at Darby's bar anymore. I've spent years upon years trying to figure out the concept of time and where my life had gone. When I was little, I wanted to be a rock star or an archeologist when I grew up. Now I was neither. Why? I spent too much of my life daydreaming about what I wanted it to be. But dreams are for people who sleep their way through life. Too much daydreaming lets fate take over.

I'm always amazed at how a familiar smell in the breeze, a mourning dove singing on a swing set, or an old familiar song on the radio can bring up feelings and images from the past, images I usually wanted to suppress. They came when I least expected them, and that scared me. I was haunted by a past I couldn't escape. I wondered how things might have been if just one or two little things happened differently back then. What if my dad had done this? What if my mother had done that? What if they had stayed married? What if Father Jacobson had never been in our family's lives? I went over "what if" scenarios in my head until it froze up or until I was too drunk to think anymore.

My earliest recollections, the good and the bad, were from the very early 1960s and our small house on Broderick Street. We moved there in the late 1950s when I was two. The chaos, tension and confusion were epidemic and hung over the house like a storm cloud. At the time I couldn't figure out why, but knew it was coming from my parents. It wasn't toward us kids but between them. I thought it was normal. I hadn't experienced life long enough to know what was normal and what wasn't. I mean, didn't everyone's parents fight constantly? Was an unfamiliar, dark-red Lincoln pulling out of my family's driveway late at night normal?

✝

There were lots of kids in the neighborhood in those days. Scores and scores of them. They ran around in groups of two or three, or in large packs. It was the post-World War II baby boom, which I was a part of.

Our neighborhood was a rectangle with houses on both sides of each street and a large, well-kept field on the north end. "The Field," as we called it, was a focal point – a strange and foreboding place. There were a few old, larger trees scattered through it and many houses whose back yards bordered it. The neighborhood was bounded by three busier streets on the north, east and west perimeters. I wasn't allowed to cross those streets on my own.

Directly south of our house was another slightly smaller field, more overgrown and wild. My friends and I used to explore it or play "army." We called this field "Little John." Toward the east end of Little John was a weird, abandoned house we called "the Shack." It was an old, run-down, two-storey wooden house that I was told to stay away from. But my neighborhood friends and I would sneak over there from time to time and stumble through the rubble and rotting wood because we thought it was cool. It was like hanging around and exploring a dead dinosaur. We always found something new about it. We heard stories of a creepy old man people would sometimes see walking around the shack, but I never saw him. Nor did I have any desire to. Further past the Shack was the no-man's land of Mrs. Gertelwitch's house.

On the west end of Little John were more normal surroundings. There was a small strip mall with Knead's bakery, some small, private, one-room businesses, and a little grocery store called Safeway where mom always sent me to pick up groceries – a pound of chipped beef, milk, or a loaf of bread. Further to the west, across one of the busy main roads, was a large strip mall complex with clothing shops, a grocery store, and, of course, the Toy and Hobby Shop – my favorite. A cool pet shop had painted turtles which, back then, were a "gotta-have" item. There was a music store where Mike and I took drum lessons for a while.

I remember one time when I rode over there in the car with my mother. She pulled up right in front of one of the clothing stores, next to the Toy and Hobby Shop. I always wanted to go in. It was torture to sit and stare into the enticing window full of cool stuff. While she ran in to get something, "Johnny Angel" by Shelly Fabre played on the radio. I sat there and listened, thinking what a beautiful song it was. I fell in love with Shelly Fabre that day in 1963. And it took my mind off the Toy and Hobby Shop. That is the primary song that takes me back to that era of my life.

✝

My parents and five kids were crammed into our tiny house. I had two older brothers, one older sister, and my younger sister Catherine.

I didn't interact with Lanny much back then. He was much older and married with kids when I was still young. Lanny went to Presser College for a couple of years, then following the path of our grandmother, joined the Bridgeport Police Department around 1963. He eventually married a woman he gave a speeding ticket to and I didn't see much of him except around the holidays.

Second in line was my older sister Karen. For some reason we never got close. She could be wintry like the Arctic air that pours over the northern plains from the North Pole. That kind of chilling air can make the sensitive skin of your tender ass stick like glue to a cold metal railing. I always attributed her coldness to the fact that I was much younger. Beyond being in the same family, we had absolutely nothing in common and didn't develop anything in common. But I loved her nonetheless.

My oldest memory of her is when I politely asked her to put some maple syrup in a glass for me to drink before she went to school. I loved to drink it. After she left for school I saw the glass on the kitchen counter. Smiling, I walked up to it, put it up to my lips, and took a big gulp. I gagged. It was raw pancake batter. I never asked her to do that again. I was never completely sure whether she'd done that on purpose. In 1964 she moved out of our house to attend a Catholic college out of state.

Closest to me in age was my older brother Mike. We were often home alone together and sometimes traveled to our dad's job sites together. Our relationship was the closest until Mike started going out with his high school buddies and partying. That became his way of escaping everything. As he got older I became too young and childish for him, and I understood. Mike was as disturbed as I was about things that were going on in our family, but he wouldn't discuss them with me until much later. He saw things from a different vantage point. I guess he figured I was just too young.

And then there was Catherine, my youngest sister. More about her later.

✝

Our house was a plain, unobtrusive, limestone single-story home built during the '50s middle-class suburban expansion. It had a one-car garage and a yard that was a nice size for playing. My dad designed the house. That always impressed me. There were six trees in the yard and I climbed every damn one of them.

It had a full basement. I was afraid to go down by myself at night. I'd stand at the top of the stairs and peer into the darkness below me, daring myself to take just a few steps downward. Or was something else daring me? Mike always told me two evil, ghoul-type people lived down there at night. Their names were Sakers and Keylock. I didn't know whether to believe him or not. But I knew Mike didn't go down there at night by himself either. He just acted tough about it.

"You're not going downstairs, are you?" Mike said.

"I don't know. Why? What's the big deal?" I didn't want Mike to see my expression of fear. He'd make fun of me.

"Sakers and Keylock are down there now. They're always down there at night. You know that."

"I was just checking to see that all the lights were off." It was a total concoction but I wanted to save face. I shut the basement door, but not before I sensed something was staring at me from the blackness.

Sakers and Keylock. I had never seen or heard them but never doubted they were down there. You could feel them. They hid during the daytime and came out in the darkness. Sometimes I could hear them walking around downstairs in the middle of the night. I wasn't sure where they came from or why they were in our house, but if I went down there by myself I felt I might never come up.

I wonder if a lot of my curiosity about the old neighborhood was because I survived it. Or liking to believe I survived, when in fact I may not have. Physically, yes, but did I psychologically? The chaos, tension and confusion hung over the house like a storm cloud. It seemed to come from my parents. But I was so young I thought it was normal. I mean, wasn't everyone's family life as chaotic as mine? All the time? I spent a lot of time alone at that house on Broderick Street. Everyone was always gone for one reason or another. But "home alone" then wasn't like it is now. It was normal, but I didn't like it.

✝

When I do travel back though, I feel very haunted. I search for answers to questions that will always remain unanswered. Sometimes answers are never meant to be found. It can be better that way. I also try to think back and imagine exactly where my childhood friends and family members were standing and what the parking lots and residential driveways looked like full of early 1960s automobiles. What stores were along here then? What did the clothing look like in the shops? Could I remember the hairstyles? Could I remember all the names of my friends? I try to take in the smell of the neighborhood and think that was the way it smelled back then. And then there was the music. The music always brought me back. I was always imposing these
nostalgic and hallucinatory reconstructions of the past on myself. I don't think I'll ever escape it. I wasn't meant to.

My favorite doughnuts back then came from Knead's Bakery, 15 minutes south of our house. Sometimes mom or dad would drive us kids there and pick up some yeast doughnuts. But one terrible afternoon completely changed the way I looked at yeast doughnuts.

"Hey, Mike, is there anything to eat?" I had been playing with some friends and I was starving. It was still a good hour before dinnertime but I couldn't wait.

Mike warned, "Don't go scavenging for food now. You know mom will get mad if you start eating before dinner."

I saw something very familiar right there on the kitchen counter. That enticing little white cardboard Knead's Bakery box. I peered into it. There were three yeast doughnuts left. Why hadn't anyone told me? I really wanted one, but decided I'd better go ask mom or there'd be hell to pay.

"Mom, there's some leftover doughnuts in the kitchen and I'm really starving. Can I have just one? That's all I'll take. I promise."

"Well, dinner will be a little late. Just one, mind you, and that's it."

Yes! VICTORY!

Back in the kitchen I opened the white box right in front of Mike.

"What are you doing?" he asked.

"Mom said I could have one."

"Now are you sure you asked her?"

"Yah, go talk to her yourself if you don't believe me." Mike then left the kitchen.

I opened the box and took one, just one. Earlier someone else had taken a doughnut, had a couple bites, and then put it back in the box. Just then dad came into the kitchen. I had little icing crumbs on my lips.

"Have you been eating these doughnuts?" He wasn't in a good mood. He never was when he and my mom were in the house at the same time.

"Mom said I could have one." Dad opened the box and saw the partially eaten doughnut.

"Why did you put that doughnut back? I told you to NEVER put half-eaten food back into the same container you got it out of!" He had that trademark loud, piercing, angry tone.

"Dad, that wasn't me. I didn't do that." My voice was trembling.

"You are the only one in here. The last time I looked it wasn't there. Don't lie to me!" dad roared.

Then mom came in. My heart sank. Here comes another fight. This would be like a scene out of *King Kong* versus *The Serpent From Outer Space*. Only this was real and much worse.

"Dean, what in the hell are you talking about?" mom demanded.

"Carl apparently took a bite out of a doughnut and put it back. Didn't you tell him not to do that? Or is that another thing you've been neglecting around here?" His voice sounded almost evil.

"First of all, he asked if he could have one. I said he could. So tell me why in the hell would he just take a couple bites and put it back? And tell me what you meant by me neglecting things around this house."

The thing I constantly feared would happen was happening. Their fights always started over some little thing, then escalated.

"You know exactly what the hell I'm talking about!" dad shouted. "And where is Catherine half the time anymore?"

"Oh, God, Dean, stop it!" mom shouted.

I quietly backed out of the kitchen and slipped into my room. I closed the door and put my hands over my ears, but I could still hear the screaming. When I finally uncovered them I sensed an eerie silence. I peered into the kitchen and dining area. No one was there. I lay on my bed and cried, terrified and confused.

✝

Not long after the doughnut fight mom and dad decided to ship Mike and me out on the train to New England to spend a couple of weeks with the Walsh's — Aunt Dora (mom's sister), Uncle Dan, and our cousins. Maybe they saw this as a chance to recover and heal, or maybe a way to keep us from the pain of witnessing what was becoming more and more obvious.

What a cool trip. I'd never been on a train. I'd never been to their house or even New England. Hell, I'd never been out of the neighborhood! It would be cool to see the countryside from the inside of a passenger car.

On the big day, mom said, "Carl, hurry up out of that bathtub. I have your things packed. Mike is all ready to go." I jumped out of the tub so fast I slipped backward and fell right back into it. As I went backward my body went down then slid forward with my feet sliding all the way up the front wall. Luckily, there was enough water to cushion the fall but it splashed all over the bathroom floor. Thankfully I didn't bang my head too hard. Oh ha, ha! God is watching out for me once again. He'll get me to that train on time. I got dressed, grabbed my suitcase, and made it to the front door.

Dad took us to breakfast at the Boxcar Grill at Union Station. (In the '80s the Boxcar Grill turned into Darby's – a very odd twist of fate.) I ordered bacon and eggs — no runny whites. Mike got a cheese omelet and mom and dad just drank coffee. It was one of those rare times when they sat together with a common purpose and didn't fight.

Riding a train was like being in a movie. The conductors were attentive and even protective. After all, how many times did they see two small boys traveling alone across half the country? What amazed me was how fast the train went. They said it went almost 90 miles an hour at full speed on open tracks. To me it felt faster — maybe 300 miles an hour. I thought we'd broken the sound barrier. About two hours into the trip, I got a taste for a hot fudge sundae. I was scared to order one because it cost 45 cents —20 cents more than Dairy Queen or the Satellite. Mike said go ahead and he'd split it with me.

"I'll take the hot fudge sundae!" The waiter looked at me and smiled.

"Coming right up, Mr. Sanders." My God. I'd never been called that before. I felt like I owned the train and these people all worked for me. I waited and waited and waited. For 45 cents I was expecting something the size of Mount Everest. Finally, our waiter and some of the kitchen staff marched out with huge smiles on their faces. It was like my birthday and I thought they were going to sing. In front of me was a small plate. On it sat a small square of vanilla ice cream (ice milk, I found out later). On top were dribbled a few squiggles of chocolate syrup. I looked at the sundae and then looked up. They were all smiling at me. I looked at them and then over at Mike. He stared at the waiter in shock.

"Well…uuhhh…thank you very much. Ummm, this really looks good. I can't wait to dig in." I managed a smile.

"Well, Mr. Sanders, if you need anything else just let us know. We're glad you're happy." *We blew 45 cents on this?*

"Listen, Carl, if we share it'll be gone in one minute. You eat it and I'll get something later," Mike said.

I felt bad and humiliated. The next time I ordered dessert from anywhere I planned to ask, "Well, sir, can you tell me just how big that's going to be?"

The trip took 14 hours. We'd been on the train about seven. I couldn't stop looking out the window. I looked till it got dark.

†

"Next stop, Oneida!" called the conductor.

"God, Mike, we're here. I hope they didn't forget to pick us up."

"So do I, but Uncle Dan is pretty good about planning." We stepped out onto the terminal.

I liked the Walshes. That family had more kids than ours so there was easily one of them for every one of us. And my counterpart was Tommy. Mike's was Don. Then there were five more of them. Their names were Sandy,

Dion and Kristi. Their ages almost mirrored those of my family. They were nice and easy to get along with. Then there was Uncle Dan and my Aunt Dora, who was my mom's other sister. They both had a nice and kind demeanor about them. Uncle Dan was an engineer who worked for a defense contractor. As a result he was usually precise about things.

I had never been to their house before, or even New England. Hell, I'd never been out of the state at all until now. Their close relationships and the general fuzzy happiness of the Walsh family was a psychological breath of fresh air. It reminded me of the Fezziwig family in the Charles Dickens novel *A Christmas Carol*.

"Hi Carl!" Aunt Dora gave me a big hug.

Right behind her was Uncle Dan. "Well hello, Carl," he said as he stuck out his hand. He was not much of a hugger.

Next to him stood my older cousin Don. He shook our hands and helped with our suitcases as we headed toward the car in the breezy darkness.

"Well, Carl and Mike, how was the train ride? Your Uncle Dan loves the train," Dora said.

"Did you get to steer it, Carl?" Don asked with a grin.

"Nooooo, but it was cool. I never went that fast before. I liked to just look out the window at all the places we passed."

"Those engines go about 90 miles per hour. That's fast. There are trains out there that go much faster than that too," Uncle Dan said.

"I'm sorry you got in so late. I know you boys are tired. But everyone back at the house is so excited to see you they couldn't go to sleep. You both look so cute!" Dora said. I didn't know what to say. Mike just smiled and cousin Don laughed.

"The train station is only about 30 minutes from our house. How was the food on the train?" Aunt Dora asked.

"We wasted 45 cents on a shrimpy sundae," Mike said. "I don't think it was even ice cream and it was about the size of a pack of cigarettes. I think it was ice milk, which I hate."

"How do you know that?" Aunt Dora asked.

"Well, I really don't. Uuhhh, Aunt Dora, can we sleep a little late tomorrow because we're getting back so late?" Mike was desperately trying to steer the subject away from cigarettes.

I was so excited it didn't matter. I just wanted to have fun and forget all the tension at home. The Walshes felt so normal and loving. I didn't want to leave and we weren't even at their house yet. On the radio I head Trini Lopez's "If I Had a Hammer." The whole time I was there that song went through my head.

It was after midnight by the time we pulled into their driveway. We weren't five feet from the front door when it burst open and everyone came rushing out in their PJs, hugging and kissing us. They were all anxious to hear about our train ride and how everyone was back in Iowa. Eventually the questions died down and the talking dwindled. Everyone started yawning.

We said our goodnights and Aunt Dora shepherded us to our room. We stayed up talking with Tommy and Don about monsters, or at least models of them.

"Wow, Don, you have a model of the Wolfman?" I asked. "That's really cool!"

"You're too young to be using that word," Mike said.

"So should I use the word neat? Tommy, do you use the word cool?"

"Sometimes, but mostly I use neat. Don says I'm not supposed to use that word till I'm in my teens."

"So I should wait until I'm in my teens too?" I asked Mike.

"You can do whatever you want. I don't care. But just don't use it around me."

"Since when is that the new rule?"

"I don't know. But whenever I use cool in front of mom and dad they think it's weird. So I just don't use it," Tommy said. The cool case was closed for now.

"Well, I'm still going to use the word man. Like, 'hey man, how's it going?'" I said.

"Yah, me too. But we can't do that with our parents," Tommy said.

"I know, man," I said. We laughed. Our conversation had dwindled to slow whispers. I could tell Mike and Don were trying to get to sleep.

We had barely 10 days with the Walshes. I loved the relaxing feeling of normalcy. I didn't think it existed.

Several cool things stood out on that trip. The first was all the monster models Don had, ones he'd made himself. I got to help him put one together. The Mummy. "Now Carl, hold the glue right over that little ridge there," Don said. I glued it as steady as I could and Don put the piece in place.

"We'll get this put together in the next few hours so it has plenty of time to dry. Then we'll paint it a creamy white like it has real bandages. We'll paint the eyes black and put some red on it for blood. That'll be neat."

We had the whole Mummy put together in a few hours. I was thrilled. I felt like an apprentice working under my older cousin, whom I considered a professional model maker. He had so many models—the Wolfman, Dracula, Creature of the Black Lagoon, Godzilla and now the Mummy. I wanted them all. I was a little uneasy that I could relate to them all so well.

The next morning we all had breakfast together. Uncle Dan was taking time off work to be with us. After breakfast Don asked, "Hey, Carl, are you ready to start painting that model? I think the glue is dry now."

"Let me wash my hands and go to the bathroom."

"Hurry up. Tommy and Mike are going to help." I raced two of my girl cousins up to the bathroom. We fought to see who could get in first, slamming the door. That caught Aunt Dora's attention and she stood there, monitoring who went in first. According to her, as a visiting cousin, I had first rights. It trumped "ladies first."

"Are you guys going to paint the Mummy with us?" I asked from inside the bathroom.

"No, that stuff scares me," Sandy said. "And Dion's not either."

Downstairs we got started. "Okay here are the colors we're going to use. I have two bottles of a cream color for the bandages. Then black for the eyes and red for blood," said Don.

"That will look cool. Just like on TV," Mike said. At the word cool, Tommy and I looked at each other. But we didn't say anything.

"Okay, here are the brushes. Mike, why don't you start painting the bandages? Then I'll let Tommy do the eyes and Carl, you can put the blood on where you want."

Mike ever so carefully took the brush and stroke by stroke painted the bandages. It took him over a half hour. Don handed me a brush to do the blood. I was really nervous. If I messed up I would never hear the end of it. I thought of my dad when he golfed. He took his time to eye the ball and line up his shot. I took my time and decided where I wanted the blood to go. I put a stroke of blood here and a stroke there. I didn't want to go too far or it would look like a candy cane. So I quit while I was ahead.

"Great job, Carl. I think that looks great," Don said. I looked up at everyone with an expression of supreme self-confidence. I was so happy. It all felt so normal.

A few nights later we played flashlight tag in the back yard. It goes like this. Everyone has a flashlight and hides. You look around to see who's moving and try to hit them with a beam of light. When you do, they're out. The idea is to knock out as many of the opposing team as possible. Aunt Dora had to referee as to who was really hit. We played in the dark for more than two hours.

The big highlight was two nights before we left. Don and Mike took Tommy and me hiking through the woods behind their house. A creepy old man lived on the other side of those woods. Sometimes he stared at us. I asked Tommy who he was.

"Oh, that's Mr. Fullerton. He just likes to stand and stare at the sky or at us. He creeps me out but I don't think he'd hurt anyone...I don't think," Tommy said.

"You don't think?"

"Well, dad says he's harmless enough. Besides, if he tried something dad would take a belt to him just like he does us." And off into the woods we went.

The four of us spread out. I went opposite to the old man's house. A grouping of stones stood in an odd place, like someone had put them there. I removed them one by one. Suddenly a small snake jumped out and slithered away.

"Hey, man, you gotta see this!" I yelled. Tommy came running up. "It was so neat. I pulled these rocks away and all of a sudden this snake comes out!"

"Really? Where is it?"

"It took off into the grass," I said. I was so sad. I wanted it as a pet.

"If there's one, there could be more. Are there any more rocks?" Tommy asked. Soon we found a larger stone. It took both of us to pull it up. Underneath, all coiled up, lay a much bigger snake. Hell, we weren't even wondering if it was poisonous or not.

"Oh God, go get Mike and Don! Get over here! Hurry, man!" I yelled. "Go get your dad. See if he can get a big box to put it in. It's gonna be mine. I found it!" Mike and Don came running over.

"And just how are we gonna get that back home?" Mike asked.

"I don't know. I'm sure Uncle Dan can figure something out. Can't he, Don?" I asked in desperation.

"If anyone can, he can. I don't think it's a dangerous one either. Looks like a big garter snake." Finally Tommy came running back, completely out of breath.

"Dad said put it in this for now. Oh, and mom said she didn't want it in the house." Tommy held out a large cardboard box. Mike carefully lowered the snake into it.

I picked up the box and we marched triumphantly back to the house. Uncle Dan, Aunt Dora and the girls all waited in the garage like a reception committee. I proudly displayed my snake.

"Uncle Dan, I really want to take it home."

"On the train? Carl, I'm not so sure about that." My heart sank. Here was the catch of the century and I can't have it. If I could get my little trophy home I'd be a big man in my neighborhood.

"But Uncle Dan, is there any way we can make a strong box to put it in? Then I can cover it up when we get on the train. It won't get out and the people on the train won't know. It would be okay, wouldn't it?" Everyone stood there, silent.

"Well, I do have an old drawer from a desk I'm going to get rid of. We could put the snake in that and nail a screen on top of it. I think that might work. Dora, what do you think?"

"I'll have to call your mother, Carl. She may not want it at your house." I almost started to cry. It was now out of my hands.

Muffled phone conversation came from the kitchen. Aunt Dora was talking to my mom. I heard her laughing. I prayed. Oh, Dear Father in Heaven, please, please, please let mom say yes. I'll be good and never lie or laugh in school or call Regina Sayer ugly ever again. I'll even....

"Okay, here's what your mom said. Your father was there too, which I think worked in your favor. It was really your father who said yes. But the snake will stay at the Shop or something like that," Dora said.

"Yah! The Shop. That is dad's business." That meant mom doesn't want the snake, but dad overrode her in front of her sister. Good God, there's gonna be a fight. I can hear them screaming at each other right now. I hope it's all over before we get back. Please make it be over.

"Yes, your dad clinched it for you," Dora said laughing. "He wants to see the snake and was proud of you for finding it. You can keep it at the Shop. But he said if it gets too big you'll have to let it go in the woods. But for now it's yours. Your mother didn't want it in the house at all."

"Thanks, Aunt Dora!" The big problem would be getting the snake past the conductors. We'd have to make it look like just another piece of luggage, like a little snake purse. So I asked, "Uncle Dan how are we going to do this?"

"Well, Carl, I'm not totally sure yet. Let me worry about that. You and Mike just enjoy the rest of your time here." Uncle Dan and Aunt Dora had a way of comforting me with their confident assurances and family strength. Uncle Dan had the love and respect of all his family.

We spent the final few days making models, watching scary movies, and eating popcorn and an occasional pizza.

When it was time to go, all the departure preparations revolved around sneaking my snake, now named Lucifer, on the train. Uncle Dan had used an old desk drawer, nailed a screen on top of it, put some grass in the bottom, and wrapped it in newspaper. Inside a matchbox he stowed some crickets he picked up at a bait store for food. Mike and I said our goodbyes. I didn't want to go home. The Walshes didn't want us to leave either.

"Now you kids be careful. We love you," Aunt Dora said. We hugged each other goodbye. We were off to the train station with my new pet tucked safely under my arm.

Smuggling the snake on the train was easier than I thought. The conductors took our luggage but I kept the snake box on the floor by my feet.

A few hours into the trip I cut open the newspaper in the top of the box and looked at my little prize. Lucifer stared up at me. I wanted to feed him and put a little water in the cage. I loosened the screen and opened the matchbox of crickets. At once the box slipped out of my hands and all of the crickets fell out. A couple landed in the snake box but most of them fell on the floor and immediately hopped away!

"Be careful, man! We don't want a bunch of bugs running around all over us!" Mike said.

"The train is a little bumpy and they just slipped out." God, I can't believe that happened. I was getting a bad feeling.

The conductors walked up and down the aisles, checking things and seeing if passengers needed anything. Suddenly, we heard a loud chirping. It seemed to come from a few rows in front of us.

Someone said, "Honey, where in the hell did that come from? Does that sound like a cricket to you? Are there bugs on this train?"

"It's down by your left foot. Step on it!" That was just the beginning of everyone trying to stomp on the annoying crickets.

Please don't make it be our crickets. The conductor was finishing up in our car and heading toward the next one.

"You have to check the box again when the conductor leaves," Mike whispered. I looked down and lifted up the newspaper. People all around us were looking in all directions and mumbling about the now more-frequent cricket sounds.

Oh.....my.....God!!! It was bad enough all the crickets were gone, but now Lucifer was gone!! A snake was now loose on the train!

"Everything's gone. The box is empty!" I told Mike.

"We have to hide it. We have to act like we had nothing to do with this," Mike whispered. The chirping was now not only in front of us but across the aisle and behind us. People were complaining to the conductor. I shoved the cage further under my seat. We both stared straight ahead, pretending nothing was going on. We were the only people doing that.

"What's with these bugs?" a man asked.

"Sir, we're not sure. They must have slipped on back at the last stop," the conductor said. Was he serious? He was as confused as everyone else, except us, of course. We knew where the sounds were coming from.

"Well, this is quite a nuisance and my wife is very upset. I'm sending a letter to your company," the man complained.

"We're sorry for the inconvenience, sir." The conductor was now as frustrated as Mike and I. Two conductors went up and down the aisle dealing with the numerous passenger complaints.

"I got it! I got one!" a woman screamed. Passengers were now stomping on the crickets all around us. We, of course, continued to nervously ignore it all.

There was so much commotion that Mike and I didn't have time to think about the missing snake. A conductor approached.

"Let me do the talking," said Mike.

"Are you boys okay? We are so sorry for this. Can I get you anything?"

"No thank you, sir. We're just fine." We were now 90 minutes from Bridgeport. The train wasn't going fast enough. We avoided any eye contact with the conductors and passengers. There was so much stomping going on we felt like we were at a Pilgrim Holiness Church Revival.

"Next and last stop, Bridgeport!" Finally!

"Make sure you hide the cage good when we get off the train," Mike said.

"I will. You don't have to tell me." With the snake cage well hidden under my arm we got up and breathed a huge sigh of relief. The snake-cricket catastrophe of 1962 was coming to an end. No one ever knew a rather good-sized snake was running around on the train. It was too bad it didn't quickly devour all those loud, chirping crickets.

Dad greeted us at the station. We were never so glad to be there.

"Hey, how are you boys? Did you have a good time in New England? Where's your snake, Carl?" Dad eyeballed our luggage.

"Dad, well, uuhh, we don't have it."

"What do you mean you don't have it?"

"Well, uuhh, it somehow got away from us on the train," Mike said.

"How did that happen?" I held out the cage while I tried to explain to dad. My eyes welled up.

"Carl, it's okay. The good thing is you didn't get caught. It's too bad. I was looking forward to seeing your little catch."

"You'll have to tell us more about your trip tomorrow. Your mother wants to hear how everyone was," dad said. All I could think of was my lost pet. Was he cuddled up under a seat cushion or was he crawling up some lady's back?

Now that we had left the stability of the Walsh's world and were on our way back home, it was like my life went from color to black and white. Dad was now driving us past the dreaded old Mrs. Gertelwitch house, which was on the way home. I'd never seen her house this late at night. There was only one light on in the side parlor, which gave it an even creepier aura. I shuddered looking at it. She was one of the most frightening human beings in the neighborhood and the world. We called her "Gertelwitch." I quickly turned away.

Chapter 3: Mrs. Gertelwitch

ONE OF THE scariest places in our neighborhood was the house of the dreaded Mrs. Gertelwitch. It was a typical multi-story, gothic-style haunted house that was as old as time itself. The house and the area around it rivaled the Field in mystery, fear, and misadventure. It was around three or four acres with overgrown brush and tall, ancient trees that seemed to be watching you.

"Mom who is that scary person?" I once asked.

"That's Mrs. Gertelwitch. You are to stay away from her house. Do you understand?" That was the end of that. But it wasn't.

We started calling her Gertelwitch. We thought she was one of the most frightening human beings in the neighborhood and the world, for that matter. There were horror stories about her chasing kids off her property. Tales abounded about someone daring someone else to sneak up and knock on the door or look in the window, then, of course, run like hell. Mrs. Gertelwitch would pop up out of nowhere, like a jack-in-the-box. Just when you thought you'd gotten away with it there'd she be. She could even scare the crap out of you from inside her house. Her croaky voice bellowing through the woods as if from a bullhorn could send you running for your life. Mrs. Gertelwitch was slightly hunched and her hair was in a kind of bun. You'd see her standing on her front porch or slowly walking around her lawn. She reminded me of Margaret Hamilton's Elmira Gulch character in *The Wizard of Oz* and was as old as the forest that surrounded her. Even my fearless brother Mike said stay away.

"She eats kids like you!" he'd say. "She snatches them out of her yard and drags them inside. The next thing you know you're on her dining room table with an apple sticking out of your mouth, surrounded by fresh oregano and a bowls of mashed potatoes and green beans. Or she'll make pumpkin pie out of you. Did you ever wonder what happened to Chris Sadler? He just kind of disappeared, didn't he?"

"I knew he went away. I mean, their family moved away, didn't they?"

"Let's just put it this way. It's better to stay away from that house."

One day I was hanging around with Greg and Tom Powell, the neighborhood tough-guy brothers and bullies. I had to be careful around them and suck up a little.

We were kind of bored standing around one day. "We're goin' after Gertelwitch!" Greg and Tom said. I didn't like the sound of this.

"Are you coming with us?"

"I don't know. I mean . . . you know what she does to kids . . ."

"And what's that? She puts them on the dinner table? Yah, but she won't try that with us."

"How do you know?" I asked.

"We're not afraid of her. We'll take sticks and rocks and throw 'em. We're gonna scare her for a change. Also John Binson is coming over."

I stood there, trying to figure out how to get out of this. Then John Binson, Billy Babick, and Scott Andrews showed up. There'd be six of us.

"Okay, is everyone here?" Greg asked. "We need everyone we can get."

"Hey, guys, I think it would be better if we went into the woods and really planned this out. Do you think anyone'll see us?"

"I'm with Carl," John said. "Why don't we head over to Little John and figure this out?"

So off we went like a gang of little Army Rangers executing a top-secret Black Ops attack. Greg was in charge of strategic planning.

"Here's how we've got it figured out," he began. "First, we're all going in from right here, through the woods, then toward Gertelwitch's house. We'll meet at the Shack where we can see her house from the back. No talking on the way. John and Billy will go around the left side of her house and throw rocks at the living room window to distract her. Carl, you and Scott go around the right side and throw rocks at the windows. Then Tom and I will go up to the front door and kick it in and throw bags of worms into her living room and take off."

"Where are the worms?" asked Scott.

Greg smiled, looked at Tom, and nodded. From his front pockets Tom whipped out two baggies of earthworms and dirt. Everyone looked impressed. But I got more worried. We fanned out, looking for good throwing stones. Everyone but me was stuffing them in their pockets. I faked it. If I got caught at least I wouldn't have any weapons on me. If mom or dad found about this I could be in deep trouble. We crept along in the overgrown field toward the staging area at the Shack. We also had to navigate a large briar patch. I'd hear an occasional "ouch!!" or "oh!!" as someone got snagged on briars and sticker bushes. All of a sudden Scott yelled "Aaahhhh!" and went face down.

"Hey, man, are you okay? Hang on. Let me help you," I said.

"No, I think I'm okay but I stepped into this hole. But, oh no, what's this?"

In the hole was a dead opossum all bloated up. It apparently had been lying in the hot sun for days. It burst and squirted all over him. Scott and I looked at it with its eyes popped out and Scott started to cry. He desperately tried to wipe off the dead animal goo with some tree leaves.

"I'm done. I'm through. I'm going home," he said.

"Oh Scott, come on," I whispered. "It's not that bad. You got most of it off. And you don't smell that bad." Inside I was thinking...YUK! He really stunk and looked like some sort of cadaver mess.

"Oh come on," Greg said. "Come on, Scott, Gertelwitch will hate it. She deserves it."

"No, I'm done. I'm going home." Scott trudged back toward Little John and home. We were down to five. This was a bad omen. The spirit of that dead opossum was trying to tell us something.

We re-grouped and crept forward. At the Shack we found a good vantage point for watching her house. One final bit of strategy remained – what to do if we got caught. We went over the basic attack plan but didn't have a strategy for *that*.

"One final thing," said Greg. "If she catches one of us don't give her any names. Just say you were cutting through her yard to get home and you're from another neighborhood. After the raid we planned to run back into the depths of Little John, hide a while, come out the west end, and then nonchalantly walk home like nothing ever happened.

We began moving away from the Shack. As we got closer I felt her house staring back at me. Even Greg and Tom seemed apprehensive. Scott was supposed to go around the right side with me. Now that little task would be up to me. I decided to fall back a bit and let the other four approach ahead of me.

We finally reached her property. We all fanned out into our pre-planned attack positions. I could feel everything change, even the smell of the air. The entire atmosphere rapidly took on a more ominous tone. There were no bug noises – no noise at all. As we got closer with rocks in hand, I decided to drop mine. I couldn't bring myself to actually throw them at her window. I also figured without rocks in my hand I'd be able to run faster.

Oh no! Someone on the other side threw his rocks. I heard the loud, unmistakable thud of a rock hitting glass. She *had* to have heard it. I froze. It's not too late to run. Just then someone shrieked, "She saw us! Gertelwitch saw us! She's coming! Let's split!"

Tom and Greg tore out from the front of the house. Billy, John, and I were heading out from the side of it toward the back. We rendezvoused in unison, running together toward the woods. All of a sudden Mrs. Gertelwitch appeared in our paths like somebody had flipped on a hologram light switch. She moved so fast! We stopped dead in our tracks. She had us. We were right up, face to face with Elmira Gulch from *The Wizard of Oz*. I was so nervous my tongue stuck to the roof of my mouth. All of us stood there fossilized. None of us had ever been this close to her.

"I saw you boys sneaking around way back in the woods. You thought you were clever, eh? Who threw that rock at my window? Which one of you did that?"

She looked from left to right and right to left, scanning our eyes for any clues. For a split second I remembered the ancient Greek mythological story of the Medusa and could not bring myself to look directly into her eyes. Her voice had a hoarse vinegar tone to it.

We stood there stunned, unable to quickly come up with any type of answer that would exonerate us. We were now about to find out first hand if all those scary rumors were true. I prayed to St. Francis very, very hard.

It had to have been Tom or Greg who threw the first rock. Were they going to admit it? This whole thing was their idea.

"Well... I didn't do it ma'am," said Billy. John said the same thing. Billy and John looked at me to say that too.

"Ma'am, I didn't throw any rocks either." I was shaking in my now filthy Hush Puppy shoes.

"Well, what about you two boys, then?" she pointed to Greg and Tom. Her fingers must have been six inches long. Her nails made her fingers seem even longer.

"Mrs. Gertelwitch, I did it," Greg admitted. The funny thing was, he was half in tears. Mr. Tough Guy, I thought. Mr. Cool. Yah.

"I knew it was you. I was watching you all along." She glared at him. He was melting.

"You're lucky that rock didn't break any glass or I'd have called your mother on you. Why did you do that? What did you hope to gain by it?"

It was kind of fun watching Greg squirm. Would the rest of us skate though? Then her tone changed as she lectured Greg. She had somehow managed to gradually corral us into a circle. She was in the middle. She had become some strange center of gravity.

"You children should ask yourself what you have to gain by trespassing on an older woman's property and trying to scare her," she said. "You're better kids than that." I smiled to myself. Not Greg or Tom. They're jerks.

"First of all, you didn't accomplish anything. And second, all you did was degrade yourselves. Again, if that window was broken, I was serious about calling each and every one of your mothers. But all I'm going to ask is please stay off of my property and away from my house, or your parents will get a little visit from me. Do you understand what I am telling you?"

"Yes, Mrs. Gertelwitch," we replied in unison. Our heads hung and we all felt embarrassed. Then a very strange thing happened. She slowly and deliberately walked up to each of us and spoke our names and kissed us on the cheek. How did she know our names? As she got closer, the fear I had felt from her disappeared. This was the most peculiar, yet calming human behavior ritual I'd ever experienced.

"Okay, you go on home now," she said. There was finality in her voice.

We slowly disbanded, bypassed Little John, and walked directly out along the streets and home in an eerie sort of bewilderment. We didn't say anything to each other but walked in silence. I was afraid to turn around and look back at her, thinking I'd turn into a pillar of salt as Lot's wife did when she turned and gazed back at Sodom and Gomorrah. Days and weeks later, we made tough little wisecracks, like, "Hey, Gertelwitch never got ahold of us." Or, "Gertelwitch couldn't catch us." But we never, ever again went near Mrs. Gertelwitch's house.

At home no one was there and I blew a sigh of relief. Mom would have asked where I'd been or why I was so dirty and scratched up. I didn't like to lie, if possible, and now she'd never know, thank God. I had to clean myself up quickly, though. I did notice something odd: the heavy scent of cigar smoke. It wasn't my dad's cigarette smoke, and anyway, he was out of town on business. I sniffed around, trying to find the source of it, but couldn't. After cleaning up I went into my bedroom and turned on the radio where "One Fine Day" by the Chiffons started to play.

A couple weeks later, with the Mrs. Gertelwitch incident mostly behind me, Rufio Binson came over. He was one year older than me and his family lived relatively close to us. Douglas was his real name, but we and the rest of the neighborhood kids called him Rufio.

"Mom, Rufio — uuhh, I mean Douglas is here. He wants to know if I can come over Friday night and watch TV." I knew if Rufio was asking, the odds of her letting me go would be better. She liked Rufio and the Binson family.

"Hello, Douglas. Will your mother be there?" mom asked.

"Yes, Mrs. Sanders. She will be there fixing popcorn for us."

"Who else will be there?"

"Well, some of my brothers and sisters, my dad, and a few of our friends. We'll be out on the back porch with the TV outside."

"That sounds neat, doesn't it, mom?"

"Well okay, what will you be watching?" Rufio looked over at me. He was on the spot and had to play it honest or no dice.

"Mrs. Sanders, my mom and dad told us it would be okay to watch *Nightmare Theater*. It starts at 10 and I think goes until midnight. We'll have popcorn and Kool Aid and of course my parents will be there. After it's over we'll be sure Carl gets home safely." Their house was only a block away.

"Well, that's pretty late for Carl. You don't think you can stay up that late do you?" At least it's not a *no*, I thought.

"I think I can, mom. The movie is the *Creature from the Black Lagoon,* which is one of my favorites."

"Alright, you can go, but don't fall asleep there. I don't want Douglas's mom calling me to come get you because I have to stay here with Catherine. Mike's staying at a friend's, and your dad is out of town again. You won't be afraid to walk home after watching a movie like that, will you? Who exactly is the Creature from the Black Lagoon, anyway?" Mom was amused.

"The Creature is a scary monster that lives under water. I'll be alright mom." However, I hadn't thought of walking home alone at midnight.

"Okay, Douglas, Carl can go."

"Mom, thanks a lot."

Friday night couldn't have come fast enough. I had thought about it all week at school. When my homework was all done I was going to get to walk over to the Binson's at around 7. It got to be 6:30 and mom said she'd take me to the store so I wouldn't show up empty handed.

"Carl, I don't want you to go over there with nothing. I'm going to run to Safeway and pick up some popcorn for you to take. They have Jiffy Pop on sale. How does that sound?" she asked.

"Mom, that would be neat," I responded.

"Let's get in the car now. Mike is coming with us because I'll need some help picking up a few other things," Mom said. Mike really wanted to ride over with us because apparently he thought it was cool I was going over to the Binson's to watch *Nightmare Theater*. He just kind of wanted to be involved in the process.

We pulled into the parking lot and mom told me to stay in the car and they would be out soon. She and Mike headed to the store. I was sitting in the back seat with the window rolled down, anxiously waiting for them to be done and drop me off. It was a beautiful summer evening. I was sitting there, just kind of staring off to my right, when a loud car pulled into the open parking space next to us. I looked over and saw the coolest two-seater convertible sports car with the top down. In the next instant I saw who was up front. There were two clowns!

What is that all about? They turned the engine off and one of them, the driver, got out and went in to the liquor store across the parking lot. The one in the passenger seat, closest to me, stayed. I stared straight ahead and tried not to make a sound. I wasn't sure if he, or she, or whatever it was, knew I was there. I didn't want it to know. I was in uncharted territory. I didn't look straight at it but stared out of the corner of my eye. After a couple of minutes the clown lit up a cigarette and started looking around. I didn't think clowns smoked, and it was really weird watching one do it only a few feet away from me.

As it perused the parking lot, all of a sudden it glanced sharply over at me as it blew out a puff of cigarette smoke. We locked eyes for a few seconds, then it smiled and nodded at me. It was a weird clown smile, not a kind one. I kind of waved back, then slowly slid down the seat so it couldn't see me anymore. A clown parked in a sports car with a cigarette in its mouth was making me a little uneasy. I stayed hidden until I heard the other clown come back. He had two cases of Falls City beer in his arms. Thank God I think they're leaving, I thought to myself.

"Hey, I think I spooked that little kid in the car next to us," one clown laughed.

"That's too bad. Hasn't the little shit seen a clown before?" the other responded.

I thought, these are bad clowns. They use cuss words. Now I was scared and stayed way down. I heard them both laughing and start their car up and slowly pull out of the parking space. I wasn't going to get up until I was totally sure they were gone.

But just then I heard a voice.

"Carl, what in the world are you doing down there?" God, I was glad to see mom, and jumped right up.

"Hey, man, what were you doing down there?" Mike asked.

"I don't know…well…uuhh…after you left, a weird car pulled up and, well, I don't know if you'll believe this or not, but there were, well, two clowns in it and one went into the liquor store but the other one stayed in the car right next to me."

"What?" mom said. She looked around the parking lot. Mike just raised his eyebrows.

"These two clowns pulled up next to me. One went into that liquor store and the other one lit up a cigarette and started staring at me and its smile was scary."

"Carl, clowns aren't supposed to be scary. They try to make people laugh. And you said the one went into the liquor store? Clowns don't drink. At least not the ones I've seen."

"Yah, and it came back with two cases of beer. Anyway, I was hiding because they really scared me."

"Okay, well, after seeing those bad clowns you're not too scared to watch *Nightmare Theater* are you?" mom asked with a smile.

"Those clowns will be in the woods waiting for you when you walk home tonight. Don't go near that line of trees across the street," Mike teased.

"No they won't! Mr. and Mrs. Binson will be there," I snapped.

"Mike, stop it. Just come straight home after the movie, Carl. You'll be fine. Mike, turn around and dry up." Mom was getting fed up with Mike trying to spook me all the time.

We pulled up to the Binson's house around 8. They had a big family and most of the older ones were going to stay up to watch the show with us. The kids I was closest to were Rufio and John. Rufio was one year older than me and John one year younger. One of their sisters, Jody, was a year older than Rufio. She was a dumb girl, though, and we didn't talk a whole lot. But she liked *Nightmare Theater* and wanted to stay up with us.

When mom dumped me off Rufio was on the porch, waiting. We immediately ran into his bedroom with John and turned on the radio. I was just getting ready to tell my weird clown story, but right then one of my favorite songs came on. It was "Little Town Flirt" by Del Shannon. It reminded me of Janet Franklin at school. But she flirted with most of the guys so it really didn't feel special. Maybe she would really pay attention me when I became an altar boy. If not, it would be her loss. The clown story could wait for now.

"Oh, Rufio, don't change the station. I really like that song. I listen to my sister's radio when she isn't around. That's how I know a lot of the songs. My mom hates this music, though. I don't think anyone's parents like it."

"They call it rock-n-roll. Our parents don't like it either," John said.

"That's why we have to keep the radio turned down. If we don't, my mom will come in and make us turn it off," said Rufio.

"It's weird. We can watch *Nightmare Theater*. But we can't listen to rock-n-roll music," John said.

"Parents don't make sense sometimes," I said. Rufio and John nodded in agreement.

Scott and Billy came in. They weren't Catholic and went to a public school, but we got along as long as we left religion out of it. They joked about us drinking blood and sacrificing animals on Sunday.

"You'll have to tell us about altar boy training in the fall," I said to Rufio. "I'll be doing it a year after you."

"Yah, I will. A lot of guys signed up for it. I think there's going to be nine in our class."

"My brother Mike's been one for a few years and really likes it. It makes him feel like a big man." Rufio and John laughed.

"The last time I was at Mass one of the older altar boys up there had on these cool shoes. They had lightning bolts cut out on the sides and his white socks were showing through like lightning," John said.

"Wow, that is cool. Maybe Mike knows him and could find out where he got them," I said.

"I don't know if my mom would ever let me wear shoes like that," Rufio said. Neither would mine probably.

All five of us sat in that bedroom and talked about meaningless stuff like the girls in class, who got in trouble, and who we thought was creepy. I'd sworn to not discuss the Mrs. Gertelwitch story it until it died down more. My parents still didn't know about it and that's the way I wanted it. So I started in on the clown story. I had just gotten it started when Mrs. Binson came in to check on us. The story would have to wait.

"How are you boys doing? You've been in there talking up a storm. Why don't you join us in the living room? The movie starts in an hour."

In the living room, Mr. Binson said, "Well, Carl, how have you been?"

"I've been okay, sir."

"Are you going to play football in the fall?"

"I'm not sure. Maybe."

"Come on, you ought to go out for it," Rufio said.

"I might if my mom lets me. My dad really wants me to."

"Well, I hope we see you on the field." I was flattered Mr. Binson thought I could play.

"So what's on tonight? Are we watching *Nightmare Theater*?" asked Mrs. Binson.

"It's *The Creature of the Black Lagoon*. It's kind of a neat movie," Rufio explained.

"Jody wants to stay up and watch too. That's okay, isn't it?"

"As long as she doesn't scream," said John.

Then Rufio said, "If she does, we're kicking her out." All us boys laughed, but Mrs. Binson didn't.

"Just be nice to her. She just wants to be one of the group."

Jody came in. "Thanks for letting me watch the movie with you guys tonight."

"Yah, it's okay if you keep quiet," John said. Mrs. Binson glared at him.

Mrs. Binson eventually herded all six of us outside to the back porch where Mr. Binson had some blankets and pillows laid out in front of a 15-inch, black-and-white television set. She then went back inside to start some popcorn. We all staked our territorial claims. None of us wanted to be next to Jody because in all probability she had cooties. So we just kept our distance. Mr. Binson had turned the TV on and was adjusting the rabbit-ear antenna to bring in good reception. It was a few minutes until the magic hour of 10, and we watched the last few minutes of a rerun of *The Fugitive*. I was a little nervous about watching *Nightmare Theater* outside. I thought we'd be in the safety of the indoors. But Mrs. Binson, I believe, thought it would be easier to sweep all our popcorn scraps off the porch when we trashed the area. She was probably right.

Although a fence around their backyard separated us from the woods, I was still a little uneasy. For a moment I stared back into those dark woods, but quickly turned away. Mr. and Mrs. Binson would be with us. They had never really sat down and watched *Nightmare Theater*. Then there was the walk home alone later, but I wouldn't think about that right now.

Then came the witching hour. The TV antenna was adjusted and the picture was as good as it could get. *Nightmare Theatre* organ music started. TV's most famous phantom appeared.

"Gooood Eeeeving, my friends. I am Sammy Terry, your host of *Nightmare Theater*," he howled. We were hypnotized.

"You are probably wondering why I look the way I do. I was conducting a veeeery frightening, yet important experiment many years ago when it went terribly wrong. I cannot discuss the details with you for your own safety. But please rest assured all is well, at least for the time being. After all, my friends, I would never want to put you in danger," Sammy Terry said with his evil smile.

"What in the . . ." said Mr. Binson in a very low voice. I looked over and watched him roll his eyes.

"Let me introduce you to our movie tonight. It is one of my favorites, *The Creature of the Black Lagoon*. I saw this thing, if you will, while I was on a research experiment project down in South America. I saw it up close as it swam across the lake. It had bright green scales and the most frightening eyes I had ever seen. It looked right at me. We stared at each other for what seemed like an eternity. I was in a transfixed state as this creature swam by. Only after it was gone did I snap out of it. I hope I never have to go through such an experience ever again."

I quickly looked again into their back yard toward the woods, but couldn't see anything beyond the darkness. If I kept looking, though, I might see something, so I turned away.

"So tonight, *The Creature of the Black Lagoon* comes creeping into our world once again. So I urge you to exercise caution and always stay away from the lake. Enjoy the show if you dare! Ha ha ha ha ha!" Sammy Terry looked so evil tonight.

Mr. Binson put his head in his hands and Mrs. Binson smiled and slapped him on the arm. We watched long after they went inside. Jody eventually got scared and went inside, too. The clock inched toward midnight. We made it through. Sammy Terry came on to wrap up the show.

"Well, my friends, it looks like you survived that magnificent monster, for now, anyway. Oh, and please tune in next time for another round of horror. Next week I am going to be visited by my good friend, the Mummy. So until then, my friends, please try to stay safe and don't wander into the dark. I do want to see you again, ha ha ha." Then came a close-up of his face. I couldn't look. He said don't wander into the dark. That's exactly what I had to do going home.

"That was a cool movie," Billy said.

"I can't wait for the Mummy next week," I said.

Mrs. Binson came out and turned off the TV. "Well, everyone, it's time to go home and get to bed. Carl, Scott, and Billy, are you going to be alright?"

"Yes, Mrs. Binson," we answered.

"We loved having you over tonight. Maybe we can do it again."

I said my goodbyes slowly. I wasn't in any rush to leave. I was hoping a slow-moving car would light the way for me.

I watched John and Rufio go inside, and Scott and Billy take off together in the opposite direction I was going. It was time to walk the eerie, dark gauntlet back home alone. It had gotten windy. I didn't think it was going to storm. The street light by our house was off but Mom had given me a flashlight. It was my best friend.

So I stepped out onto the street and started walking as fast as I could. I had to keep *The Creature of the Black Lagoon* out of my head or the walk home would be worse. I hadn't gotten very far when, out of the corner of my eye, I noticed a dark figure trailing me cattycorner to my right side. I turned around and saw it run behind a big, double-trunk tree in the Carson's front yard. Filled with apprehension, I stopped, thinking or hoping it was maybe Rufio playing a game with me. But it wasn't like him to do that, and at this late hour his parents wouldn't have let him out again. So who was out in the neighborhood after midnight following me? None of the kids I knew in the neighborhood would have still been out at this time.

I shined my flashlight at the tree I thought this person was hiding behind. There was a chalk-white face peering back at me from between the two tree trunks. My light was right on it. Whoever it was had a very pale, white face with a shiny, almost waxy look to it.

The person was staring directly at me. Now I was much more scared than I had been during the movie. That was it. I turned around fast and broke into a hard, dead run for my house. I ran as fast as I could and didn't look back. I ran until I came right up to the front porch. Luckily, mom had left the porch light on. Only then did I turn around and look back toward the area of that tree. I saw nothing and I thanked God that person, or whatever it was, didn't follow me. I pounded on the door as hard as I could. Through the glass I could see mom coming.

"Carl, I'm right here. You don't have to knock so loud. Are you okay? You're as white as a ghost." I rushed inside, almost tripping over her shoes.

"My God, what's wrong with you? Was the movie that frightening?" I sat on the sofa trying to catch my breath. I couldn't believe what I'd been through. First, those terrible clowns, then lying around outside in the dark watching *Nightmare Theater*. And finally, walking home by myself and being followed by some sort of strange whatever it was. I looked up at her. I couldn't bring myself to tell her what I saw in the trees. That would scratch future overnights watching *Nightmare Theater*.

"Yah, the movie was pretty bad. I don't think I could have watched it alone."

"Bad? Scary bad? You looked like you'd been running hard. Are you sweating?"

"After the movie I just wanted to get home, so I ran a little bit." I hoped that would derail further questions.

"Get ready for bed. You've had a long night. Mike will be home tomorrow and, of course, your dad isn't coming home. He's out of town again," she said.

"When did he leave?" Dad, Mike, and I slept in the same room and now none of them would be here.

"He's still somewhere in Ohio. The irrigation project at that country club doesn't finish until tomorrow." She was very matter of fact about it.

I trudged into the empty bedroom. My fear turned into sadness. I was looking forward to dad being here. I put on my pajamas, crawled into bed, and tried not to think about what was following me home, or dad being gone yet another couple of nights. On Monday I'd be back at school. We'd have recess in the Field. St. Micaelis was putting new blacktop on the playground. I couldn't wait. Dad would be back soon and all would be right with the world. It would be fun to go hang out at the Shop. I drifted off to sleep and dreamed about the Field.

CHAPTER 4: THE FIELD

TO THIS DAY, I still drive by the old neighborhood, cruise up and down the streets, and look at the homes of childhood friends. I park at the Field. I still recall those beautiful, calm summer mornings in the early '60s. I turned five in 1960, my first year of real consciousness. I can't remember much before that. A dove always sang from the top of the swing set in the early morning. Its main mission in life, I guessed, was to let me know everything was all right in my little world. Why do I remember that? I'm not sure. It's been in my head most of my life. Every time I hear that same kind of dove it brings me back to that time. I really liked to be by myself back then. Sometimes I would do little-boy things in the back yard, or walk around the neighborhood, seeing who I could play with, or sit alone in the Field, but only in the daytime. I used to lie on my back and look up at the clouds drifting across the blue sky. Sometimes I imagined someone was lying on top of those clouds peeking down at me. The clouds calmed me just like the dove. It was my own little version of the Drifters' "Up On the Roof."

The Field was a six-acre rectangle between my house and St. Micaelis grade school. It was the neighborhood's main "go-to" area. My friends and I were always in the Field playing, or cutting through like it was some sort of worm-hole-type portal. To a small boy it was the ecliptic plane. I was free there. It was a gathering and social place, a magical place, and sometimes I didn't want to leave it. When I ran away from home for an hour or two, it was first on the list for refuge and escape. It was a quiet place where my dad sometimes took me just to walk. At the back was a swing set and a dirt bicycle track where Mike and I raced bicycles. When we beat our friends we went home feeling like we'd conquered the world. But in later years the Field morphed into a state of mind. It symbolized my early life in that neighborhood and the developing family chaos.

In the Field I learned the truth about Santa Claus and the Easter Bunny. One Saturday morning I ran into my friend Scott Andrews. He was a straight-A student and a year older than me. It seemed like every time I talked to him I learned something. He wasn't Catholic, though, so I had to be careful. He was one of the kids I watched *Nightmare Theater* with.

I said, "Hey, Scott, look what Santa Claus brought me for Christmas!"

"Who gave it to you?" Scott asked with one of his famous smirks.

"Santa Claus." I wasn't liking this direction.

"You don't believe that do you?"

"Well, yah, kinda."

"Don't you know there *is* no Santa Claus?"

"That's not true, is it? I mean, that's what mom and dad told me."

"Carl, I'm gonna tell you something and I don't want you to get mad at me. And *don't* tell your parents I said this. But, well, uuhhh, there is no Santa Claus," Scott hammered out.

"Are you serious?" I was shocked. I didn't want to believe it, but deep down I suspected he was right.

"Yah, I'm serious. My parents finally told me last year and my older brother said so, too. Besides, it never made sense to me. I would have figured it out anyway. I mean, how can he get around to all the homes all around the world in just one night? And he's too fat to fit down a chimney." I didn't know what to say. I looked down at the ground and then back at Scott.

"What about the Easter Bunny?" I asked, fearing his response. Scott just looked at me and shook his head. I could tell he was getting uncomfortable. "I have to get going now," he said.

"Don't worry," I reassured him. "I won't tell anyone what we talked about."

"I hope not." And off he went. I stood in the middle of the Field, staring up at the sky. This was a huge turning point in my life. Now I began trying to figure out just what was real in my life and wasn't.

There was one lone tree right in the middle of the Field that is still there to this day. There were also a couple of isolated tree stumps that always seemed out of place. At the west there was a small slope where we sledded during the winter. Also it was the St. Micaelis school playground overflow for noon recess, at least when the weather was good.

It was also a place where monsters came out and walked late at night. I didn't like to go in it or even walk past it in the dark, alone. The deeper I stared into the Field at night the darker it got until the middle was pitch black. Something always stared back at me. Was it my imagination? I'd like to think it was.

Dad told me stories about what happened when the Field was just virgin forest many years ago. An unusual amount of ancient-type weapons had been found— arrowheads and spearheads. They were of Indian origin. The area had always attracted historians and thrill seekers.

One of dad's stories really unnerved me. At story time before bed, dad asked, "Did I ever tell you about the time long before our house was here that they discovered three bodies of some kids?"

"Dad, no. Are you kidding?" Mike asked.

"I don't know if I want to hear this," I said

"My father told me the story," dad began. "This area, way back when, had a reputation as a kind of scary place. In the '20s when this whole area was one big forest, they found the bodies of three high-school kids at the south edge of the Field, almost right across the street from us. They'd been hiking, and apparently died of some sort of cardiac arrest. They were found several feet apart from each other."

"Oh God!" I shrieked. "I won't ever go across the street again. What's cardiac arrest?"

"Neither will I," Mike chimed in "So they died kind of mysteriously? How did all three have heart attacks at the same time? Is that what cardiac arrest is?" Mike asked.

"Well that was what the police reports said. And yes, that's what cardiac arrest is. They don't know why they died like that. Their eyes were wide open. Kids ventured into the woods from time to time, thrill-seeking or even looking for ghosts."

"You said this area back then was, like, haunted?" I asked.

"Yes, if you believe in that sort of thing."

"Dad, I don't want to talk about this story anymore."

"Yah, I think I've had enough too," added Mike.

"Okay, you scaredy-cats. That's the end of it," dad laughed. And that *was* the end of it. The story was never brought up again.

I rolled over and tried to get some sleep. It didn't come easy. In fact, that story scared me so much that during the night while I was sleeping I pooped in my PJs and started to dream. I dreamed I was running away from something in the Field that smelled really bad. Some stinky monster was chasing me. In reality the smell was coming from my pants, no thanks to my dad.

✝

Sometimes we kids did things as a dare to prove how brave we were.

"Hey, Carl, you're not going to believe this," said my friend Eddie.

"What?"

"Ellen is going steady with Tom Anderson and they really kissed!"

"There's no way. I don't believe it. And who does that anyway? My parents don't even do that."

"Well, you believe what you want, but I heard it from Tommy himself. He's been walking around in the hallways holding hands with Ellen when they think no one's watching. Ya know, I'm not supposed to say anything."

I stared down at the ground and then looked around at the kids playing in the Field. It took time to process this information.

"Promise you won't tell! Not anyone! Tommy and I are best friends."

"Of course I won't tell. And besides, if that story got to the wrong person I could get into a lot of trouble."

Eddie again swore me to secrecy. I pondered this new and exciting information. Of course I was bursting at the seams to tell someone. And I found just the right person. One of the tough older kids was walking by. I wanted to impress him. Tony was a few years older than me and an altar boy, which I aspired to be one day. I wanted to impress an altar boy. We knew each from passing in the halls but that was it. I was about to find out just how un-cool he really was.

I tugged at his shirt and said, "Tony, you're not going to believe this."

"Carl, oh hey, how are you? What are you talking about?"

"I just heard that Ellen Sims and Tom Bosworth are like going steady. They've even kissed!!"

55

"Carl, are you sure? When did you hear this?" Tony barely knew them but it didn't matter.

"Yah. I just heard from….well I can't tell you."

"Wow, they kissed….really…? How gross!" His mouth resembled a yeast doughnut" with a hole in the middle.

"That's what I heard."

"WOW!" exclaimed Tony.

Tony reached into his pocket and pulled out a little pocket knife. It might as well have been a machete—we weren't supposed to have those in school. My parents would have cracked me a good one if they found me with a knife. These days that would be called child abuse but then it was just seen as discipline. I was cracked or spanked many a time and probably was a better person for it.

"Tony, what's that for?"

He said, "You know what would be fun? If you walked down to the football goal posts and carved 'Ellen Sims + Tommy Bosworth' into one of them. That would be funny. I won't tell anyone."

"You won't?" Here was my chance to impress Tony. I took him up on the dare.

"Recess is going to be over soon so you better do it quick," Tony said.

I hid the pocket knife and snuck down to the goalposts. I thought about it for one more minute. Then, as fast as I could, I carved "Ellen Sims + Tommy Bosworth" and put a crude heart shape around it all.

Shoving the knife into my pocket, I ran away from those posts as fast as I could. I pulled it off! However, this quickly became hot news, a little too hot. Within 20 minutes a large crowd was huddled around the goal post. I stood watching in horror from afar. You would have thought Vince Lombardi had shown up to give a speech or coach the proper procedure for kicking a field goal. But no, they were flocking to see my artwork. But then from a distance I watched in horror as one of the nuns went to see what all the commotion was about. It was surrealistic as she looked like something out of an André Breton novel. Scores of children followed her. It was the dreaded and feared Sister Ande. She taught third grade at St. Micaelis.

At over six feet, she was the tallest nun in the school. She was gaunt, always pointing her finger at someone. She looked like a 70-year-old grim and austere nun version of Queen Victoria. With my luck I would wind up in her class one day. Thank God I was only doing the pre-school part of it now.

My first instinct was to run further toward the safety of the breezeway up at the school. No one would be there at that time. I ran as fast as I could before the commotion started, then froze like a Popsicle, a very tart and bitter flavor. I hid in the nearby bushes. I had never in my life wished for the end of recess. I thought I would die and go to hell. Confession on Sunday would be too late.

Then came the sound of the first bell. In St. Micaelis in the early '60s, the first bell was a signal for you to freeze no matter what you were doing. It could be comical. The more clownish kids literally froze in whatever position they held. If someone was bending over, they froze. If they were hitting someone or standing there with their mouth open, they froze. We always talked about who had the funniest freeze position. But you had to be very careful. If one of the ever-watchful nuns caught you in a silly freeze, you could get publicly reprimanded. And to be quite honest, watching someone get publicly disciplined on the playground could be hilarious but unfortunately you couldn't laugh. You always knew when it was happening because the nuns made a graphic loud example of it. It was like watching a slapstick comedy skit. You know, when someone slips and falls in the mud or gets a surprise smack in the face. When a second bell sounded you had to unfreeze and go to your respective class line-up to head back inside to class.

I had just heard the dreaded second bell go off. I could see some of the kids shuffle toward the school building. I snuck around from behind the bushes and stealthily fell into line at the rear, hoping not to be noticed — a little football razzmatazz on the backend, if you will. We all moved toward the school entrance in perfect synchronicity. I continued to pull it off for a little longer but there were hostile witnesses, I found out. And they were starting to talk. I could tell by the weird stares and giggles of the returning kids.

Now, in those days, the Catholic school judicial system doled out harsh punishment for those who didn't come clean in the face of clear evidence. So I figured it would be better to confess than to have Sister Ande actually come after me. My soul started to swell up with guilt. I couldn't hold it in anymore. I did the most embarrassing thing I could think of. I started crying and ran up to Sister Ande and confessed on the spot. It would have been much worse to try to defend what little honor I had left in the principal's office. That would have been a disaster. I did not want to be at the mercy of the school principal, Sister Carabella. She was the meanest nun ever to enter the convent. And too, spending any kind of time in her office for disciplinary action was like having a felony on your school disciplinary record.

"Sister, I'm sorry, I'm sorry!" The all-knowing, all-seeing Sister Ande knew what I had done. To avoid a public spectacle, she asked one of the lay teachers to shepherd the rest of the children inside. Then she took me aside and gently scolded me for publically embarrassing a couple of fellow classmates and damaging the school goal post.

For my proactive confession though, Sister Ande seemed proud of me and the case was eventually dismissed.

My relatively light sentence was to privately apologize to that poor couple and scrape their names off the post. She didn't even tell my parents, thank the good Lord on high. After a week or so it all seemed to settle down. The knife was never found. As I'd raced toward breezeway, I'd thrown it as far as I could into someone's back yard.

The episode traumatized me for the next few days and of course it happened in the Field. But I got over it as I daydreamed, one day at home, while Chad & Jeremy's "Summer Song" played on the radio. And best of all, my parents never ever found out. That was my first traumatic experience in the Field, but not the last.

✝

A few weeks later, when I came home from playing outside at a friend's house, something didn't seem right. I heard strange noises. When I asked mom and dad, they acted like I didn't know what I was talking about. Then Catherine said, "Carl, do you hear something?"

"I'm not sure. Do you?"

"It sounds like someone's crying."

"Shhhh. Let's listen and try and see what it is."

"Woooowwww…eeeeeeeee," it went, faint and muffled.

"Did you hear that?" said Catherine.

"That's what I heard a little bit ago. That is what it sounded like."

"But where is it coming from?"

"Shhh, let's keep listening."

"Woooowww…eeeeeeee," it went again. It sounded like a cross between a bark and a howl.

"It's coming from the front closet!" That closet was always filled with junk and I was never allowed to even peek into it.

"Let me ask mom before we open it or she'll get mad," I said. She was in the kitchen making dinner.

"Mom, there's some funny sounds coming from the front closet. Is it okay to open it up and see what's in there?"

"Well, I don't know, Carl, are you sure?" She didn't sound concerned at all. And dad was still downstairs.

"Yah, Catherine and I both are sure. Is it okay to open the door?"

"Yes, go ahead. Catherine, stand back when Carl opens it up," mom said. Well that was a weird thing to say. What would I find? I approached the closet with mom and Catherine close behind and slowly opened the door. Out sprang a male toy poodle! I was taken totally by surprise and instinctively slammed the door shut. Now, however, behind the door came distinct growling and barking. Catherine started crying.

"Mom, I'm afraid of that thing. I think it was going to bite me. Can we just keep it in the closet for now? Where did it come from? It's not ours, is it?"

I was confused. Why was some strange, mean dog locked in our closet? Then dad came upstairs. On his way out to the Shop he glanced at mom with a look that said "I told you so." Apparently he didn't want anything to do with this dog. Hunting dogs were more his type.

"Carl, don't open that door!" mom yelled. Just then Mike came home from school. He saw the three of us standing there with weird looks on our faces.

"What's going on?"

"There's a mean dog in the closet," I said.

"This closet?"

"Mike, you open it. I don't think it likes Carl and I don't want it to hurt Catherine," mom said. The dog was barking and scratching the door. Mike carefully opened the door and into his arms sprang this obnoxious, mean, curly-haired animal.

"Whoa, where did this come from?"

"Grandmother gave him to us as a gift. If we're going to keep him we all have to take care of him," mom said.

"What are we going to name him?" I asked.

"How about Mickey?" said Mike. The name stuck. Now we had a hyper toy poodle added to the already redlined household chaos mix. Maybe grandmother thought it would add some joy to our lives. I never totally got along with Mickey and tried to avoid him. Maybe he could sense he wasn't the right thing for our family. He was kind of a big pain. He crapped and peed all over the place and we forever had to clean up after him. Forget potty-training him. It didn't work. Then when his ass itched he'd rub his hind end up and down the hallway and into the living room. There were those perpetual shit streaks we occasionally had to deal with. Mike was the only one he seemed to like.

✝

Halloween was one of my favorite times. It was one of the few times I got to run around after dark in a kind of scary atmosphere. But I found out the hard way that fear isn't always amusing. In those days kids went trick-or-treating alone with their friends. It wasn't the protected process it is today where adults have to act as escorts.

The first truly frightening incident that happened to me in the Field was on a Halloween night. I dressed up as the Wolfman, one of my favorite monsters. Mom had laid my costume out on my bed like a prom tuxedo. As twilight approached I suited up and met some friends on the street corner. Off we went. We worked the houses, door to door, until we covered the whole neighborhood. Not everyone was nice. Some of the neighbors left their lights off which meant stay away. Those people were weird, mean, grumpy, or just didn't like kids. We didn't want their candy anyway.

We were on the last leg of a row of houses on the south side of the Field. It was after 10 and there weren't many trick-or-treaters left that we noticed, just me and my friend Hal Sargent. The rest of our friends went on home.

"Hey, Carl, it was really fun tonight. We had a great haul," said Hal.

"I know, one of our best Halloweens."

"Uuh…Carl…you want to cut through the Field and walk over to my house?"

I sensed Hal was a little bit afraid of having to walk back home totally alone. Now we'd have to go in opposite directions. I lived just down a few blocks on the street but Hal would have to go through the Field. That was the fastest way for him to get back to his impatiently waiting mother. The later he got back the madder she'd be. But he didn't want to walk through the Field alone at night.

"Hal, I have to get going. My mom said to be home no later than 10. It's about that now. What will we do when we get to your house anyway?" I said.

"My mom might let us stay up and watch a late movie. The Wasp Woman is on channel 6! Or we could watch that John Wayne movie on tonight."

That might be kind of cool, I thought. Then reality set in. I knew I couldn't stay. It would have been nice to spend the night and not have to walk back home alone but that wasn't going to happen either.

"I can't, Hal. My parents will be looking for me. And besides, we have to go to school tomorrow."

I actually wasn't sure if anyone would be home but I couldn't take a chance. I needed to get back quickly as well. Hal seemed desperate and was clearly trying to bribe me any way he could. He reached into his Halloween candy and pulled out three king-size Zero bars. My favorite.

"Will this change your mind?"

I looked hard at those Zero bars. God, I wanted them. I gazed up at the sky, then out at the dark, foreboding Field and then back at the Zero bars.

"Okay, you got a deal, but I can't stay at your place long, man."

So I took those Zero bars, tossed them into my bag, and nervously stepped into the creepy, dark Field. We just stood there on the dark edge of it like Dorothy, the Scarecrow, the Lion, and the Tin Man in *The Wizard of Oz* as they started their journey through the Haunted Forest. The Field held an eerie silence tonight. This would be my first time navigating it in the dark.

"Well, Hal, are you ready?"

"Yah, let's just get it over with."

"Okay, on the count of three: one, two, three!"

Away we went walking as fast as we could. We didn't say anything to each other but just looked and walked straight ahead. We weren't exactly sure where Hal's house was on the other side, but had a good idea of the general direction. We would recognize it more the closer we got to that general line of houses. We could barely see them from where we were. We would be navigating almost on blind dead reckoning but moved forward.

The more we ventured into the Field the darker it got. We were quietly ignoring our uneasy feeling and the fact that the air seemed to be getting heavier. I distinctly felt we weren't alone out here and I sensed Hal was feeling the same thing.

We quickened our pace and the straight line we started out with was quickly turning crooked. We were now panic-walking in some sort of weird diagonal direction and not toward our original destination. I didn't want to tell Hal but I started feeling we were being followed. I was afraid to turn around. We were now walking very rapidly — just short of a run. I didn't want to start running and panic Hal.

I'd lose him. Then his parents would somehow get involved and I'd be the bad guy. He'd start crying and I would have to explain it to his mother. All of sudden I heard Hal cry out.

"Ooohhhh, aahhhh!!!" he screamed.

I was frightened out of my mind, thinking something got hold of him. I still felt someone was close behind us. I had to stop! I had to turn around and see what happened! And it was completely dark!

"Hal, what happened? Are you okay?"

He didn't respond but I could see him lying on the ground. I put my candy bag down, went over to him, and discovered he'd walked right into a small tree stump and had tripped, twirled around like a ballerina, and had fallen down on his back. His candy was scattered all around him and the tree stump. I could see little bits and pieces of it in what faint moonlight there was. It would be impossible to gather it all up quickly. I kneeled down beside him.

"Hey, are you okay?" I asked.

"Yah, I'm okay, but I want to get out of here now." Hal nervously said.

"Okay, get up and let's get your candy together. Is there any at all left in your bag

"A little bit, I think, but so what? I don't care! Let's get out of here!" Hal hoarsely whispered back.

I helped him up and found his candy bag, or what was left of it. I knew there was still a lot of candy scattered all around but we were going to leave it and get moving. We continued our fast pace and finally hit the line of houses on Hal's side of the Field.

But to our horror we discovered that we had missed his house by quite a bit. Finally we realized where we'd come out and crept along the house lines toward Hal's house. At last we arrived in his back yard. We were in the Field for only about 10 minutes but it seemed like an eternity. Now Hal, knowing he was in the safety of his house, ran up to the back door, quickly opened it, and found his mother standing there.

"Hal, honey, you look flushed. It's about time you got home. Did you have a fun time trick-or-treating?"

"No, mom. I fell down. I walked into a tree stump and tripped in the Field."

"You're not hurt are you? You seem okay. Did you collect any candy?"

"A lot of it spilled out of my bag when I fell down. I don't care." Hal was angry.

"Carl, why don't you get along home now? You can go out the front door if you want."

"That's fine, Mrs. Sargent thank you." Then I wished her a Happy Halloween, which she took kind of funny. I saw her look at me weird as I headed for the door.

I walked out the front door of their house and snuck into their back yard. I stood there and wondered. All that candy is still out there, lying on the ground. It won't last long. The animals will take it by morning. I think I could find its location in the dark again. It's by that tree stump on the left side of the swing sets. There's no one out there...right? Be a big boy, Carl. Be a grownup. Make it fast. Run in. Scoop it up. And run out as fast as you can. I'm going for it! I then whispered a little prayer to St. Hubert of Liege, the Patron Saint of the Fear of Werewolves.

I timidly stepped out of the Sargent's back yard into the dark Field once again. Then I broke into a hard run. I ran as fast as I could. At last the fuzzy dark outline of the swing sets was in sight. As I approached the spot where the candy and tree stump were I thought I saw some shadows off to my right. I couldn't make out in the darkness exactly how many there were but one was enough for me. I thought I heard menacing laughing, too. It sounded like some creepy girl or girls trying to scare me, but I didn't think it was. Girls wouldn't be out here this late at night.

I started running even faster, trying not to spill the candy I already had. Here I was in the middle of the Field at night, and on Halloween, no less. And just for a pile of spilled candy. This was a surrealistic and terrifying situation. I contemplated simply running past the candy and getting out of there as fast as I possibly could. Finally, I got to the tree stump and the candy. I had to be careful so I didn't also trip and fall. I got to my knees and started looking down very closely and feeling the ground like someone who'd lost their glasses and couldn't see. I felt around, and around, and around.

I know it's here. Ahhhhh yes, there it is! I was relieved.

The lode was substantial. God, Hal dropped most of what he had! I quickly set my bag up next to the pile and started frantically scooping. I was scooping up candy, grass, dirt, twigs and who knows what else. I wouldn't get all of it but I would get most of it. I had finally corralled it all up in my bag. I didn't feel guilty taking Hal's spilled candy because he never did give me those Zero bars he promised.

I continued kneeling, catching my breath, when again I heard something. And this time I saw something move out of the corner of my eye. It was a shadow-type figure of some evil nature manifesting itself in the ever-so-faint moonlight.

Okay, now this is getting way too scary and real! Was this someone just passing through the Field close to me, or was this someone actually watching and following me? Whoever, whatever it was off several feet behind me just staring toward me.

I decided I wasn't going to stick around to find out. I oh so slowly got up off my knees with bags in hand. I was afraid to look in the direction of what I feared might be there. I had to quickly decide what direction would take me out the fastest. It would be toward the nearest bright lights.

I was going to start diverting myself away from these shadows and point myself where I needed to go. I would start out very slowly and then break in to a very fast run. To my horror the shadow figure, or whatever it was, started toward me at a fast pace.

There was more than one, I thought to myself in horror.

That was it. I started in a dead run toward Moreland Avenue on the west side of the Field, and the safety of the porch lights. It was difficult holding onto the now very heavy bag of candy. Much of it was spilling out over the top. But I ran as if my life depended on it. I ran as fast as I could but the shadows were closing in on me. Running ever faster, I heard them laugh like it was a big joke. I was praying that they would go away.

As I started to approach the porch lights, I looked behind me. Now I could make out two figures dressed as some weird clowns with masks. They were definitely bigger than me. Wasn't I supposed to be the monster? I had left my own mask way back by the tree stump but now it didn't matter. They weren't funny clowns, but evil ones. Were they after my candy? Were they after me? Did they just want to scare me? Were they human? My God, were they those two weird clown people I saw in the parking lot a while back?

As they chased me, I started to cry, but managed to keep running toward my destination. Finally, exiting the Field, I reached the sanctuary of the porch lights. My heart was beating so fast and irregular it sounded like popcorn popping. Would they continue to pursue me even here? Again, I looked behind me, but now didn't see anything but the eerie darkness of the Field.

Where did they go? God, I hope they'd stopped. Make them go away! I frantically thought.

I looked all around me and saw nothing. I appeared to be the only one left out in the whole neighborhood. I saw

67

no one. I'd stopped trying to catch my breath and wiping away the tears. I looked back again into the Field but couldn't see much in the pitch black.

I don't see them. And where did they go? Who were they? I still wasn't sure if I was being watched from some unknown place by some unknown entity out there. I didn't look toward the Field anymore. I walked as fast as I could back home.

✝

Thank God I reached my house. I was never so glad to get there. But something strange . . . a red, late-model Lincoln was just pulling out of the driveway. That car belonged to the man who sometimes took Catherine out for the evening. He was a Catholic priest. Mom was waiting for me.

"Did you have a good time tonight, Carl?"

"Yah, it was okay, mom. Can I just go to bed now?"

"Sure honey. Mike is in watching TV. You can watch it with him but don't stay up after that. You have school in the morning."

"Mom, who just left our house?"

"Oh, that was Father Jacobson. He just dropped off Catherine."

I didn't know whether to be confused or alarmed or both. Why wasn't dad taking her out?

I went into the bedroom in silence. I poured all the candy onto my bed for inventory. What a haul. But what really happened out there? I never found out and I never discussed it with anyone. That was the last time I went into or even near the Field by myself at night.

And what about that house I came home to? What about a house that bred nightmares and fighting between my mom and dad? Home could feel as bizarre and ghostly as the Field at night. A house can take on a character of its own and transmit that character to its inhabitants. Or do the inhabitants transmit character to the house?

I was so exhausted I fell right asleep, maybe because Mike was there, watching TV and I felt safe. Dad was still out of town, but I knew Mike could probably keep at bay whatever was in the Field out of our house that night.

The next morning the alarm clock went off like a freight train whistle.

"Hey man, get up. It's time to get ready for your pre-school." Mike shook me a little. "Mom's gonna get mad if she finds you lying in bed. And then she'll get mad at me because I didn't get you up. Hey, can I have a little of your candy? You did pretty good last night." I rolled over and looked at him like I just got out of the dryer with both my eyes and hair puffed up.

"Can you just give me a couple more minutes? Just two?"

"Two minutes! That's it." I rolled over and tried to rest but was so nervous about going over the two-minute mark I couldn't close my eyes.

I stood under the hot shower until my eyes opened all the way. I was still tired from last night's trauma. Mom put out some breakfast but I wasn't very hungry. Mike was waiting impatiently at the front door.

"Let's go. We can't be late or you know what the nuns will do to you. They're the enforcers, you know."

"I know, I know." Mike ran into a friend on his way and went on ahead. My friend John Binson was behind me and yelled for me to wait. He caught up with me. One more block and we'd walk right past the Field.

"Did you get much candy last night?" John asked.

"Not too bad. I got a whole big grocery sack full. You didn't do too bad either."

"You're not gonna believe what I heard last night," John said.

69

"What? Not about me is it?"

"No. Jody had one of her friends over for Halloween last night. You know that Kelly Johnson that's in her class.

"Yah, I think I do. What happened?"

"Well, she spent all last night at our house with Jody. When we got back from trick-or-treating they were still up watching TV so we sat with them for little bit. Jody and Kelly were talking and someone cut a fart! Man, it was Kelly!" John couldn't contain his laughter and I couldn't contain my shock. This changed everything.

"What? Wait a minute. Girls don't fart. There's no way." I was seriously troubled.

"No, man. I swear to God she did. I wouldn't have believed it either but I heard it. Rufio heard it, too. You can ask him. I guess she was laughing so hard at some dumb thing Jody said she couldn't hold it in. She was laughing and farting at the same time! It was so loud I know mom and dad heard it too."

"I can't believe it! I mean, gross!"

"And then Jody went and….." But I started tuning John out. We were passing the Field. I gazed out at it as my pace quickened.

"Hey, man, why are you walking so fast?" I stopped and stared out at last night's scene. It looked so normal in the morning sunlight.

"Okay, so Jody's friend farted real loud. Then what happened?"

But John interrupted, "What just happened? What did you see? You just stopped and looked out there. What were you looking at?"

"I'm not sure. It happened last night. It was weird."

"You mean Halloween? Were you out *there* last night? On Halloween? Even we don't do that."

"Billy, Scott, Hal and I went trick-or-treating together. It was getting late and Scott and Billy had to go home. Then it was just me and Hal. We were right about here and Hal was afraid to cross the Field alone to get home. So I said I'd go with him because he promised me three Zero bars. But Hal walked into that tree stump because it was hard to see in the dark. You know the one out I'm pointing to out there. We were walking really fast. I thought someone was following us. When Hal hit the stump he lost a lot of his candy. It just spilled out on the ground. When I got him back home I was thinking about all that candy just lying out there. I decided to go back after it.

"You did? Oh, that was crazy."

"I know. I've never been in the Field at night. Anyway, I found the candy and scooped it into my bag as fast as I could. But then it really felt like something weird was out there. I could kind of see someone weird close to me."

"Wow. Let's get out of here," John said. "It's scaring me now, even here in the morning. Can you tell me the rest of it later? We have to get to class or Sister Carabella will nail us to that big pine tree."

"OK, but don't tell anyone about the candy and especially not Hal."

We walked through the front door of St. Micaelis. I needed to forget about last night. I'd never do something like that again, even for candy.

CHAPTER 5: DEUS SERVO MEUS MATRIS

THE JOHNNY ANGEL car radio story three chapters ago now brings me to my mother, Madeline. I loved her. I felt terrible for her. I cried for her. I praised her and I prayed for her. I desperately wanted to help her but I couldn't. Back in the early '60s, when everything was changing and our family was struggling to find sanity, I couldn't even save myself. Every time I hear the song "I Was Born A Woman," by Sandy Posey, it reminds me of her.

My mother was fundamentally a good woman trying to survive in what was back then a very male world. She was desperately trying to raise her remaining children at home as her marriage and husband's financial support crumbled. Born in the northeast into a very hardcore Irish Catholic family, she was tossed onto the Catholic bandwagon from the start. She was strong and conservative. She was one of seven children raised by a fiercely devout Irish Catholic mother, my grandmother, who reminded me of Auntie Em from *The Wizard of Oz*.

I loved my grandmother. She was a great cook and knew how to keep secrets better than anyone. Her political Christian modus operandi was to have a *Bible* in one hand and a poker in the other. What was unusual was that she was a policewoman in New England and then in Bridgeport. She and my grandfather moved to Iowa in the early '30s during the Great Depression when he lost his job there. My grandfather found a job at a silk factory in Bridgeport. Grandmother worked there too until 1943, then she became a policewoman. Silk was a big commodity during World War II and the work was plentiful. A housekeeper called Deilia took care of their seven kids.

Italian cooking was one of her specialties. She'd lived in an Italian neighborhood while they were in New England. She was an Irish woman who had become a great Italian cook.

Mom's early years were relatively calm and uneventful. She went to the local Catholic grade school. After graduating she worked at the Iowa Bell phone company as a secretary-receptionist. Somewhere in this time period she met my dad. Where and how they met remains one of the great Sorrowful Mysteries of the Rosary. They must have met in 1941 because my older brother Lanny was born in the early 1940s. Whether or not that was an accident or not planned we'll never know. But they were married in haste and before my dad was shipped overseas during World War II.

No two people could have been more different. Mom was very conservative and like her mother had a forceful personality. But the primary conflict, in the early years of their marriage anyway, was the fact that my mother was Catholic and my dad wasn't. My grandmother had a fit about that. God forbid a non-Catholic should sneak into the henhouse and steal one of her prize hens! Later, under duress, dad converted to Catholicism. And what a good Catholic he made, for a little while anyway.

Catholic upbringing permeated every cell of my mother's being, and for many years, mine, too. Most all family actions and decisions were seen and made through the Catholic prism. Whether she was an innocent victim of the intense psychological upbringing or Catholic views became her own preferences in life I still don't know.

In the late '50s she worked in the St. Censurius High School cafeteria. The school principal at the time was Father Jacobson. They eventually developed a strong friendship. I got to know him too, more than I wanted.

One of my very first memories of my mom was in the very early 1960s when she called from the hospital after she gave birth to my youngest sister Catherine.

"Carl it's your mother, she's on the phone and wants to talk to you." Dad pushed the telephone toward me.

"Hi, mom. Are you okay?"

"Yes, Carl, I'm fine. Are you behaving for your dad?"

I weighed my response carefully. If I told her the truth I'd piss her off. I certainly couldn't tell her about the toilet paper I overloaded the toilet with a couple of days ago after doing something no one in the house wanted to talk about. So I went with the standard, expedient response.

"Yah, I am."

"It's yes, I am. And by the way, you have a new younger sister."

"What does she look like?"

"You'll see her when I come home."

"Did you name her yet?"

"No, did you have something in mind?"

I thought to myself, good God, she's asking me? Why? I would have suggested something way out there like Ginger, Sheila or Tammy. Those were my favorite names at the time. But I knew they weren't Catholic enough.

"I don't know yet, mom."

Since I couldn't come up with anything serious she said, "Okay, we'll see later. You be good and I'll be home soon."

"Okay, mom, goodbye."

"Goodbye, Carl. I love you." I gave the phone back to my dad. Dad lowered his voice and they continued their conversation. That was my cue to leave the room.

I wasn't sure why she was in the hospital at all. Maybe she went there to meet the stork. I didn't know. All I knew was she had to go away for a while. Then she magically returned with a new female family member who, incidentally, was brought home from that hospital by a Catholic priest. Why didn't dad bring them home? That didn't make sense to me. But back then Catholic priests had a high degree of unquestioned carte blanche.

My sister was baptized by that same Catholic priest. I wasn't at the baptismal service but I ran to the door to greet mom and dad when they returned.

"Well, how did it go? Is she okay? Did she get hypnotized?"

"In a manner of speaking, Carl, yes," dad chuckled. Mom gave dad a very dirty look.

"Carl, the word is baptized. *Not* hypnotized. Don't ever use that word again."

Only a few weeks later she was staffing the money table at the Ice Cream Social at St. Micaelis Parish playground. She had on a green dress and was wearing white pearls. I was so proud of her and glad she was my mother.

✝

I was always riding around in the car with her. She was a nomad. Running to someone's house here, shopping here, dropping off something here, another errand on the other side of town. I got to know most of Bridgeport really well that way. I waited in the car a lot. I waited in the car in every parking lot in town at almost every time of the day. It was usually my decision to stay in the car. Mom seemed to get her business done faster without me tagging along. But I didn't understand why she had to do this all the time. Anyway.....

One Saturday the order came down without warning. "Carl, get in the car."

"Mom, Rufio is coming over soon," I whined. I was hoping I wouldn't have to go on yet another endless round of errands on a Saturday. Rufio and I were supposed to go target shooting with his new toy gun.

"Call and tell him you have to leave with your mother. He can come over later this afternoon if he wants." She was very casual about all this but I was despondent.
Rufio's line was busy so I ran the half block to his house with the bad news. I explained about mom's errands and asked, "Do you wanna to come over later this afternoon?" Rufio paused. "Let me think about it. You know you did this last month." He had kind of a sour expression on his face. But he was right as I was probably running errands with her then too.

"I know, but it's not my fault. You can talk to my mom. I really want to see your new gun."

"When you get back home just call me and I'll try to be here."

Mom was waiting in the car with the motor running. Her hands were on the steering wheel and she was staring straight ahead.

"What took you so long?" She didn't even look at me.

"I ran over to Rufio's house to tell him we couldn't play today."

"Get your seat belt on."

And we were off.

"Mom, where are we going?" I dared to ask. I had noticed we were heading toward my grandmother's house and St. Censurius Church and Rectory, which were in very close proximity. St. Censurius High School and St. Angeles Academy were in the general Catholic education complex as well.

This was where all my older siblings went to school. I assumed I would one day attend here. It was also where the mysterious Father Jacobson resided behind the heavy, medieval, wooden doors in the rectory. He was the superintendent of the high school.

"We're going to the St. Censurius Rectory. I want you to run up to the side door and drop off an envelope for

Father Jacobson. But be sure to say that to whoever answers the door. Don't just say Father. Say it's for Father Jacobson," mom said. There was an insistent tone in her voice.

She handed me the sealed envelope. I squinted from the bright sun and looked straight ahead. If she didn't tell me what was in the envelope I certainly wasn't going to ask. It really didn't matter anyway, or did it? She pulled her station wagon up to the side door of the rectory. I ran out with the envelope in hand and knocked on the foreboding wooden door. A few seconds later it slowly opened and a kind, older lady answered.

"May I help you, young man?" she asked in a sweet, polite tone.

"This is for Father Jacobson," I said. As I handed her the envelope she looked around, wanting to see who brought me. Although she didn't say anything, I knew it was possible she'd seen my mom's car parked a little way down the street. Then she looked back at me with the envelope in her hand.

"Thank you," she said with some abruptness. I was curtly dismissed as she closed the door. I ran back to the car.

"Did you say to give it to Father Jacobson?" mom asked.

"Mom, yes," I responded with an ever-so-faint tone of impatience.

✝

Next stop was the house of my grandmother and grandfather, always a welcome refuge. I always felt a sense of peace around them. She and mom started their usual mother-daughter conversation, so my grandfather asked if I wanted to help him take the trash down into the basement. It was a creepy place with a lot of old boxes full of stuff I liked to peek at. I wasn't allowed to go down there alone.

There was the old, gigantic, coal-fired furnace, an imposing, ancient, fiery thing I was afraid to get near. It made a lot of spooky noises. My grandfather burned the paper trash in it. He also sharpened knives down there. That's also where he hid the Old Grand Dad bourbon back behind a stud in the wall. But it was relatively easy to see with its bright orange label.

"Granddad, what's that?" I asked, pointing up to the odd location of the bottle.

"What are you pointing to, Carl?"

I continued to point at the bourbon. The orange label intrigued me.

"Well Carl, it's kind of like Geritol. You know the healthy blood booster your uncle Harold takes?"

"Ooohhhh." Geritol, sure, that makes perfect sense. Yah, I see Uncle Harold taking that sometimes." I now felt much more educated about other alternate formulations of Geritol.

I helped granddad bring three bags of trash down for the furnace.

"Carl, I'll hold the door if you throw those bags into the fire."

"Well, okay but we won't catch fire will we?"

"Of course not. I'm right here watching," he laughed.

He opened the heavy iron door and I peered into the flames. I carefully tossed the bags into the inferno. The flames got hotter and more flamboyant. As the reflection of the flames danced in my eyes I was transfixed, staring into the jaws of hell.

Trudging upstairs I turned around and looked at the monstrous furnace with its huge, protruding air tubing. It looked like a huge, fire-breathing octopus.

Back in the kitchen I admired my grandmother's freshly-made sugar cookies. I could eat one after the other like potato chips. She was one of the best cooks on the planet.

"Carl, do you want to take a few of them with you?"

"Mom, would it be okay?"

"Yes, go ahead. Mom, can you wrap some up for Carl?"

"Why of course!" Grandmother said winking at me.

As we left, my grandmother said, "Goodbye, Carl. We love you. Make sure you take good care of your mother."

I would painfully find out in later years exactly what she meant by that. Mom and I moved on toward the next errand stop. I had just finished brushing the cookie crumbs off my lap when I realized, with utter dread, where our next stop would be.

Our next stop was the unique clothing store, Jane Bryant. It catered to hard-to-fit women, but my mom liked it for the styles. Because of this, you'd see a lot of funny, strange-looking people in there. This was always a killer errand and one that could really get me in trouble if I wasn't careful. It also typically was where my mother would spend a lot of time. As we pulled into the parking lot I started to moan softly, knowing what lay ahead of me. The parking lot was full and we had to park in the very back. That was a bad omen. It was clear this would be another long, drawn-out affair.

The atmosphere was a like the movie set of *The Blob* combined with Cirque de Soleil. It was a funky arrangement unlike any other clothing store. Shopping was like being on the trading floor of the New York Stock Exchange. I had to stand up and wait with the rest of the angry, disgruntled husbands, kids, and other women. It was like standing in a room of wall-to-wall people listening to a lecture on dichlorodiphenyltrichloroethane by a monotone professor and you have to pee real bad but aren't allowed to leave the room. They never had enough chairs for the people that just waited around.

Here's how the shopping process at Jane Bryant worked. You sat at a large, rectangular table and browsed through catalogs. When you saw something you liked, you filled out a slip of paper, gave it to the sales lady, who gave it to someone else, who went back to the warehouse and brought it back in a box. You could reject it or try it on. And if you liked it and the price was right, you bought it. This cycle went around and around and around.

With mom it took a good couple of hours, going through more and more clothing catalogs. I didn't own a watch and there was no clock. I painfully watched the sunlight move across the furniture in the room like time-lapse photography. And in my mind, I turned the coat rack off to my left into a sundial and watched the sun's shadow move across it. I was careful not to pout or let mom see me make faces. That turned an innocent, boring, routine situation into something volatile. The man next to me was getting very impatient, sighing and talking to himself. He'd shoot me disgusted and sympathetic looks every now and then. Oh, wait a minute! Is she getting ready to leave? Yes! I got off this time with only about two-and-a-half hours, thankfully.

I helped her carry two boxes out to the car. "Where are we were going next?" I hoped it would be home.

"I have to return something at Sayers. After that we're going home."

Inside my head I did a two-step, end-over-end, Russian Irish Slovenian African acrobatic yee-haaa jig. Outside I gave her a calm and plain stare.

L.S. Sayers department store was another one of her favorites. It even had a metal charge card that my mom called a charge-a-plate you could use like money. It was one of the first consumer credit card systems.

We parked and mom said, "Carl, you wait here while I run in."

I felt like a trapped weasel.

"Oh, and make sure the doors are locked."

She got out and I locked the doors so she could see me do it. Alone in the car I sat. How will I entertain myself this time? Oh wait!! She left the keys in the car. I can play the radio. But what if runs the battery dead? I would be dead too.

It was getting hot so I rolled the window down for some fresh air. As I sat there with my right elbow on the arm rest, pulling at my upper lip, I got an uncomfortable feeling. It felt like I was being watched. I did a 360-degree tactical scan of my surroundings. Nothing but parked cars.

Then something odd caught my attention in my rear side-view mirror. A weird man stared back at me. On his face was a bizarre grin. He was looking directly at me!! I turned away from the mirror and stiffened.

My God! Someone is watching me!

I stared straight ahead, hoping, praying it would go away. I sat there for what seemed like hours, afraid to look in the mirror. I was stiff and getting sore. I glanced in the mirror again. Oh, thank God. It's gone! I relaxed. But when I glanced out the car window I couldn't believe what I saw.

Directly to my right on a bench not 20 feet away was a midget staring straight at me and laughing! I jerked my head back and stared straight ahead, petrified. What was he doing there? And where's mom? I think it was the same person who was looking at me in the car mirror.

What made things worse was the fact that my car window was down all the way. If I could simply close it that would help, but I was afraid to move.

I decided to try. I slowly moved my right hand toward the window handle. I looked out the right window again. Now the midget was standing up and still looking at me with that weird smile. Danger was staring me in the face. This was worse than being caught by Mrs. Gertelwitch, much worse. I kept searching for mom, hoping she'd come out. And there she finally was. Come on mom, HURRY!! Relief and rescue were finally within sight. As mom started to open her car door, sweet relief rushed into my soul. Feeling more confident and safe, I looked out the right window. To my horror the midget now was walking toward me with that awful smile!

"Mom there's a midget after us! He's coming toward the car!"

"What in the world are you talking about, Carl?"

"Look out the window! LOOK!" I screamed. The midget inched closer.

"Who is that? Oh! Did you ask him over here? What does he want? Have you been talking to him?"

"How do I know, mom? NO! We need to get out of here!"

"Does he want something with you?" She was now quite panicked herself.

"I hope not and please, mom, let's don't stay here to find out!"

Mom, as unnerved as I was, quickly started the car as the midget crept closer. Mom attempted to pull out of the parking spot. But another car was blocking us.

"Mom, why can't we move?"

"I'm doing my best, Carl, but the car in front of me is stuck because the car in front of him is trying to get out. And he can't move because there's too much traffic on the street!"

"But mom…"

"Be quiet Carl! I can't think with you yelling!"

We were both close to panic. The midget was approaching just a few feet from my window. I turned toward it.

"Carl, don't look at it!! Don't look at it!! Don't look into its eyes!!" mom screamed.

It now stood within inches of my face. I couldn't take my eyes from its hypnotic gaze. I dumbly stared straight at it. My Catholic grade-school education really kicked in. I instinctively started to pray, "Hail Mary, full of grace, the Lord is with thee; blessed art thou amongst women, and blessed is the fruit of thy womb, Jesus. Holy Mary, Mother of God, pray for us sinners....."

"Carl, what are you doing? My God, don't let it touch you!" Mom started honking the horn at the poor man in front of us who was completely unaware of the utter chaos behind him.

I couldn't respond. I was mesmerized by the midget's stare and frightening smile. I couldn't even finish my Hail Mary. Suddenly it raised its right hand and pointed its index finger at me, twirling it clockwise about six inches from my nose, then five inches, then four inches, then three, then two, then one. What is it going to do?? My eyes crisscrossed as I fixated on his finger.

"Carl, roll the window up *now*!! We're getting out of here!" Our hearts were pounding like jackhammers.

Mom's continued screaming finally snapped me out of the midget's trance. It was about to put its finger right on my nose. Suddenly the parking lot logjam opened up. Mom sped out of the parking lot like we just robbed a bank. The resulting G forces yanked my head so far back I saw the car ceiling. As we turned onto the street, I looked back at that frightening little guy who was still staring at our car.

"Carl what was that all about? Why did he come up to the car toward you like that?"

"Mom, I don't know! Maybe he thought I was cute and wanted to ask me to the dance at the K of C this Saturday night. I don't know!"

"That's not funny! You could have been hurt. From now on you're not staying in the car. You're coming in with me."

Was this my fault? Or the midget's? Right then Leslie Gore's "It's My Party" played on the radio. I could certainly identify with the line "cry if I want to."

At home I forgot all about calling Rufio. I silently went to my bedroom and sat on the bed, traumatized from that day's fantastic and surprising midget assault on me and mom.

✝

My mother was a very beautiful woman. She wore white pearls a lot and looked great in them. A good spanking was part of her disciplinary regimen. It could come quickly and without warning. Events at the dinner table were always unpredictable. The least little thing could trigger a fight between mom and dad. Sometimes I acted silly around them to keep the atmosphere light. One evening a few months after the tragic midget incident we were all at the dinner table.

"Carl, can you pass the roast beef?" dad asked.

"Sure, dad, hold on." I picked up the heavy, unbalanced platter with both hands. But it started to wobble up and down and left to right. I knew I was in trouble but wanted to save face.

"Carl, be careful. Go slow." Dad's tone was soft yet stern.

I tried to balance the platter and keep it moving across the table. My brothers and sisters, instead of offering to help, just sat there as if watching a slapstick comedy where the main character is about to fall on his ass. I extended my quivering arms ever so carefully toward my dad's outstretched arms. By now the gravy was leaking over the edge of the plate and onto my mom's cherished lace tablecloth.

"Carl, please be careful," she said in a low shriek.

"Uuhhh anybody, can you get up and get this?"

"Don't move, Carl. I'm coming!" Dad jumped out of his chair and started to run around to my side of the table. But the platter full of roast beef and gravy tilted over forty-five degrees to the port side and most of the roast beef and gravy covered the table and the large bowl of mashed potatoes. If you wanted gravy on your potatoes you sure as hell had it now.

"*Shit!*" I instinctively blurted out. KAPOW to the right side of my face came my mother's hand. It felt like someone took a pizza paddle and hit me in the cheek. After a few seconds of recovery I looked in shock at the mess, then back at my mom.

"Don't you *ever* say that word again here or anywhere else!"

"Mom, I'm sorry. I don't know why I said that." I was more upset from the slap than the humiliation of ruining the family meal. This time I would have welcomed a shot of Novocain in my jaw.

"Do you want me to clean this up?" I was crying.

"Carl, we'll clean this up." Dad tried to sound soothing. "Just go to your room and I'll come talk to you in a little bit."

I sat on my bed awaiting further chastisement. Dad came in.

"How's your face? You took quite a crack there." I heard disgust in his voice. Was that tone meant for him or my mother?

"I'm okay now, dad. I'm sorry about spilling the food and more about what I said."

"Well I'm not going to say any more. I think you got the message from your mother. I thought we'd go see a movie this weekend." I could tell he was trying to dilute a stressful situation.

"That sounds good, dad."

"Okay, we'll check the paper tomorrow. In the meantime go finish your dinner."

"Thanks, dad. I'm starving."

"But there's one more thing. Can I ask you a question, just between us men?"

"Yah, dad, what is it?"

"Have you talked at all to this Father Jacobson that keeps coming around when I'm gone? Have you seen him around the house yourself? Has Mike said anything to you about him?" I could tell he was really concerned.

"No, dad. He never talks about him. All I know is he comes around at night sometimes and takes Catherine out to places, but I'm not sure where. He seems to come when no one else is around. He picks her up and brings her back later. I've come home a couple of times now and have seen him just leaving. I know he drives a dark-red Lincoln. Why are you asking? Is something wrong?" I, of course, knew because of the increased level of tension, suspicion, and fighting between my parents over the past couple of years. I was also worried if this little conversation would reach my mother. The ramifications of that would be quite frightening.

"Well, I've heard a few things from other people. That is all I can say now."

I was aware of Father Jacobson's growing presence in our home. I was unclear where he was from or why he was around. He had a knack for showing up when dad was out of town. And of course no one offered any explanation. All mom would occasionally say is he's a good friend of the family, and yes, he was there to take Catherine out for the evening. But no one ever talked about it.

When I could I liked to ride my bike over to the Shop where my dad had his business. It wasn't all that far from our house. These days, he seemed to be spending more time there, or on the road at job sites, than at home.

CHAPTER 6: THE SHOP

I KNEW my dad for barely seven years of my life, from 1960 to 1967. That was nowhere near long enough, which I considered another one of the Five Sorrowful Mysteries of my family Rosary. I was close to him and loved him very much. I could relate to him and I think he related to me. I always had lots of fun with him. His mysterious, gradual, then final departure left deep psychological scars on me for years to come. Many, many unanswered questions linger to this day.

My dad's upbringing and general background are shrouded in obscurity. His name was Dean. Born in 1918, he grew up in inner-city Bridgeport. He was an unassuming man of average height and build. I wasn't sure where he went to school and knew almost nothing of his parents or family. The exception was when we went down to see his mother in southern Iowa. She had a pond way out in the back part of her property that I loved to play around. She also made the best fried squash leaves I've ever had.

Dad made a great Catholic, at least for a few years. He converted in order to marry my mom. He dutifully went to church with me, in the beginning, and he even coached the St. Micaelis table tennis team.

The Shop is where my dad had his office and irrigation business, the Automatic Field Irrigation Company, one block from our home. He simply called it the Shop, so that's what we called it, too. It was in a small, unassuming house converted to an office up front and a work area in the back, with tools, work tables, power equipment and general outdoor irrigation contractor supplies. He had irrigation projects all over Iowa, Wisconsin, Oklahoma, Illinois, and beyond. In the back was a small yard where he parked his utility work vehicles. In that yard stood an apple tree that had the tastiest Golden Delicious apples I've ever had.

The Shop was synonymous with my dad. He spent a lot of time there, as well as on the road. I constantly rode my bicycle over to the Shop to see dad. I loved to visit his job sites. He liked to golf, hunt and fish but not always for animals. I loved him as much as any son could. He was fun to be with, made funny faces and had great stories. And he had a spontaneity I liked.

One afternoon Mike and I were riding around in his work van.

"You know I was talking to Dwayne down in Williamsville last week and you know what he told me?" dad asked out of the blue.

"What?" Mike and I asked. Dwayne was one of his friends and was always part of interesting and bizarre situations. He owned and worked a farm in southern Iowa, where dad's mother still lived. Dad had to turn down the radio, but I was torn between the story he was about to tell and the song he was about to turn off— Sonny James' "Young Love." He was a big lover of country music.

"Dwayne told me he found one of his cattle dead out in the north field."

"Wow! What happened? Did a wolf kill it?" asked Mike. I like the way my dad looked into the rear view mirror to make sure I wasn't left out of the conversation.

"He doesn't know. They're still trying to figure it out. The strange thing was that whatever killed it didn't try to eat it, which is very unusual."

"So it probably wasn't a wolf, coyote or big dog was it?" Mike asked.

"No, they don't think so because of the way the animal was killed."

"Dad, what do you think it was? How was it killed?"

"Well, they really don't know. The cow had several sharp incision-type cuts and its heart was missing. It was taken clean out and hardly any blood was on the ground."

"Dad, what does incision mean?"

"That means it was cut very neatly and cleanly, which a wild predator-type animal wouldn't and couldn't do."

"Well, dad, who or what do you think did it?" Mike's eyes were now as wide as the headlights on our van.

Just then we felt a big bump at the back of the van. The person behind was going too fast and hit us. Well, that was just enough to distract dad from the rest of the story just when it was getting really good.

"Dammit, I don't believe this!!" Dad looked angrily in the rear view mirror.

He and the poor other fellow pulled over to the side of the road and he and dad talked. When dad came back he was totally on another plane. He started up the car and drove in silence. I wanted him to finish. I decided to open my mouth.

"Well dad, can you finish the story?"

"Not right now, Carl. I'm dropping you and Mike off at the house then I'm heading back to the Shop." Mike and I never did hear the end of that tale, though later on I read about such incidents in the newspapers. It had something to do with farm animal mutilations.

One time dad and his right-hand man J.A. Filctar were going to drive dad's Ford Thunderbird sedan all the way to Wyoming on a hunting trip. I wanted to go.

"Dad, are you sure I can't come?" I whined.

"Carl, no. You're right in the middle of school and that is the most important thing for you right now."

"But why couldn't you wait till I'm out of school?"

"This is the only time J.A. and I can go together because of the business. We're very slow for the next few weeks. Besides, it might be a little dangerous for a boy your age and you certainly aren't old enough to handle a gun. I promise we'll go on hunting trips and even go back to Wyoming when you're older. And I'll bring you a surprise. J.A. and I will be back before you know it."

About two weeks later, just before bedtime, I was in bed listening to Terry Stafford's "Suspicion" on the radio when Mike came bursting into the room. "Hey man, get up! Dad's back and you're not going to believe what he has!" Mike practically screamed. Mom was up, too. I ran up and hugged him. But I sensed mom wasn't too thrilled.

"Hey Carl, remember that surprise I promised you?" Dad looked the happiest I'd seen in a long time.

"Yah, I do. What is it?"

"You're not going to believe it, Carl," mom said. Even she sounded excited and a bit shocked. Dad led me out to the front porch. Tied to the front hood of his Ford Thunderbird was a dead deer. Tied to the top was another one. Tied to the rear hood was a third deer. I was utterly flabbergasted and just stood there with my mouth gaping wide open. Mom was doing the same thing. It was the coolest thing I had ever seen in my life. Dad seemed larger than life.

"Wow, dad, how did you get them all back here like that?"

"Well," said J.A., "Your dad and I had some help in Wyoming and we got 'em lifted up onto the car and tied 'em down good."

"And you drove all the way back from Wyoming like that?" Mike asked.

"Isn't Wyoming way out west, dad?"

"It's pretty far out there and yes we did." Just then J.A.'s wife Ruth came over. She looked like she'd just seen a UFO touch down.

"My land, honey, did you drive all the way back with those on the car? It's a wonder you didn't wreck." A few neighbors came out to see what all the commotion was all about.

"Well, honey, we almost did wreck a couple of times. We took turns driving and here we are," said J.A. in a matter-of-fact tone of voice. He nervously laughed and scratched his chin. Ruth's facial expression indicated she didn't think that was funny.

"We're going back to the Shop and get these hung up. It won't take too long, will it Dean?" J.A. asked.

"No, we'll need only an hour or so. Mike, you and Carl get back to bed. I'll be back soon. Madeline, I'll see you in the morning."

"Well, I can't sleep now," I said.

"Neither can I," agreed Mike. "But let's go back in. Dad will tell us all about it in the morning." We trudged back to the bedroom and kept talking in the dark.

"Do you believe they drove all the way back from Wyoming with those deer tied up on the car like that?"

"I know. I can't wait to hear the stories. I can't wait to tell everyone at school."

"I'm glad tomorrow is Saturday and we don't have to get up right away."

We finally drifted off to sleep. When I opened my eyes the next morning I heard dad on the phone, telling someone about his hunting trip. Sounded like a business acquaintance. Mom had gone somewhere with Catherine. Mike and I wanted to hear as much of the story as we could.

"Well, are you both all rested?" dad asked.

"Yah, we want to hear the rest of the deer story. With his cup of coffee, dad motioned us to follow him into the living room.

"Well, guys, there's really not a whole lot to tell. J.A. and I got into the hunting lodge in Caspar, Wyoming, about 10 on Sunday night. There were two other hunting parties besides us. We figured that was the best way to go deer hunting out there. The lodge had hunting guides who worked with us. They knew the area and where the best hunting was. I've always wanted to go out west for a big hunting trip."

"Did you see any bears, dad?"

"Yes, we did see a couple of them but they were far away and didn't bother us. Also, we rode horses."

"That is so neat. You rode horses!"

"Well, we were up in the mountains and on that terrain that's the best way to get around. Our guide was on horseback and he knew the trails and deer paths really well."

"It was really funny. One of the first deer I saw was about 100 yards away and I decided to take a shot at it. I put my rifle up to my shoulder and got the deer sighted in. It started to move and I followed it with my scope. It walked to my right and I kept following it, when all of a sudden there's J.A. in my sights. Well, of course I couldn't shoot him. I had to put the gun down." The three of us started laughing really hard. It really wasn't funny but it was the way dad told it.

"You mean you almost shot J.A.?"

"No, not really. But I missed one heck of a good deer shot. It was a big one. But it got better. And J.A. apologized for being in the way!" Dad laughed hysterically. And so did we. His laugh was contagious.

"The next day the guide kept pointing off to our right. I put the scope out there and a huge buck stood out at about 150 yards. It was that big one with the antlers tied on the top of the car. I had to move before the buck heard or smelled us. I hoisted the rifle and got it in my sights."

"So, dad, J.A. didn't want it. That was nice of him," I said.

"Well, yes, but here was the tradeoff. If I got that buck, he got the next two does. He'd get more venison, but I'd get the trophy antlers."

"What is venison?" I asked.

"It's what they call deer meat. Right, dad?"

"Right. Anyway, it took a few seconds to get the deer in my sights. I had to aim steady and quick because the wind was starting to really blow. Well, I squeezed the trigger and got the shot off. The deer went right down."

"Good shot, dad!" I yelled.

"I was lucky because I probably wouldn't have gotten a second one."

"We cleaned it and threw it over our pack horse. J.A. got his two later that day and the next morning. So he was pretty happy, too. He loves deer meat. We're going to go hang them in the Shop, then take them to someone who'll cut them into deer steaks, burger, and roasts and make some gloves out of the skin."

"I've never had deer meat before," said Mike.

"Dad, so you can ride a horse? How did you do?" I asked.

"It's not that hard once you get the hang of it. They were pretty well trained. And the deer meat is good. It's a little drier than the meat at the store. I think you'll like it but I'm not sure your mother will."

"Good, more for us." I smiled.

"Yes, that's right Kingosabee!" said dad, tickling me.

"What did people on the highway say when they saw the deer tied to your car?" Mike asked.

"We got a lot of stares and honks from truck drivers. The funniest thing was when we stopped to eat. We pulled over at this diner outside of Kansas City around 8 at night. The place was crowded. J.A. always said if a place is crowded it means the food is good. We could the see people inside staring at us. A bunch of 'em got up and came outside. Then the owner ran outside in his apron and ran over to us. 'How are you boys tonight?' he asked.

'Wow, you got a load there! Just follow me over here, gentlemen! This way! This way!'"

He guided us to the very front of the restaurant and told us to park there and cut the lights. He shook his head in total awe. Then more people came out to see. We stood around for a while and they took pictures and asked us all kinds of questions. But all I could think about was going to the bathroom! Well, finally everyone had seen enough and we all went inside. The owner gave us our meal on the house!" Dad laughed and laughed.

"Dad, what does on the house mean?" I asked.

"It means they give it to you for free."

"Wow! That's neat! On the house! That sounds cool!"

"So, anyway, people kept coming over, wanting to know about the deer hunt and our driving all the way back to Iowa with them tied on the hood. You'd have thought J.A. and I were Carl Newman and Rock Hudson." Dad kept laughing. Mike and I did too.

Dad telling that deer story was one of my happiest times with him. His eyes had a twinkle. And we ate deer meat for the next six damn months. However, after he and J.A. took the deer over to the Shop, dad did not come home that night.

†

Thankfully, I had fallen asleep quickly. Sometime during the night I started to dream vividly. Dreams can reflect a macabre version of conscious life experiences and one's mental states, or a reaction to those states. I dreamed I was on the living room sofa watching TV. A strange, almost evil feeling filled the room, then the entire house. As this feeling increased in intensity I started to freeze both physically and mentally. Whatever it was had completely taken over my immediate environment. I could now sense someone or something was in the kitchen. The light in the dining room was on but very dim and the rest of the house was dark. The evil feeling became more intense. All of a sudden an eerie light emanated from the kitchen. It was accompanied by a weird, low sound of half music and some other sound I couldn't identify but scared me. I was afraid to look. Whatever was in there wasn't one of my family. It didn't feel human. The show I had been watching on television was now forgotten.

I was getting the impression it was getting ready to walk out of the kitchen. It did. A skeleton ever so slowly walked out of the kitchen. It didn't look at me but walked straight ahead with a wicked smile that was meant for me. It knew I was out on the sofa and knew the slower it walked the more frightened I would be. It was white with a sinister, blue-black hue, and carried some sort of box or small chest in its hands. I just saw it from the waist up as its legs, if it had legs, were hidden behind the sofa where I lay terrified and motionless. It walked ever so slowly and deliberately into the dining room.

Then all of a sudden it turned off the dining room light and with an evil laugh, ran toward the basement door and down the steps. The basement door then quickly and on its own shut behind it. Everything happened very slowly at first then very fast. For the first time in my life I knew the feeling of evil.

I woke suddenly, terrified, and looked at the clock. It was 2 am and of course still dark outside. What was real? My bedroom still held an uncomfortable atmosphere. Only mom, Mike, Catherine and I were in the house. I tapped Mike's bunk bed below.

"Carl, what do you want?"

"I just wanted to see if you were there."

"Well, yah, I'm here. Now go back to sleep!"

"Okay, sorry Mike." It was worth the price of waking him up. At least I wasn't alone, for now.

From then on I was afraid to ever go into the basement alone again. What was that scary creature? I didn't even want to guess. Did it roam around the house when I couldn't see or feel it? Was it watching me? Did it walk into my bedroom at night when I was sleeping? Why did it go downstairs?

A couple weeks later I made the mistake of telling Mike. To my horror, he confirmed everything. He said *that* was Sakers, the monster that lived in the basement with Keylock. He always reminded me about Sakers and Keylock being real for a long time after that. I pretended I didn't believe him. But I was never sure he didn't believe it himself.

✝

One Friday afternoon I came home from school and slapped my books on the table.

"Mom what's for dinner tonight?"

"I don't know. You'll have to ask your dad." She was smiling.

So I asked dad. "I'm not sure, Carl, maybe a big bowl of beans for you." He laughed. I shook my head in confusion and found Mike outside in the back.

"Mike, do you know what mom's fixing for dinner? I'm starving and mom and dad are acting weird about it."

"Didn't they say anything?" Mike looked puzzled.

"Do they ever tell me anything?"

"Well not really. They hardly tell me anything either. I have to guess just about as much as you do. Don't tell them I said anything, but you and I are going with dad up to Michigan tonight. Then mom, Karen, and Catherine are driving up separately tomorrow. I think we're leaving right after dinner. I think mom's fixing something quick like hotdogs and baked beans. Dad wants to get going as soon as we can."

I was pleasantly shocked. I wasn't big into surprises but I did like this one. I ran back upstairs almost too excited to eat.

"Dad, is it true? Are we really driving to Michigan tonight?"

"Well yes. I was going to tell you as a surprise but it appears someone beat me to it. Did Mike say something?"

"Well yah, because no one would tell me anything." I was laughing and in a really upbeat mood.

I just picked at my dinner. I was way too excited to eat. But of course I instantly snarfed down a piece of cake. Mike and I rushed to finish packing. I packed things like tennis shoes and a football while my mom made sure I packed my toothbrush and deodorant. I hated brushing my teeth and had to be forced.

We raced to the car, almost knocking each other down. I wanted to sit between dad and Mike. It felt safe. I felt protected. It also gave me some control over the radio. I turned the radio up when "I Will Follow Him" by Little Peggy March came on. It was late at night and we were in the Thunderbird, cruising north on Highway 31. I can remember hearing that song on the radio like it was yesterday. We drove for hours. When we got there Mike and I were fast asleep.

Dad had rented a really cool older house right on the lake. It was gray and had two stories. The back yard led to a long boat dock and a little beach.

We spent the weekend fishing, cooking out, and riding around in a pontoon boat. I loved the spontaneity of it. It was one of those getaways with dad that I cherish. I didn't want it to end. But I noticed mom and dad didn't sleep in the same bedroom, just like at home. As we drove home Sunday night I cried quietly in the car.

✝

A few months later I was playing in the back yard and accidentally hurt Catherine. She ran in the house crying. I went into a tailspin. I didn't know what to do. So I headed for the safety of the Field where I hid and prayed. I lay by the tree in the middle of it and thought about how to approach my angry mother.

Finally I decided to go home and face the music. Then I saw dad coming toward me. We met in the side yard. I was scared to approach the house and started crying. I told dad it was an accident. Dad held me, saying it was okay and Catherine was fine.

"Just don't take off like that again without saying anything," he said.

"I won't, dad. Thanks for coming to get me." I was relieved and stopped crying.

"It's okay, you big lug. Let's go back inside now."

CHAPTER 7: ST. MICAELIS AND THE SHOP

WHEN I STARTED first grade in the halls and classrooms of St. Micaelis grade school it was the fall of 1961. I had briefly gone to pre-school there. I had no clue what to expect and I clearly wasn't ready for the dramatic culture shock.

Built in the late 1940s, St. Micaelis was a grand structure rising three stories and made of a beautiful dark-red brick. It held classrooms, offices, a cafeteria in the basement and the office of Sister Carabella, the school principal. The cafeteria and the playground were my favorite places. On the east side of the property stood the school. The halls had green tiled floors with matching green and white walls. On the west end, and connected to the school through a breezeway, was the imposing cathedral-like church.

Directly in back of the church was the rectory where all the priests and brothers stayed. This was the residence of the parish Pastor, Father Kramminnion. He was a tall and soft-spoken priest who seemed a little distant and eccentric and seemed old to me even back then. I would get to know the good Father once I started my training as altar boy. When we greeted the priest in the hallway or the classroom, he responded with limited warmth. When I greeted him alone his response was relatively cold. He looked at me as though he had no clue who I was or what I was doing there. I always wondered whether I'd greeted him the right way. And if I hadn't, I was afraid of the nuns finding out.

Behind the rectory was the Convent, which housed the nuns. This was a forbidden no-man's land where you would be watched if you ventured near it. No one dreamed of going anywhere near it, not even on a dare. It was as if a supernatural benevolent force field kept us kids far from that mysterious building. The most feared room of the entire parish was the office of the dreaded Sister Carabella, the stern, no-nonsense, no-mercy principal of St. Micaelis. Rumors were told of children going into her office and never coming out.

I vividly remember my first day of first grade. St. Micaelis was an extremely disciplined environment I wasn't quite ready for. We were all very, very apprehensive. Some were even sick to their stomachs. We went from beating each other up, playing in the dirt, and attacking old ladies' homes, to this. The moment I walked inside it felt like stepping onto a conveyor belt. Various lay teachers herded us down into the cafeteria and organized us by grade level. My first-grade class was on the west side of the dining room. By the time we were all in there, it was packed to the hilt. We weren't allowed to talk. God forbid you had to pee.

All of a sudden a fearsome and intense black-robed figure came out of nowhere. It floated in front of us all with a menacing stare. Even the eighth-graders looked nervous.

"Okay, children, my name is Sister Carabella, the school principal. I want to say a few words before we send you into your classrooms. Step over here and don't run... and I mean don't run, and no talking." Her stern look would have turned the Medusa herself to stone. Recalling Greek mythology, I tried not to stare into her eyes.

"First graders, you will go with Miss Tussell." We were set upon by an army of nuns and lay teachers who acted as enforcers. They molded us into a single line proceeding up two flights of stairs and onto the main floor toward our first-grade classroom. Miss Tussell herself led our group as another nun, Sister Romano, kept us in a perfectly silent straight line. We were herded into the classroom and on to our pre-assigned desks. On that desk sat my very first name tag. This would be one of many for years to come. We were told to stand by the desks until instructed to sit down. Once the nun saw that Miss Tussell's class was secured into the classroom, she stood before us.

"Well, class, you did a very good job of walking to your assigned classroom with no incidents. This is one of the best-behaved groups of students I have seen so far today. Please keep up the good behavior."

"I will have to agree with Sister Romano. It all went perfect," said Miss Tussell.

Then Miss Tussell said, "Now, class, here is how we'll say good bye to Sister Romano. We'll all say 'God be with you, Sister Romano.' Can you repeat that together?"

"God be with you, Sister Romano," we repeated in perfect unison. Sister Romano smiled.

"God be with you, children, too. I'll be back to check on you later." I was thinking, we're not out of the woods yet. If that nun pokes her head in here later and we're misbehaving in the least its curtains for us.

"Okay, class, you may all sit down now. You may introduce yourself to your partner next to you. And remember, you are not allowed to talk in class until given permission," Miss Tussell said. I was thinking how much better to have a lay teacher for first grade than a hardcore nun.

The desks were arranged in rows of two. Most pairings were usually boy/girl except for the lucky guys whose partner was another boy. I was paired next to a creepy girl I didn't like right off the bat – Amanda Pessler. I just didn't like the way she looked at me with that sour, cry-baby face of hers. I tried to be nice and talk to her but she barely responded. I looked around and saw most of the other paired students were having some form of conversation except us. I also noticed Amanda wasn't assimilating too well. She wasn't talking to anybody or even looking at anybody.

"Hey, my name is Carl Sanders. You're Amanda, right?" She looked dismally over at me and shook her head. She didn't like this at all and I was getting a bad feeling. All of a sudden Miss Tussell stood up to talk.

"Okay, class, I'm sure most of you have gotten to know your neighbor a little better. Now I want each of you to stand up, introduce yourself, and tell us a little bit about yourself. You don't have to talk long, just a couple of minutes. Elizabeth, why don't we start with you?" This was a complete surprise to all of us and we were not prepared.

Oh my God, our desks were right behind Elizabeth. Amanda and I would be up next. Elizabeth stood nervously and looked around the room at all the other apprehensive faces. Then she looked at Miss Tussell. She opened her mouth to speak but only stuttered. Some of the kids snickered but I kept a straight face as I was right behind her and in Miss Tussell's direct line of sight.

"Class please! Elizabeth, go ahead," Miss Tussell said.

"Uhhh, my name is Elizabeth Randall and I live on Sahara Drive over by the shopping center. My dad is a lawyer and my mom stays home and takes care of the family. That is all, Miss Tussell. Thank you."

"Okay Elizabeth, thank you. You may sit down now. James, you're up next." I was next. I felt like the Lion in *The Wizard of Oz*, right before the Wizard asks him to come forward. Oh please, don't make me look stupid, I thought. As I was listening to James give his little talk, I noticed Amanda next to me. She was frozen, white as a ghost and had a look of sheer terror in her eyes.

"Are you okay? Do you want me to go first?" She didn't respond at all. This wasn't a good sign. James droned on for what seemed like an hour and then abruptly stopped.

"And that is pretty much what my dad does," he concluded.

"Well, James, that was very exciting and I'm sure the class was thrilled to learn that. You may sit down now." I was so preoccupied with what I was going to say and distracted by Amanda's meltdown, I hadn't heard a word James said. I thought if I went next, Amanda would have a few more minutes to pull herself together. When Miss Tussell said, "Well, okay, let's see who's next" I quickly raised my hand. This was an early lesson I learned in how to get unpleasant things out of the way quickly. Just raise your hand and go first.

"I'll go, Miss Tussell."

"Well, Carl, that will be fine. You must have something really exciting to tell the class. Go ahead and stand up." Man, I can't believe she said that, I thought.

"Not really, Miss Tussell, I just wanted to be next and get it over with." I heard a few muffled snickers. Miss Tussell faintly smiled.

"Now I don't want anyone to be nervous when they're standing up. Part of what we're doing here is to help get rid of the butterflies when we're talking in front of our classmates and other people. And as I said earlier, I want everyone to get to know each other a little better too." I quickly looked down at Amanda. There was no change in her expression.

"Okay, Carl, you may continue."

"Well, my name is Carl Sanders and I live just a block away on Broderick Street. Uhh, I have four other brothers and sisters. My dad owns an irrigation business which is kind of close to here. It's neat sometimes because I get to go and stay with him on some of his job sites. And I get to go fishing with him, too. I like to read, play army, watch *The Twilight Zone* and go hunting with my dad. Oh, and I collect skulls too."

"You said what, Carl?" Miss Tussell had a nervous smile on her face.

"About the skulls?"

"Yes. Do you want to tell us a little more about that?" Now I had the full attention of everyone in the class. Some of the girls grimaced. This would be a good chance to gross them out.

"Well, it's simple really, and my dad helps me."

"Carl, may I ask how many of these uh, skulls, do you have now?" I looked up and started thinking.

"Right now I have only about seven."

"What animals are they?"

"I have an opossum, a pheasant, a deer, a raccoon, some birds and a rabbit. Yah, that's it."

"Well, Carl, now I'm going to ask what you do to make them into skulls. Do you have some sort of process?" Wow, she really wants me to make the class sick. Well here goes, I thought.

"What I do first is cut the head off the animal whose skull I want. It's okay. They're already dead. Then I bury them in my back yard or in back at my dad's shop. I like to do it right after it rains because the ground is easier to dig. Then, well, I wait for probably three months or so while the maggots eat at it and then dig it up. And all the fur and skin and everything else is pretty much gone. All you have to do is rinse the dirt and gunk off with the hose." There was dead silence. Finally Miss Tussell spoke up.

"So Carl, let me get this straight. You bury them in the ground for a few months then dig them up again?"

"That's right, Miss Tussell. It's kind of like baking a meatloaf in the oven but leaving it in for three months." Now more of the boys started to snicker.

"Well, not the kind of meatloaf I prepare," Miss Tussell said.

"I'm sure of that, Miss Tussell. I'll bet yours smells a lot better, too." The class now broke out in loud laughter. Miss Tussell reluctantly started to laugh.

"Well, Carl, I sure hope so. I must say I like my recipe better than yours. But I want to thank you for sharing that very interesting and somewhat macabre hobby of yours with the class."

"My dad wants me to enter my collection in the Hobby Show here next year," I said.

"You know, I would like to see that. I'm sure the rest of the class would be very interested as well. Carl, you can sit down now."

"Miss Tussell, what does macabre mean?"

"I'll tell you after class, Carl."

I was about to say thank you Miss Tussell when the principal, Sister Carabella, stormed in out of nowhere. Miss Tussell ran her finger across her mouth for us to be quiet. Sister Carabella stood sternly at our classroom door. She was like the school bouncer wandering the hallways, always on the lookout for commotion and misbehavior. I immediately sat down. She scanned the room with a look of consternation. We couldn't look at her directly for fear of being turned into stone. She indeed was the Medusa. The sudden arrival of Sister Carabella intensified Amanda's nervous condition. Now she looked like a body on the mortician's table that had been propped up and a final layer of wax applied to the face.

"Class, I could hear you all the way down the hallway! Miss Tussell, is there a problem?"

"No, Sister. We were going through our first class introductions and one of my student's stories was of particular interest to the class. We didn't realize we were being loud and we promise not to have it happen again, won't we, class?"

"Yes, Miss Tussell."

"I am sorry, Sister," Miss Tussell said.

"All the noise from this classroom was disturbing the other nearby classes. I can understand it's the first day and we're all trying to get organized but please make sure it doesn't happen again. May I ask who told the story that was so interesting?"

"Carl Sanders did, Sister." I cringed and slowly turned my head away from everyone.

"Well, perhaps I can hear it someday. But in the meantime, please remember to respect your fellow students in the classrooms next to you. That is all for now." She actually smiled this time. I breathed a sigh of relief. I wasn't quite ready to repeat my little hobby story. Then mercifully she turned around and whisked away. Miss Tussell recovered from the intrusion. Even the lay teachers feared Sister Carabella.

"Well, class, from now on we must be a little quieter. We certainly don't want Sister Carabella coming in here like that, do we? I know some of your stories might be a little bit humorous, but we do have to be considerate of the other classes around us. Is that understood?"

"Yes, Miss Tussell," we responded in monotone unison.

"Now, why don't we continue? Let's see who is next. Oh, Amanda, I believe it's you. Can you stand up, please?" By this time Amanda looked like she had indeed gazed into the Medusa's eyes and turned to stone. There was no response. Oh no, here it comes. Please be okay, I prayed. Amanda did not respond to Miss Tussell but looked straight down at her desk.

"Amanda, honey, the class would love to hear about you."

"No! I won't," she replied. I moved my chair a little further away from her. I didn't want to be close to what I thought was going to happen. Miss Tussell began walking slowly toward Amanda and me.

"Well, sweetie, there's no need to be nervous. Why don't you just give it a try? I'll bet you'll find it's easier than you thought. You don't have to stand up if you don't want to." Amanda just sat there. Now came a brief impasse. Miss Tussell stood, staring at Amanda and Amanda still sat staring down at her desk.

"You know what, Amanda? You don't have…" she started to say. Just then Amanda swelled up and started to sob. She jumped up from her desk and yelled, "I don't want to be here. I hate this! My mom and dad made me come here and I hate it!" She then stormed crying from the classroom. Miss Tussell didn't have time to react. She simply watched in shock. I sat spellbound. This was the first time in my life I'd seen someone really freak out. The class was in a state of shock as well. Everyone stared at each other deciding whether to laugh or just keep quiet. Another outburst of laugher would surely alert Sister Carabella.

"Amanda, honey, come back," Miss Tussell called. Amanda was already in the hallway and probably heading out of the building. Miss Tussell was still recovering from the first incident and now this. In Sister Carabella's eyes, this would make it look like she had no control over her class. Miss Tussell quickly refocused.

"Uhhh, class, I want you to remain quiet and I will return shortly." She darted from the classroom in the direction Amanda ran. We tried to grasp what had just happened. In a few minutes she returned. Amanda's escape attempt had been thwarted by a couple of nuns standing at the front door. She was escorted to Sister Carabella's office. We weren't told what happened after that. I not want to know.

"Class, I'm sorry you had to see that. Some of us just get nervous in a new environment. You leave your homes and your family to learn new things and it can be quite an adjustment. It's natural for us to be nervous, especially on a first day. Let us continue with our introductions. Karen, I believe you're next." I couldn't listen anymore and tuned the rest of it out. It was sad. I hoped Amanda was okay.

There was a woman at St. Micaelis I knew I didn't like. She wasn't a teacher. I think she was some sort of teacher assistant or secretary. She'd pop into a classroom all of a sudden and drop off something the class needed. She gave off evil vibrations. I always looked away when she came into my classroom. I never mentioned her or my feelings about her to my family, friends, teachers, or other classmates.

But we certainly had fun on the playground. The nuns called the church the most sacred place in the school complex, but to me it was the playground, with the cafeteria a close second. Our favorite games were kickball, foursquare, tag, and catch-me-if-you-can. Or we just stood around with our friends, talking and trying to look cool.

For a boy, one of the most venerated and important occupations was that of cootie doctor. As school life went forward, we had many reasons to believe some of the girls at school were infested with cooties, at least the ones we didn't like. You could tell if a girl had cooties just by looking at her or by certain ways she acted. The cootie scene at St. Micaelis in the early 1960s was a little like the Salem Witchcraft Trials of the late 1600s. If one of the boys just didn't like a girl he could simply spread it around that she had cooties and she instantly became a social pariah, at least to the rest of the boys. However, many of the girls considered it an honor to be a cootie carrier. It kept some of the creepier boys away. I personally witnessed some girls chasing boys around the playground, trying to infest them with cooties.

What exactly cooties were, or why or how certain girls contracted them, remains unknown to medical science to this day. But that's how we isolated the girls we didn't like. It was an engineered social disease, so to speak. You caught cooties simply by being touched by the infected girl. Immediately an imaginary painful rash would form on the skin of the male victim. The only way to remove the cootie infection was to find the cootie doctor.

I was one of the school's handful of certified cootie doctors. With one carefully administered needle shot in the affected area, the cootie infection magically disappeared. There were two types of cootie shots. One shot would immediately cure the affliction. Then there was a second vaccine-type shot. If you were attacked again, you could get infected again without getting the vaccine shot. I took no payment for my treatments. Not candy, baseball cards, school supplies, Twinkies, or anything else. I was simply happy with the prestige and high social status of being a cootie doctor and being able to help heal my friends. It kept the male population at St. Micaelis healthy, happy, and free of the ever-threatening cootie pestilence.

"Carl, you gotta help me!" cried Tom. "Ellen Fulton just touched me on the neck! I don't think I'll make it until the end of recess." All the boys knew that Ellen was one of the biggest cootie carriers in school. And she made the most of that fear.

"Over here, Tom!" I led him off to the side and administered a healing shot to the affected area. After just a few minutes the symptoms diminished and he was feeling better. He thanked me and went on to finish his last game of kickball with a higher level of enthusiasm and confidence.

"Hey man, thanks. I'm never getting near her again!"

"Amen to that, Tom. I'm glad you learned your lesson. You really have to be on your guard for some of these girls around here."

I would discover in later years that some of the women I dated as a young adult were infested with more complicated mental strains of cooties. I thanked the Good Lord I self-vaccinated in grade school.

✝

One night a knock on the door announced John and Rufio Binson.

"Hey, Rufio, what's going on?"

"It's going to be a nice night. Do you want to do some bat hunting? They just put some fresh tar on the street by us. Can you go?" It was the perfect night for it. It was just before dark and a warm evening breeze was setting in. Bats loved to fly around in that kind of weather at that time of night. I desperately wanted to join them.

"Mom, Douglas is here. Can I go over to his house for a little while? My homework's all done."

"What are you going to do?"

"Well, I was going to go over to the Binson's and maybe watch a movie."

"Tell Douglas you have to be back in a couple of hours."

Rufio and I looked at each other and smiled. It was bat hunting time once again. I snuck into the garage and got out the long bamboo fishing pole we kept for that very purpose. Then I grabbed an old tennis ball.

"Okay, let's get out of here. Don't say anything." I had to move quickly. We snuck out of the garage and around toward Rufio's. It was just starting to get dark – the perfect time to hunt bats. In front of Rufio's house we started to prepare our main weapon. John joined us as a spotter. With a pocket knife Rufio cut a small circular hole in the tennis ball. Then we rubbed the tennis ball in the street tar until it was really gooey and stuck it on the end of the 10-foot-long bamboo pole.

"Okay, Carl, pick the pole up and I'll help you lift it from my end," Rufio said.

112

"Hurry up, guys. I can see them. They're all over the place! Oh wow, hurry!" John screamed. Rufio and I maneuvered the fishing pole into place. As I hoisted it up it fell back toward John, who started to run.

"Hey, what are you trying to do? If it hits me I'll never get that out of my hair!"

"Sorry. Rufio, grab that other end and don't touch the tar ball."

"It's getting darker and harder to see. We can't turn the porch light on or my parents will see us. They think we're just outside talking," Rufio said. I hoisted the pole up with Rufio's help as far as I could. That was enough leverage to get it all the way up in the air.

"Hey, Carl, keep it up there. Now walk into the street away from the street light. Maybe you'll get one," John said.

"There are three of them flying around just above you. Hold the pole as steady as you can." I could see the bats flying all around it but none got close enough to stick to the tar ball. They were too smart. Or we were too stupid. I held the pole as steady as I could but my arms got tired and I had to lower it. It was now Rufio's turn.

"Okay, Carl, I've got it. Go ahead." I began to lift the tar ball end up as far as I could to give Rufio leverage. I had to keep the tar ball as far away from my face and hair as possible. It would be a disaster if I got any on me. None of us were supposed to be out doing this. We could get in big trouble. Rufio finally got the pole up in the air and held it steady. Bats continued to swirl around the tar ball but none were getting too close.

"Rufio, how much longer can you hold it up?"

"A few more minutes but not much more." All this was kind of dangerous—people said most bats have rabies and if you get bitten, the shots are painful. Also we had no clear-cut plan as to what we were going to do with the bats if we ever did actually catch one.

"We're not really having any luck are we? I'm surprised no one's come out and asked what we're doing," John said.

"Shhh. Don't talk or we'll scare them away. Give Rufio a little longer."

"This isn't really working. They just keep flying around it. They're not as dumb as I thought they were," Rufio said.

"Aren't they supposed to be blind too?"

"Yah, I think so."

"You know what? I'm getting tired of holding this pole and nothing happening. What if I swing it into them as they fly by?"

"Yah, give it a try." Rufio started swinging the tar ball actually toward the bats. They were still too quick. I could tell they were now appearing agitated because their flight patterns were more aggressive. Then they started diving down toward us and then swooping back up. It happened so quick I couldn't react.

"Rufio, maybe we ought to stop. It seems like they're mad at us now," I said.

"Let me just try once more. It's getting darker anyway and soon we won't be able to see them at all." Rufio swung the tar ball hard and at least bumped one of them just below the tar ball. That was it. The bats had had enough. They started swooping down toward the three of us in full force.

"Rufio, look out! They're coming! I'm getting out of here, man!" I yelled.

"We need to get out of here!" John cried. We were trying to keep as quiet as we could. But Rufio panicked and swung the pole down. The bats flew right down after it. Then he frantically swung the pole around, hoping to make the bats go away.

What was that? I heard a swishing sound right by my ear. My God it's a bat trying to bite me in the neck!

"We gotta get outta here now! They're after us!" I yelled. We could barely see them and they knew they had more advantage the darker it got. I could hear them! The swooshing sound of their wings was right by my ear! Rufio was still frantically trying to swing the attacking bats away with the pole. But he was now swinging in the dark. He swung so hard the tar ball flew off and hit John smack in the head. Because of the tar it stuck to the right side of his face. We started to run.

"Oh man, no! You hit me with that ball!" John said. He couldn't get it off. Rufio threw down the pole and we ran, trying to flee the attacking bats. Everyone was in full panic mode and John had a tar-covered tennis ball stuck to his right ear.

"Oh God, the last I saw they were right over your head!" I yelled.

"Man, I hope I don't get bitten!" Rufio screamed.

"We gotta stop! I can't get this ball off my ear!"

"Keep running. We have to get to the Safeway store. They won't follow us in there," Rufio yelled.

"But Safeway is in the other direction!"

"I'm not going back there!" Rufio meant it. "We'll just have to run around the block." We followed Rufio, running past house after house, then turned the corner onto my street. We sprinted by my house, praying my mom wouldn't see us. We ran on through the Moreland Street stop sign and made a hard left all together in perfect formation. We ran past Mrs. Carson's barking dog Wilbur, hoping he'd shut up. The Carsons were sitting out on their front porch watching us. We appeared like we were in some sort of military exercise.

"Where the hell are they going in such a damn hurry?" wondered Bill Carson. "Are they running from something?"

"Oh, don't worry about it. They're probably just playing a game or having a race," said his wife Betty.

"They're not running like they're having fun. Was that something sticking out of John Binson's right ear?" Ken asked.

"I'm not sure, they're going so fast." Their dog Wilbur must have got some of the other dogs riled up because several dogs in the neighborhood started to create a howl fest. That prompted some of the loose dogs roaming around to now start chasing us. They were closing in on us quickly, too. It looked like a couple of poodles and a schnauzer.

"Oh my God! Those dogs are right behind us! Please God, not now! Doesn't anyone chain their dogs up anymore?" I screamed. One of the poodles started nipping at Rufio's heels but he managed to kick it off. The other poodle picked up the pace and tried to bite John on the calf. It got one little nip in but appeared to be moving closer for a bigger bite.

"God, get it off me!" John cried. I bent over and seized a good-sized stick. I hurled it behind John in front of the dogs, who thankfully started tripping over it.

"Keep running! Don't stop! Safeway's right over there!" Rufio screamed.

John was crying but still running. We ran faster down the street, hooked a hard right back on Halifax Drive north, then cut over left through Mrs. Brown's front yard. This would usually have gotten is us in big trouble from Mrs. Brown herself. But this was an emergency. Half the animals in the neighborhood were after us.

We ran out of her yard and past Kelly's Bakery into the relative safety of the Safeway parking lot. The dogs finally abandoned their chase. When we reached the sanctuary of the store we banged into each other as we tried all at once to squeeze through the front door. We looked around to see if bats were flying in the doors behind us. We stood there panting and puffing, bent over, hands on thighs, trying to trying to catch our breath.

One of the cashiers was looking at us weird. She took a long look at John and the tennis ball he was trying to pull off his ear. Then she walked away from her cash register. Before we knew it, the store manager was there.

"Are you boys okay?" We all three looked up at him.

"I'm Ted Arnold, the store manager. Are you okay? Hey, is that a tennis ball sticking out of your ear there? Whoah! How did that happen? Was someone chasing you?" He was laughing. We had to think quickly. There was no way we were going to tell him what really happened. Rufio recovered the quickest.

"Mr. Arnold, uuhh, we were racing on a dare to see who would get here first. We really like to run a lot. Also we had to pick up some chipped beef for my mom." I flinched. None of us had a dime to our name but I had to make something up.

"I see." Mr. Arnold looked at each of us and the unconvincing expressions on our faces. And he kept eyeballing the tennis ball on John's head. We knew he didn't believe a word we said. But I think he wanted to get us out of there and away from the customers.

"Well, let me ask you this. No, on second thought I don't want to know. Would you like me to remove that tennis ball off your ear? I can do it so it won't hurt." John glanced nervously at Rufio, who nodded.

"Okay, sir, that would be nice."

"You guys follow me to the meat counter. I'll take your friend to the back and get him fixed up. In the meantime there's the chipped beef. You tell our meat manager there how much you need." The manager then took John into his office and got out some turpentine. That took care of the stuck tennis ball. He led John back out to the meat counter.

"I don't know how your friend got that ball stuck on him but he's as good as new. Did you get your chipped beef?"

"Well, sir, what you have isn't the kind of chipped beef we need. We'll come back another time. Thank you for everything but we have to go now," I said.

"Now, you kids take care and stay out of trouble," the manager said, smiling. We left the store as fast as we could, covering our heads and continually looking up at the dark sky until we all got home. It was the last time we went bat hunting. We were through.

✝

I remember when third grade was getting ready to start. I spent some time mourning the end of summer vacation. I remember the day I learned who my third-grade teacher would be. I waited anxiously for Mike to come home from school. Drum roll, please.

"Hey, Mike, did they say who my third grade teacher is?" I'd heard rumors that it would be the horrific and feared Sister Ande. She was the tallest and meanest nun at St. Micaelis. She was the teacher nobody wanted. I'd managed to block it out of my mind all summer.

"I have some bad news for you." I stared at Mike, not wanting to hear anymore. I put my hands over my ears. Mike gently pulled them away.

"Your third grade teacher, its Sister Ande."

If I hadn't been so afraid to use the word "shit" again I would have said it right then and there. But I just closed my eyes, opened them, and stared at the ceiling. The nightmarish goal-post story from a couple of years ago was still fresh in my head and I feared in hers. Will she remember that?

I went to my bedroom and turned on my beloved Popeye & Olive Oyl cartoon show so I could forget about the cruel world I found myself in. I loved watching Popeye beat up the bully Bluto. It made me feel strong and proved that good still triumphed over evil. For a while I forgot school would start in no time.

A tragic event from third grade stands out even to this day. It was November 1963, the Friday afternoon before Thanksgiving week. It was art class, one of my favorites, and the atmosphere was laid back. It was fun because all the kids in the class were allowed to talk to each other. The closing school bell would ring soon. All of a sudden Sister Carabella got on the public address system and made an announcement. We could tell she had been crying.

"Boys and girls, I have a very sad announcement to make. President Kennedy has been assassinated." We all looked around in confusion as nobody knew what "assassinated" meant. But I could tell from the tone of the Sister's voice that it wasn't good. Sister Ande was getting ready to explain it to us. But then Sister Carabella came back on and said, "I now have some terrible news. President Kennedy is indeed dead." She practically sobbed.

We certainly knew what that meant. The classroom became very somber. We were dismissed about 30 minutes later. I walked home, completely confused as to why anyone would shoot the president of their own country. At home, mom appeared upset.

"Honey, are you okay?" she asked.

"I think so, mom. What happened? Why did they shoot the president?" I asked.

"Carl, I just don't know. I don't know," mom replied. Catherine and Mike were already home. Karen and dad would be home shortly. We all sat down in front of the TV, watching the commentators trying to explain what had just happened.

Back then I had no clue about why it really happened and how it would transform our country. I did realize, though, that that day was one of the few times most everyone in my family was in the same room together, especially my mom and dad.

✝

One Sunday afternoon a few months later I rode my bike over to the Shop. It was January of 1964 but unseasonably warm this particular day. I hung out for a little while looking at all the cool equipment and machines. After a while dad took me out for a Coney at the drug store next door. Dad had a small black-and-white TV in the front office and sometimes he and I would watch *The Ed Sullivan Show*. He'd installed a tubular heating system under the floor to keep it warm. I could lie on the floor with a fluffy pillow and stay really cozy.

Tonight dad asked if I wanted to watch Ed Sullivan.

"Hey, dad, that would be cool. Who's on?"

"Well, one of the acts is some rock-n-roll group. I think that's what they call it, rock-n-roll. I can't remember their name but it's on the tip of my tongue. Uhhh, let me think. Oh I know! They're called the Beatles. Now that's a funny name. Have you heard of them? This is their first appearance in this country."

"Yah! They had a song on the radio the other day. Someone at school said they have really long hair."

"Let's turn it on. I want to see what they look like. I don't know much about rock-n-roll. I can't understand it. But everyone is talking about them." Dad looked a bit bewildered.

"I can't understand some of the words with that thick English accent. But I kind of like the beat. And anyway, people don't dance to the words," I said laughing. Dad gave me a funny look when I said that. Then he nodded his head in agreement.

120

At that moment we heard Ed Sullivan make his historic announcement, "Ladies and Gentleman, The Beatles!" Onto the national stage came four Englishmen with nice smiles and really long hair. We didn't know this was to be a defining moment, not only in music history, but in American history. That night also signaled the end of national mourning of the Kennedy assassination, and the start of a new plethora of changes in social mores, politics, entertainment and society in general. The leave-it-to-Beaver era was fading fast and being replaced by a less innocent blame-it-on-Beaver era. The Beatles played "All My Loving." Dad almost screamed, "My God, Carl, did you see their hair?" It was hard to hear the song over the hundreds of screaming girls.

"Carl, have you heard that song before?" dad asked. "That's a lot different than what I grew up with."

We watched them play "Till There Was You" and "She Loves You." I was getting a headache from all the screaming and I couldn't read dad's expression.

"Well, dad, what did you think?"

"I don't know. I'm not sure everyone is going to like all that hair. Your mother certainly won't." Dad grabbed me and started tickling me. I laughed hysterically, trying to get him to stop.

"Okay Ringo, have you had enough?"

"Dad! Put me down! Put me down! I give up! You win!" I almost peed in my pants. But after *The Ed Sullivan Show* the fun was over. I didn't want to go.

Mom was up and seemed mad because I'd been at the Shop for so long. Catherine was asleep. Mike was still over at a friend's house but would be home soon. Karen was over at a friend's house. And God knew what time dad would ever get home. I went right to my room and hid under the covers.

✝

Well, I was a proud survivor of Catholic school, third-grade boot camp with Sister Ande. It was now the fall of 1964 and I was starting fourth grade. I was daydreaming at my new desk when, on the very first day of school, my fourth-grade teacher introduced herself as Miss Wiwi. It was all we could do to keep from howling. What made it doubly funny is that she had a straight, serious-looking face. Oh no, Sister Ande the year before and now this?

"Can the class pronounce Wiwi?" she asked as she looked around at us with a straight face. We couldn't believe our ears and we couldn't believe *she* wasn't laughing too. But we had to respond.

"Weeeweee," we all chimed in. I didn't dare look at anyone. I knew I'd burst out laughing. Somehow we all got through the introduction. But Miss Wiwi's next exercise was much worse.

She asked us to stand up and introduce ourselves, one by one. I was dreading my turn and started to pray to St Francis. The kids around me had various kinds of surprised smirks on their faces. I couldn't look at them. I lowered my head and continued to pray for guidance and sober discourse.

Oh St. Francis, please don't make me laugh. Please don't make me laugh. Please don't make laugh. I'll be good. I'll be good. St. Francis... that big bag of worms I dumped on the floor in the kitchen two years ago at mom's card party... that won't ever happen again. Please don't make me laugh. Please don't make me laugh. Please don't.....

"Okay, who is next? Carl, I believe it will be you."

Feeling once again like the cowardly Lion in *The Wizard of Oz* I grabbed my tail and looked up from my prayerful meditation. I stared right at Miss Wiwi. If I looked around, my now straight and solemn face would

122

turn into a snickering mess. I had to give a generic response and not speak her name. That is what my classmates were doing and it seemed to be working. Not one of them had broken down laughing, yet. I thought: This is a character test. This is a big hoax and the school system is testing us for mental turpitude. This cannot be true. *No one* has a last name of Wiwi.

"My name is Carl and I'm nine years old. I have four brothers and sisters and a couple of them went to school here," I said. I stared straight ahead at the chalkboard in a self-induced trance.

"Is that all you can tell us about yourself?"

"Yes ma'am," I said. I was ever so careful not to utter her name or it would be all over and I'd wind up in the principal's office.

"Class, I want to make something clear right now. From now on, I want you to address me as Miss Wiwi. Is that clear? I think that's a better way to get to know one another. Don't you agree?" I was now in gripped in horror. Was this a cue for me to speak her name?

"Don't you agree, class?" Her tone of voice was a bit more stern.

"Yes, Miss Wiwi," the class barely responded in unison. Thank God my response was concealed in with the rest of the class.

"So Carl, before you sit down, what do you do?" What? Oh, Dear God, please, no! I slowly stood up. My legs were shaking and I felt like I was going to throw up.

"When I say something I must respond with your name." I now had to speak her name alone, and in front of the class. I was on the spot. I couldn't think, just had to blurt it out.

"Yes, Miss Wiwi." But no sooner had I got Wiwi out of my mouth I made the mistake of looking over at Kelly Brown, who, of course, had a big smirk on her face. Two weeks ago I had publically accused Kelly of having cooties and she vowed to get back at me. This was now her open window of revenge. I looked away from Kelly as fast as I could, but the damage was done. I made a feeble attempt to hide a graphically deformed smirk.

"What is so funny, Carl?" I wiped the smile off my face and got my act together. If I didn't I'd be sent to Sister Carabella's office and might never return.

"Miss Wiwi, I'm just happy you're our teacher this year. You seem really nice." How had I managed that? Miss Wiwi didn't completely buy it, but she let it go. She gave me an E for effort that morning.

"Okay, Carl, that is very sweet of you. You may sit down now." I breathed a huge sigh of relief. I was off the hook. Kelly Brown just looked at me and stuck out her tongue. The cooties issue with her was now front and center again.

Somehow, the class introductions went on without further incident. Instead of listening, I paid attention to a favorite song running through my head: "Sukiyaki," by the Japanese singer Kyu Sakamoto. It was a beautifully melodic song that was number one on the U.S. charts. But because the song was in Japanese I had no clue what they were singing about.

In October of that year I'd begin one of the major rites of passage for any Catholic boy of my age: training for the venerated position of altar boy. I couldn't wait. In any Catholic grade school, that is the ultimate social position. A new chapter in my life was about to begin.

"Mom, when is altar boy training going to start? I heard it was going to be next Monday. We're supposed to stay after school."

"Father Kramminnion put out a memo in the church bulletin. Didn't your dad tell you?"

"No, I don't think so."

"After class next Monday all of you have to go down to the cafeteria. Father Sweeney will talk to you about the classes. They're supposed to go on for six weeks. And you have to learn the prayers in Latin. Father Sweeney is going to teach most of the class but some of the older altar boys are going to help."

"I have to learn Latin?" There was a trepidation, no, fear, in my voice.

"You hear the priests speak it all the time during Mass. I think you'll do fine. You have to make me proud of you."

"I will. Miss Wiwi is real excited about me doing it, too. Not all the guys in my class are doing it. I think it's just me and five other guys."

"You'll be okay."

"Mom, what nationality is the name Wiwi? I can't believe that's really her name."

"I'm not sure about the nationality. I've never heard that name before. It's a little odd. Maybe it's French."

The following weekend I was extremely nervous. I stayed in my room most of the time. I came out to eat, use the john, and watch *The Twilight Zone*, *Combat!*, and *Gunsmoke* with my dad. Would I be able to hack it? Could I memorize the mysterious Latin language and prayers? Would I screw up during training? Or worse... would I screw up in front of the church congregation or my classmates and nuns? I had stage fright to begin with and this would put me in the spotlight big time. What made matters worse, I found out who the older boys were that would mentor us. Some of those older boys could be mean and unforgiving. It worried me.

As Monday's class with Miss Wiwi wound down, I was almost ready to walk out and skip the altar boy class. Then Miss Wiwi announced who was staying.

"John Sims, Andy Presser, Andy Wildman, and Carl Sanders are to follow Sister Carabella down to the cafeteria."

Oh God, Sister Carabella, I thought. There's no way out! At the exact instant the dreaded Sister Carabella

125

whisked into the room with her usual ominous presence. She seemed like she was pissed off all the time.

"Boys, come with me." We rose in unison like Stepford children, staring straight at her.

"Yes, Sister Carabella," we responded in choir-like tones. If we were a singing band, we'd be called the Monotones. All four of us lined up in single file and followed her down to the cafeteria. She led us to a long table where four other boys were seated. There were eight total in this upcoming altar boy class.

"I'll leave you all with Father Sweeney now. Father, the boys are all yours. I'm sure they'll do just fine for the next six weeks," the good Sister said, smiling. That was one of the very few times I'd ever seen her smile. I took it as a good omen. I needed one.

"Thank you, Sister Carabella." Then she whisked away with her long, flowing robe swaying to and fro. She didn't walk, she floated wherever she went. They all floated. Father Sweeney and two older boys turned toward the nervous altar boy candidates.

"Well, young men, you have taken a big step in your desire to serve the Mother Church," he began. "You volunteered to be trained for this highly respected position that has been created to serve God." Father Sweeney paced back and forth as he talked. "This vocation is not to be taken lightly and bears a great responsibility. You will be aiding your priest in the execution of the Holy Mass. Not everyone who volunteered was chosen for this position, though many were called."

No one called our house. At least if they did, no one told me. I looked across the table at fellow trainee John Sims with a "They didn't call you, did they?" look. John returned the same confused expression gently shaking his head *no*.

"I'm going to pass out the training agenda." Father Sweeney took a stack of papers and gave it to Rich

Geoffery, an older altar boy helping with training. Rich walked around the table handing out the agenda. He seemed to give me a "your-ass-is-mine" look. I didn't know Rich very well. All I knew was that Rich was big, strong, not very nice, and an eighth-grader, a big boy. The rest of us started looking over the agenda.

"Let's start with page one. Don't get ahead of yourselves, boys." Father explained, "You'll notice that actual training starts on Wednesday and lasts six weeks. It will be the most rewarding six weeks of your life. Training will be three nights per week, Monday, Wednesday and Thursday evenings, two hours a night. You'll be expected to keep up with your studies during this time as well. The first three weeks will be devoted to learning the Latin language. As you all know, this is the language of the Mass. It was the language of ancient Rome in Jesus' time. Most early Christians in and around Rome spoke Latin. You will learn how the language is constructed and pronounced and you'll learn every one of the Mass prayers in Latin. You must memorize the basics of the language, the prayers in your Missal, and with the English translations. I'm seeing some looks of apprehension among you. It's not as bad as it seems."

My God, what have I gotten myself into? I don't know if I can do that. I don't know if I even want to do that. What in the world does the word apprehension mean anyway? But it's too late to get out of this now. I tried to hide my fear with a look of confidence. It was too late to run. If I walked out now it would be the walk of shame.

"Moving along down page one, you'll see we'll spend weeks four and five learning the ceremonial movements of the Mass, coordinated with reciting the Latin prayers you will hopefully have memorized by then. And then of course, in week six, you'll start serving the Mass with but groups of more experienced and older altar boys.

Man, he's using a lot of big words, I thought. I again looked across the table at John Sims, who just subtly rolled his eyes in confusion.

"Okay, boys, that is basically the schedule. Are there any questions?"

"Father, what does coord- coordin- coordinated mean?" Paul Presser asked. Now I didn't feel quite so stupid. If the other boys were as confused and nervous as I was, maybe this would all work out

"Well, Paul, the word coordinated means you combine one element or action with another at the same time. In other words, put different things together so they all work at once. Do you understand what I am saying?"

"Yes, Father."

"Are there any other questions?"

I piped up. "Yes, Father. Are we really allowed to touch the wine? It's going to be a long time until I turn 21." Father Sweeney smiled.

"Yes, Carl. Remember you're not the one drinking it. I am." Everyone laughed.

"One last question?"

Andy asked, "Father, do we get to go to the altar boy picnic next year too?" The altar boy picnic was the envy of the school— *the* social event of the year. It was a cookout at the local CYO camp and the food was great. Plus, altar boys got out of a day of classes. The altar boys were the rock stars of the school.

"Yes, Andy, of course you do." Father smiled again.

The weeks of training and preparation passed. The Latin part came easier than I thought. I also managed to stay on top of my studies in Miss Wiwi's class. Everyone was getting more comfortable pronouncing her name without laughing. But I couldn't wait for the six weeks to be over. Outside of bumping into each other and forgetting some of the ceremonial lines, we got through the ritual practices rather uneventfully. That last week, as Father

Sweeney said, we would serve our first Mass in front of everyone with the more experienced and older altar boys. We new recruits would be in the least active positions in the Mass ceremony and gradually work our ways up to the venerated "pole position." This was the altar boy who did most of the work, like pouring the water and wine, serving communion, leading the ceremonial prayers, and of course, bowing a lot.

I passed training with a high score, higher than average. My first Mass was right before Thanksgiving vacation. I showed up for the 7 am service with my hair combed, my pressed casual slacks and Redball Keds tennis shoes. I was damn nervous, but I got most of the movements right and recited the Latin prayers rather well. The only stupid thing I did was slightly trip over my ankle-length black robe as I was still getting used to it. But at least I didn't fall. The 7 am service had two altar boys serving but the 8 am one had four.

The good thing was that we trained only at the 7 am Mass. It had the fewest people and none of the teachers or students. The 8 am Mass drew the big congregation. The entire school was obligated to attend. You could absolutely not screw up at that one. All your friends would see you. Your lay teachers would see you, your classmates would see you and the nuns would see you. Then there were the Masses on Sunday morning. That was when the entire parish would see you. No altar boy was immune from an occasional misstep or full-blown screw up. It was a question of how badly you screwed up and how well you socially (or religiously) survived such a catastrophe.

As an altar boy, I soon learned the ancient ways of covert communication through our secret sign language and intricate system of facial expressions while actually on the altar. It was the altar boy's version of belonging to the Masonic Order. Only another altar boy could understand it. We used it when someone forgot a line or a ceremonial gesture. You had to pray that the celebrating priest didn't notice. Usually he was too busy saying the Mass to pay attention to anything else. You had to be very, very careful about how you gave the help. It took real acting talent and complicated, stealthy gesturing to keep the congregation from noticing as well. And sometimes you messed up so bad it was beyond correction. But you always helped in such a situation because you never knew when you'd need help yourself. That was the reason for the fraternity of it. We watched each other's back.

God help you if your fellow altar boy forgot something and you decided **not** to help, just to see him mess up. It was okay to be a bit adversarial in class or on the playground, but once you were dressed up in that sacristy, ready to hit the stage, you were best friends. It took skill and a cool head to assist. Every altar boy had his favorites he liked to serve with. If you were up there with your favorites, the Mass would go much smoother and faster.

One of the altar boy's greatest fears was the dreaded laugh or snicker. One wrong sound, gesture, or movement and the laughing would start. The sillier the screw-up the worse it became. Oh, that laughing and the stomach cramps and tears that went along with it! Then, trying to cover it up presented a whole new set of problems. If one altar boy seriously screwed up, dropped something, or tripped, it could turn into a chain-reaction snickering-type situation. But the torturous part was that you absolutely could not show it. We would become well versed in the fine art of religious acting in the next few years.

CHAPTER 8: IN THE NAME OF THE FATHER

FATHER Samson Clyce Jacobson was born in the 1920s on the south side of Bridgeport. He was brought up by a stern father of German heritage and an Irish mother. Even though during World War II Father Jacobson was prime draft age, he didn't enlist, get drafted, or serve in the military. But he considered himself a warrior of sorts. He was always engaged in philosophical and religious battles. He entered the seminary soon after the war.

He was one of the last great steak-and-potato men. He loved to eat at nice restaurants and would take our family out a lot. He was never more at home than when he sat at the head of the table at a fine eating establishment with a stogie in his mouth, a menu in one hand, and a martini in the other. For some reason he was keenly tuned in to what I ordered, usually lobster or steak, and these he approved of. When I got something a bit less macho like baked chicken or God forbid just a salad, he'd blurt, "You mean you're not getting steak tonight?"

"No, Father. I ate a lot for lunch and I'm not that hungry."

He badgered me at the table whenever he could. "Come on, Carl. You're a big eater. Aren't you the human garbage disposal? You mean you can't finish that?" Father Jacobson mockingly asked.

"Father, no, I can't finish the spinach and ice cream together. I'm full and it won't taste good together. I'll throw up." It was dinner time. He'd had a couple too many Scotches. Again.

"Well, you know what my ole' daddy used to say," Father Jacobson said.

"No, what?"

"It all gets mixed up in your stomach anyway," he chuckled.

"But you don't have to taste it down there, unless you throw it up from eating too much," I said. Father Jacobson took another sip of Scotch. Then my mother said something and his attention immediately went to her. No matter what conversation he and I were having, whenever Catherine or my mother spoke up, he immediately turned his attention.

He always wore black. Black slacks, black sport coat, black hat, black shoes, and black shirt, with that trademark Catholic white collar. Jeans were for hippies and prisoners, in his view. He was generally friendly and jolly, with his trademark fat cigar sticking out of his mouth. His laugh was intoxicating, for a while anyway. He was also one of the most narcissistic human beings I'd ever met.

Father Jacobson drank more around my family than he did in front of other people. I didn't know what to make of that. Whenever he got a little too tipsy it took on nasty overtones or sometimes it was flat-out embarrassing. I could never win an argument with him, no matter the topic. He loved sports, especially football. He had more respect for athletes than for most of his own peers and superiors in the Holy Mother Church. He had befriended many wealthy and powerful people. And he was politically well connected, served on several boards, and was the chaplain of the Bridgeport Police Department.

He was an incredible orator and could sound very sincere and convincing in any setting. He could have been the top salesman at any car dealership in the city. His sermons held the congregation spellbound. He could have given a Sunday sermon about chocolate pudding or the weather on Pluto and the congregation would have been mesmerized. Some of the best sermons he ever wrote were after a few Scotches at our house. He would even recite the same exact sermon a year or two later. The flock loved him and didn't seem to notice. "How many people remember what you tell them half the time anyway?" he said. "Hell, people don't listen anymore. You can tell them anything. They're so damn gullible."

Father Jacobson was one of the most politically astute individuals I've ever met. He'd say, "Always be nice to that son-of-a-bitch because one day you may need him."

I once listened in on his end of a phone conversation with someone he apparently couldn't stand. He said, "I know. You're exactly right. That makes more sense than anything I've heard lately from those knuckleheads." Then he looked over at me and rolled his eyes. "You hit the nail on the head, Bob," he laughed. "Hell, I was thinking the same thing. Yep, no kidding. Well, I'll say one thing. You could run that organization better than any of those clowns on that board now. None of them know what the hell they're doing." Again he rolled his eyes at me. "Yes, absolutely. I'm in total agreement." Now he was even making faces. "Well listen, Bob, I could discuss this with you all afternoon but I have to get ready for Mass in 30 minutes." Mass wouldn't start for another two hours. "Okay, Bob, I will. You tell Carol and the kids I said hi. Take care now." His face showed a mixture of relief and frustration as he slammed down the phone.

"That son-of-a-bitch!" he muttered. "God, am I glad that damn call's over with. What the hell's the time?"

"Father, it's around four. You have Mass in two hours. I thought that guy was a good friend of yours," I said, confused.

"That jackass? Not a chance," he said. "I don't trust anyone except your mother. At least I have enough time for a drink before Mass."

That incident colored my view of the politics of people, institutions and organizations. And it forever changed the way I saw Father Jacobson and the Catholic Church.

I wasn't around him much at first, but he was always there, lurking. Clues had been everywhere at our Broderick Street house. There was the lingering cigar smoke, the red Lincoln in our driveway. When I came home from school or playing with friends and saw the Lincoln's tail lights disappearing down the street, I'd ask myself, did that car just leave our house? Who in the heck was that?

I started to piece things together. I think mom first met Father Jacobson in the late 1950s when she was in the St. Censurius High School Women's Club. She then worked in the cafeteria there, too. Father Jacobson was a religion teacher at the school and later became the superintendent. My mom's stunning looks caught his attention, then she somehow started doing secretarial work for him on the side. She probably had started to confide in him at some point about developing marital problems.

I first met him when I was around seven or so. In fact, after my younger sister was born, it was Father Jacobson, not my dad, who brought her home from the hospital. No one ever volunteered any information they may have known. The truth, whatever that was, seemed to be perpetually one step ahead of me.

Father Jacobson and my dad couldn't have been more different. Dad wasn't politically suave or sophisticated. And he lacked strong family, political, religious, and financial connections. His immediate family was not large, just him and a brother. He did have a keen knowledge of how to run a business, was full of practical engineering knowledge, and generally dealt with people rather well. Father Jacobson, on the other hand, had no real business acumen or any idea how to run a business. He knew how to run a church, though. He could fill the church pews up like the Rolling Stones filled up soccer and football stadiums. Father Jacobson was a moral, religious and philosophical warrior; dad was a pragmatic realist. Father Jacobson interpreted the world and dictated to it according to his own brand of morality and his interpretation of the Catholic religion to everyday living. He viewed the world as he thought it should be. Dad saw and enjoyed the world for what it was. Father Jacobson tried to change the world. Dad was more than happy to let the world sometimes change him. Father had two college degrees and dad had none. But both had great personalities and wit, and told good stories. Father's stories involved his experiences as a young seminarian and as a chaplain with the Bridgeport police department. He also loved to tell stories about Catherine's funny behavior. He'd often end his many stories with, "Hell, I could write you a book." Dad's stories involved something spectacular someone had told him or a funny experience he had.

As my fourth-grade year at St. Micaelis droned on and 1964 turned into 1965, dad was taking more and more business trips to his company's job sites. True, business was good. But as Father Jacobson ever-so-steadily encroached, dad steadily retreated. He was feeling more isolated from his family. He had to make a choice. He could ask Madeline for a divorce or he could take a stand and fight, but he'd have to extricate Father Jacobson once and for all. He decided on the latter. But he couldn't do it alone. He finally made the decision to go to the Pastor of St. Micaelis, have a hard conversation with Father Kramminnion, and lay the cards on the table. He wouldn't give Madeline any warning. It would be better that way, or so he thought.

The battle lines would be drawn and Dean would finally fire back against Father Jacobson's ever-increasing intrusions into his family. So he called Father Kramminnion and set an appointment for a face-to-face talk.

"Hello, Father. This is Dean Sanders. Do you have a minute?"

"Yes, Dean. How are you? We really appreciate what you've done with the table tennis team this year with 12 wins and only two losses. That's quite a record. Would you be interested in coaching again next year?"

"Well thank you. I might. But it would depend on the outcome of our conversation tonight." He could feel the thickness of Father Kramminnion's silence on the other end.

"What can I help you with, Dean?"

"I'd like to meet with you in your office in the next week or so to discuss, well, the behavior of another Catholic priest with respect to my family."

"He's not one in our parish, is it?"

"Well no, but this person is well known around the city." There was another uncomfortable silence.

"Why don't we meet at the parish office next Wednesday at 6? How does that work?" Father Kramminnion sounded nervous. Dean had the distinct feeling this was no surprise to the good Father.

"That's fine, Father. See you then."

On Wednesday dad drove to the parish office, but parked behind the building to keep things discreet. He took a deep breath and got out of the car. The genie was now out of the bottle. There would be no going back. Father Kramminnion's housekeeper, Ellen, answered his knock on the large wooden rectory door. "May I help you?"

"I'm Dean Sanders here to see Father Kramminnion."

Ellen was gone for what seemed like hours. "Mr. Sanders, you just follow me." This was dad's first time in the rectory. He followed Ellen down a long hallway to Father Kramminnion's office. Ellen ushered him right in.

"Father, this is Mr. Sanders."

Father Kramminnion greeted him, "Well Dean, how are you? I want you to know what a great job you've done with our table tennis team. The kids really seem to like you." He had already said that over the telephone and Dean had immediately noticed that.

"Thank you, Father. They've been really easy to work with. Two of my best players are graduating so I'm not sure we can win the Archdiocese championship again."

"Well, I do hope you'll return next season to coach."

"I will try, Father. I'll get right to the point. There are serious things going on with my marriage that are testing my faith. That is what brings me to you this evening."

"Yes. I was very concerned and curious after your phone call. Go ahead and explain everything to me now." Curious? Interesting choice of words, Dean thought.

"Well, I don't know how to begin this or how to properly explain it so I'll just come out and say it. Do you know of a Father Jacobson?"

"I know he's the superintendent of St. Censurius High School." At first Father Kramminnion mentally shit his pants, then almost physically shit them.

"I have to tell you something in complete confidence and I need your assistance," Dean said. "I probably should have come to you sooner. Now I think it's gone too far. I'll get right to the chase. For the past several years Father Jacobson has been coming around our house quite frequently, mostly when I'm gone."

"When did this start? Do you know why this happened?"

"As best as I can piece it together, it began after my last daughter was born. In fact it was Father Jacobson, not me, who brought them home from the hospital, behind my back. I let it go; don't quite know why. Maybe just to keep the peace. But why was he involved? My wife started working in the cafeteria at St. Censurius High School around 1957. So I'm guessing that's when and where they met. As far as why this is happening . . . it could be a number of reasons. Madeline and I have had our ups and downs as all marriages do. I admit I'm not a saint. And with my business I travel out of state sometimes for several days at a time."

"Umm hmm." Dad couldn't read Father Kramminnion's responses. He just stared back at him.

"At first Madeline never mentioned him. I wasn't aware she was associating with anyone other than her friends at the cafeteria. Hell, Father, I didn't know how much he was involved with our family until he brought Catherine home."

"So you weren't at the hospital when your wife delivered?"

"I was, but Father Jacobson brought them home the next day. They must have planned it behind my back. Once Catherine was born, my wife became even more detached from me and our marriage."

"Did you confront him then?"

"I did. He just said he was at the hospital anyway, as priests often are, and thought it would be more convenient for everyone if he just brought them home. I didn't buy it. But if I didn't go along with it, Madeline would have gotten all bent out of shape."

"What other events took place? Did other things make you suspicious of him? Did other people see things?"

"Well, she started doing various secretarial projects for him even though he has a full-time secretary at the school. I'd see boxes of papers and reports around the house that seemed to be associated with St. Censurius High School. I'd ask her about them and she'd say she was helping the school out for some of their projects. There were other causes for suspicion. I'd come back from being out of town. My foreman, who lives not far from our house, said he'd seen a dark-red Lincoln parked in front of our house sometimes when I was gone. He got me the license plate number. Here's a copy with the report from the Bureau of Motor Vehicles."

Shit, thought Father Kramminnion. He then let out a faint but audible fart and now ever-so-slightly pooped his pants. He prayed Dean didn't hear or smell anything and managed to continue listening like nothing ever happened.

"I traced it to Father Jacobson. My foreman has seen it there more often since my daughter was born. I have no reason to think he'd lie. Then there were other signs, like the butt of a cigar in our driveway. In the house, I'd pick up the faint scent of cigar smoke sometimes. No one I know smokes cigars. Have you seen Father Jacobson smoking cigars at any of your get-togethers?"

He slightly shook his head, no. Mother of Mercy, thought Father Kramminnion.

"And when I return from business trips, Catherine has new toys and clothes. I certainly didn't buy them. All my wife can tell me is that they were gifts from St. Censurius cafeteria ladies. As I said, we haven't had the perfect marriage and our sex life has been virtually non-existent for years. We don't even sleep in the same bedroom. But right around nine months before Catherine was born, Madeline suddenly wanted to have sexual relations. I was surprised but went along. Then, to my surprise, she was pregnant almost immediately. We had never discussed having more children. And quite frankly, with the condition of our marriage, it wouldn't have been a good idea. But I won't pursue a paternity test. Madeline would never agree and it could cause a lot of embarrassment and negative publicity. So, Father, in light of this evidence, what are your thoughts? Is there anything you want to tell me? Would you be willing to talk to me and my wife together?"

Father Kramminnion paused. The numerous rumors he'd heard in some inside circles were apparently true. This could be a significantly huge scandal for the Archdiocese. He just remembered at a priest's retreat a few months ago he had seen Father Jacobson smoking a cigar. And thank God Dean isn't pursuing a paternity test.

"Dean, would you like a drink? Some wine or a bourbon? I'm going to have one."

"No thanks, Father. I have to get back to work."

Father Kramminnion went to his makeshift bar, threw some ice in a glass, and poured himself a double shot of Old Fitzgerald. With his back to dad, he downed a big swallow. Then he turned to face dad.

"Dean, do you have any idea how long this relationship, so to speak, has been going on?"

"Catherine is almost five, so I'd guess a year or two before she was born. So let's say it started in 1958 or so. I'll probably never know. But our marriage is in shambles. Madeline and I fight constantly. It's taking a toll on our children. I'm at my wits end. Is there someone higher up who could reprimand this Father Jacobson or at the very least talk to him? I didn't grow up Catholic but I converted. My wife's family is all very ingrained in the church and in St. Censurius Parish, so I can't personally confront this man. But if you said something to the right person it could put a stop to this. Would you be willing to do that, Father?"

"Well, I'll see what I can do. So you haven't confronted him personally yet?"

"No, I've just put up with it. I feel overwhelmed by his power and political contacts. And I think Madeline's family would react badly. Even if any of them knew they certainly aren't going to admit it. If something came internally from his own hierarchy it would make a bigger impact than anything I could do."

"Let me see what I can do. This has to be handled very discreetly. If it came to that, would you be willing to talk to the archbishop?"

"Whatever I need to do. Just let me know."

"Okay, give me some time. I'll have to get an appointment with the archbishop. He's on vacation. I'll call the first day he's in. We'll see how he wants to handle it."

"That is all I can ask, Father." Dad extended his hand nervously and they shook.

Father Kramminnion stood behind his office window curtain and watched dad drive away. Then he poured himself another bourbon. The archbishop wasn't on vacation. But Father Kramminnion needed time to think. He stared up at the ceiling as if seeking guidance from the Almighty. This was very serious.

Dad wondered if he'd done the right thing. There was no one else he could talk to. Did his older children know what was going on? Lanny was married and away from the day-to-day problems. He never could tell what Karen was thinking, and she was now away at college. He sensed Mike knew things. But he wanted to leave his kids out of it. If they were dragged into it that could cause another whole set of problems. They all had been hurt enough with all the arguing going on in the house.

After a week of contemplation Father Kramminnion called and arranged to see the archbishop, briefing him on everything. Father Kramminnion was used to routine marriage counseling but this was much different. He didn't know Father Jacobson very well but knew about his power and political connections. The last thing he wanted to do was make enemies. That could ruin his shot at a position for Monsignor down the road. His best hope was to discreetly pass on Dean Sanders' confidences, then like Pontius Pilate, wash his hands of the whole affair. That would be the most politically expedient solution.

Then they met to discuss the issue. "Good afternoon, Theodore," said Archbishop O'Mally. He, too, had heard stories about Father Jacobson and a certain woman at St. Censurius. He had hoped, though, that this conversation would come on another archbishop's watch, not his. He was full of trepidation about the impending conversation.

"Good afternoon, Most Reverend Excellency," Father Kramminnion said.

"Oh, cut the crap, Theodore. I get tired of all the bullshit formality. That's what I hate about this position. Relax. We have enough on our plate."

"Uuhhh, sorry Bob. I haven't relaxed since Dean Sanders left my office last week."

"OK, recount the whole conversation for me. He didn't threaten a lawsuit did he?"

"No, and I found that funny. A lot of other husbands would have if we didn't step in right away."

"Well, good for us. Do you want, or need, a drink?"

"Thanks. I'll take you up on that." The archbishop poured himself a Scotch and handed Father Kramminnion a bourbon.

"I picked this up in Scotland a couple of years ago. It's a 16-year and very smooth. You can't find it over here. Sure you don't want to try it?"

"No thanks. I never really developed a taste for it." They sipped their drinks as Father Kramminnion recounted his meeting with Dean Sanders and rumors he himself had heard over the years.

"It's the same rumors I've been hearing," said the archbishop. "God knows how much of this story has gotten around certain circles even outside the parish."

"Dean thinks his wife and Jacobson began a relationship sometime in 1958 or so, and it continues to this day. He is not sure how far it's actually gone but would like to see an end to it."

"So the rumors are true. My God, it's taken him this long to come to terms with it."

"People can be in denial for years. I've seen it many times in counseling. He didn't want to rock the boat or alarm his children, hoping it would end. Also Madeline's family are strong Catholics in St. Censurius Parish. Her parents are well known there. Her mother, Doriana McCarney, is on the Bridgeport Police Department and as you know, Father Jacobson is the department chaplain. Her older brother is deep into Bridgeport politics. He also serves on several high-level boards. So there's a lot he's up against. He doesn't have anywhere near the family support she does. Not to mention Jacobson's own political power."

"That all makes sense. Now he wants to know if we can do something. I know Sam and what he can be like, but didn't figure he'd go so far with something like this," said the archbishop.

"Mr. Sanders also has eyewitness reports of a dark-red Lincoln parked in front of his house at night while he's was away on business. According to the Bureau of Motor Vehicles it's Jacobson's car."

"This is such a pitiful and potentially explosive situation. But I'm curious about one thing. If the relationship did indeed started sometime in '58, a full two years before his last child was born, how did they conceive a child if things were so bad?" asked the archbishop.

"Brace yourself, there's more."

"Oh no. You're not going to say what I think you are." The archbishop stared at Father Kramminnion, who stared right back.

"I'm afraid so. Mr. Sanders didn't come right out and say it. But he alluded to the fact that his daughter really isn't his. About nine months before that birth, Madeline demanded they make love. Then mysteriously nine months later almost to the day, she gave birth. That's the way he told it anyway. That was his side of the story."

"And there's been no paternity test?"

"He said no, and there won't be, and I believe him. And thank God for that."

"Well thank God we don't have to worry about any paternity lawsuit. But the other issues remain. We now know the rumors are true. I've seen similar situations in the Church but none with this high a profile. And shame on us for letting it get this far. I suspected and did nothing. This hasn't been one of the bright spots in my career as a steward of the Holy Mother Church. I don't know why in the hell they won't just let us marry! It doesn't make sense anymore." Father Kramminnion looked at the archbishop with some compassion.

"I did nothing either, Bob, and it involves my parish," said Father Kramminnion.

"Don't blame yourself, Theodore. What's done is done. There are lessons for us here and we have to move forward. We have to show Dean Sanders we're doing something. I'll think on this for a few days. Just let him know we talked, and that I'm contemplating the next course of action. I'm going to have to be discreet with Sam Jacobson as well. Too bad he's the superintendent at St. Censurius and a good earner. A lot of church donations come in thanks to him – inheritances and so on. And all the high-profile organizations he is involved in. Hell, he's the chaplain of the police department."

"Let Mr. Sanders know we talked and that we'll handle the matter in the most efficient manner possible," the archbishop said. This meant keeping it as quiet as possible.

"Well," sighed Father Kramminnion, "that's a big load off my shoulders, Bob. Again, I am sorry it has come this far. I'll leave it to your good judgment, and with the grace of God the outcome will be good for all involved."

"Let's hope so, Theodore. You get hold of Mr. Sanders, tell him we did talk, and I'll keep you apprised of

THE ALTAR BOY — STEPHENS

things from my end. I'll have Sam Jacobson over here for a meeting. I want you to be there and relay your conversation with Mr. Sanders."

"That is fine. Just let me know. Do you want Mr. Sanders there as well?"

"Not at this point. Let's just see what Sam has to say and we'll go from there."

In his office the archbishop mulled over just how to approach Father Jacobson. Surely it won't be any surprise that his questionable behavior has come to the attention of his office. With such a rock-solid reputation Jacobson must have felt bullet-proof. The archbishop picked up the phone. On the 10th ring Father Jacobson himself answered.

"Sam, its Archbishop O'Mally. Sorry for calling so late. How are you this evening?"

"Still among the livin', archbishop. How are you?" Father replied as he put down his drink. He was relieved he got the phone before any of the other priests did.

"Well, I'm as good as an old archbishop can be. Listen, I'll get right to the point. Father Theodore Kramminnion from St. Micaelis came to me with a story about one of his parishioners. Are you familiar with the Sanders family?"

"Yes I am. A Madeline Sanders worked for me in the St. Censurius cafeteria a few years ago and we developed a friendship. She was having trouble with her husband and I've counseled her several times." Father Jacobson chose his words carefully.

"I want to meet with you and Father Kramminnion to discuss what I consider a very, shall we say, sensitive situation. We have a complaint against you and we need to get to the bottom of this."

"I'd be happy to discuss it with you. When did you want to meet?"

"My house next Thursday evening at 6. The three of us can have dinner together."

"I can do that. I look forward to it."

Father Jacobson hung up the phone, wondering how this had reached the archbishop. Did one of the other priests know something? Who went to Father Kramminnion? Oh shit! It had to be her husband. But he's been out of town most of the time I've been there. A thousand thoughts swirled around in his head. He'd quickly have to talk to Madeline. He had a little over a week to prepare his story. He was tired. He had to get some sleep. He took the usual two sleeping pills and grabbed two more, just in case.

The next day Father Jacobson called Madeline at home. She sensed something was up from the tone of his voice and flat-out asked what was wrong.

"I got a call from the archbishop last night. He wants to meet me and Father Kramminnion from St. Micaelis. It appears Dean talked to Father Kramminnion about you and me, but the archbishop didn't go into detail. But that is what I have to anticipate."

"I didn't think he gave a damn. This burns me up. Dean hasn't even been around here half the time for years. He's been with a couple women that I know of. And he doesn't give Catherine the time of day. God, I can't believe this."

"Where is he now?"

"He's at a job up in South Bend. He'll supposedly be back this weekend."

"Let me deal with this end of it and I'll let you know what happens. In the meantime let's not meet or even talk anymore just to play it safe."

"Everything's going to be alright isn't it?"

"I think so. Don't worry. I'll talk to you next Friday. Remember, I love you."

That next Thursday Father Jacobson pulled up at the archbishop's house at precisely 6. He had thought over every question he might be asked. Unfortunately he had no dirt on the archbishop or Father Kramminnion, so he'd be in purely defensive mode. He would speak in generalities and shift the attention from him to Mr. Sanders.

The archbishop and Father Kramminnion were already on their second round of drinks.

"Well hello, Sam. I haven't seen you in a while. How have you been?" asked the archbishop.

"Fine, Bob. How are you?" His response carried his usual finesse and warm good humor.

"Good, Sam. Of course you know I asked Theodore to be in on this."

"How are you, Theodore?" asked Father Jacobson. His eyes lacked some of their usual sparkle. That son-of-a-bitch, he thought. Why the hell didn't he talk to me instead of dragging in the archbishop? He could have kept this a little quieter.

"Fine, Sam." Both men were a bit ill at ease. Father Jacobson, however, was as cool as a cucumber.

The archbishop handed Father Jacobson a generous pour of the premium Scotch. "It's a single malt ten-year called McTaffy's," he said with some pride.

"Don't think I've ever tasted anything quite this smooth. It's excellent," Jacobson said after a long swallow. He had tasted hundreds of single malts in his career with the Church. Frankly, this one seemed overrated and probably overpriced.

"Good. Why don't we all have a seat? As I mentioned on the phone we want to discuss this complaint from a parishioner, this Dean Sanders. He visited Father Kramminnion's office two weeks ago and in so many words, Sanders implied you of having some sort of relationship with his wife."

Father Jacobson didn't even flinch and managed to pull out a cigar. The way he held it out and lit it exuded power and confidence. He held eye contact with the archbishop and maintained a personable, friendly smile.

"He said your car has been seen at his house while he's away. Someone even wrote down your plate number. He's smelled cigar smoke in the house. He claims his daughter has new toys and clothes every time he comes home from a business trip. He even told Theodore that before his daughter was born, their sex life was practically non-existent. And you brought the infant home from the hospital. He infers you may be the girl's father. I'm going to give you a chance to explain. There was no talk of lawsuits or paternity tests, by the way."

Father Jacobson chuckled, puffed his large black cigar and gracefully blew smoke up into the air. It took on an almost menacing shape as hovered over Father Kramminnion and the archbishop. Father Jacobson had prepared for one of the greatest sermons of his religious career.

"Well, Bob, first of all, Theodore and I didn't get a chance to discuss this before it reached your desk. Mr. Sanders' visit was news to me." Father Jacobson shot Father Kramminnion a menacing glance. Kramminnion now seemed uneasy as he had just made a powerful enemy.

"Yes, I do know the Sanders family and especially Madeline and her daughter Catherine. She worked in the cafeteria at St. Censurius for a couple of years and that's how I got to know her. She seemed very distraught during those years, which caught my attention. Just prior to her giving birth to her daughter she did leave her job at St. Censurius. And now she does part-time secretarial work for me on the side. She used to be a secretary at a local business and she's good at what she does.

"At first we had brief greetings in the mornings then a bit more conversation as time went on. Then one day I noticed her crying by herself in one of the storage rooms and of course I went and talked to her. She said she had just learned of her husband's infidelities. Mr. Sanders has a business in which he travels out of town and even out of state much of the time. I suppose if a man wasn't in love with his wife he would, shall we say, stray in a situation like that.

"Anyway, in the course of our subsequent conversations and my counseling, she told me that she knew of his indiscretions on the road by what she would find in his luggage sometimes and his trousers. When she would confront him all he would say is that particular person was a client or somehow connected to whatever project he was working on at the time. However, she knew in her heart it wasn't true. Mr. Sanders' affections had all but disappeared after Catherine was born. As far as their sex life being in bad shape around the time she was born, I knew no first-hand account of that.

"Madeline did convey to me that many a night he forced himself on her, which of course contributed to their marital problems as well. He also has a bad temper and was very verbally abusive toward her. He had absolutely no affections or feelings toward the little girl. Madeline didn't want to burden her parents about her problems. So at that point in her life, with what she had to deal with, she felt the only person she could confide in was me. For some reason she felt I had the spiritual strength, education and experience needed to help her get through this extremely difficult period in her life."

Father Jacobson concluded his remarks. He gently shook the ice in his Scotch glass, took a sip and then took another puff of his cigar as he continued to convey an expression of genuine concern toward the archbishop and Father Kramminnion.

"So naturally we started to develop a friendship of sorts. And I do admit I've got a soft spot for the girl whom I felt had been totally disregarded and abandoned by her father. So how did this marriage start to deteriorate? I would have to say, again based on what Madeline has told me, it started with Mr. Sanders' immoral behavior on his many business travels.

"As Madeline started to confront him more and more he became angry and defensive. There were a few times she feared for her safety because of his hostile temper. After many months of counseling with her, that is the conclusion I came to. There were times I personally felt for her safety. Now do I visit her home from time to time? Yes I do. Do I do things with Catherine from time to time? Yes I do, as her father doesn't give her the time of day and he is gone so much of the time now. To be quite honest I don't know where they'd be if I hadn't offered counseling and friendship for these past several years."

The archbishop and Father Kramminnion were utterly spellbound by Father's presentation. They had just witnessed a performance of Macbeth given by none other than Shakespeare, himself, or on a lesser scale, a scene by Robert Young in the sitcom *Father Knows Best*. It all made sense now. Why had they even slightly questioned or doubted the integrity of this fine priest and upright steward of the Church? Once they began to regain their composure the archbishop thought, Thank God I really don't have to carry this any further or at least take any drastic action. Father Kramminnion was now slightly embarrassed he had even dragged the archbishop into this at all. He should have just had a private discussion with Father Jacobson and that would have been the end of it, at least from his standpoint.

"Sam, hey, I do appreciate your honesty, candor and sincerity. Mr. Sanders apparently has a lot of soul-searching to do. Theodore, I'm not sure he should be coaching our kids on the table tennis team next season. Is he for sure scheduled to do it next year?" asked the archbishop.

"He was on the fence about it, but I'll see he doesn't," said Father Kramminnion.

"Sam, I'll get you another Scotch. Dinner is ready. I hope you're hungry," said the archbishop.

"Being a priest and bearing the burden of God's work does build up an appetite," said Father Jacobson. He had succeeded in putting his accuser on trial while in the same conversation totally exonerating himself. He completely destroyed the reputation and credibility of Dean Sanders.

✝

The next day he called Madeline. "Well good morning, ma'am," he said with a laugh.

"Hi. How did it go?" she asked.

"More or less as I expected. Dean filed a formal complaint against me. He accused me of being romantically involved with you and playing dad to Catherine when he was away."

"Well, that burns me up," she said. "It'll be all over the parish before you know it! I won't be able to show my face. All my neighbors will know about it! All of them!"

"Calm down, my dear. It will be okay. We'll get through this like we always have. The archbishop and Father Kramminnion are convinced of Dean's bad behavior toward you and Catherine. We should lie low for a couple of weeks while things settle down."

Mom sat at the dining room table, put her head in her hands, and cried. How would she face anyone in St. Micaelis Parish again? Or even in her neighborhood? Her family would certainly find out what Dean had done, as if they didn't already know.

When dad finally got home around 10 that evening he found mom sitting on the davenport. She glared at him. "I'm not surprised you didn't call last week. Hell, I don't even know where you went," she said.

"Please don't start again."

151

"I need to ask you something. Did you go to Father Kramminnion and spread lies about Father Jacobson and me? Did you? And the damn archbishop too, of all people?"

"Yes, I did, as a matter of fact! I'm damn sick of this Father Jacobson coming around when I'm gone! This has got to stop."

"Did you tell Father Kramminnion we were having an affair? You son of a bitch! How could you start this with the Pastor of St. Micaelis Parish, where all our friends and neighbors live? I can't even show my face outside this door anymore!"

"Oh, don't pretend with me! How long has this been going on? How damn long? You can't tell me it's innocent! People know about it! They've seen his car here at night! Don't fucking pretend nothing is going on! And by the way, how in the hell did you even know I met with him?"

When I got home from school, Mike and Catherine were outside in the back yard. Mike looked solemn.

"What's going on?"

"Mom and dad are fighting again. This time it's really bad."

"What happened?"

"I can't really say. Dad went to see Father Kramminnion yesterday. Whatever it was, mom didn't like it. She found out today and started yelling at dad the minute he walked in the door." I cautiously stepped inside to listen. The yelling was so loud the neighbors could probably hear it.

I asked myself, What was it about? Why did he go see him? The shouting was extremely unnerving. But, of course, this wasn't the first time. I kept hearing Father Jacobson's name. My parents were accusing each other of terrible things. All I could do was try to block it out.

I put my books down and went outside to get away from it. I ran to the Field to try and clear my head. Why were they fighting again? God, will they ever stop? I'm so tired of it. I had forgotten about telling them how excited I was at serving my first Mass.

Exactly who is this Father Jacobson who has been creeping into my family life? I noticed him more frequently, especially when dad was out of town. And why was my dad around less and less?

That night I tossed and turned, trying to sleep. Then a song came to mind—the Shirelles' "Will You Still Love Me Tomorrow?" It came out in 1961 but it was on the radio every now and then. Shirley Owens will never know how gently she lulled me to sleep that night.

Catherine came into the living room, crying. Mom continued, "Now look what the hell you did!" She scooped up her daughter and headed toward her bedroom.

"I hope you're happy now. I hope to God she didn't understand any of this."

Dad headed toward our bedroom and prepared for bed. Mike and I pretended we were asleep. I quietly cried for both of my parents that night.

Meanwhile, the archbishop continually mulled over the meeting with Father Kramminnion and Father Jacobson. His explanation did seem sound but something started nagging at him. Would the meeting embolden Father Jacobson and Mrs. Sanders to take their "friendship" further? Should he appease Dean Sanders to keep him from pursuing more damaging action? Maybe there was an out. The position of principal at St. Augustine High School would be open soon. If Father Jacobson transferred there it would put some distance between him and St. Micaelis Parish. It might slow things down. It would get him away from Mrs. Sanders' parents as well. The idea gained some traction in his mind. He'd start the ball rolling on the transfer in the next few weeks. Father Jacobson wouldn't like this, but it wasn't his choice. The archbishop was now in full damage-control mode.

Chapter 9: Leabor Road

IN LATE 1965 the archbishop transferred Father Jacobson to the position of principal at St. Augustine High School. He was doing a fine job as superintendent at St. Censurius. So why was he transferred? What would the official reason be? The Archdiocese claimed his talents were needed to build up the relatively new high school. With the growth of the Catholic population of Bridgeport after World War II, more Catholic schools were needed. St. Augustine was one of three new ones built in the early '60s. His new parish included St. Augustine High School, a grade school, church, priest's rectory and a convent for the nuns who taught at the facilities. Two other full-time priests were already assigned there. Father Jacobson would preside over its first graduating class.

This brought difficulties for Father Jacobson and my mother, which, of course, was the plan. St. Augustine was now further out of the way. St. Censurius was expedient. Her parents were members of that parish and when Madeline would visit them it was easy to stop in his office. And her son Mike was still going to high school there. This new arrangement meant they'd have to plan more carefully in getting together. This new parish was a busier and more open place with nowhere to hide, and more important, nowhere to hide someone. Father Jacobson didn't like it one bit. People would talk now more than ever.

There was another thing Father Jacobson didn't like. St. Augustine High was coed. He didn't agree with a coed educational system. He had no experience teaching in it. There would be a new set of moral behaviors and "distractions" where he would have to be steward. Were it

155

up to him, all Catholic schools would be male-only or female-only, just like St. Censurius and its sister high school next door, St. Angeles. The nuns could have the girlie girls but leave the educational, moral, physical and spiritual development of the boys up to him. He was, for the most part, a stern, macho, old-school disciplinarian. He firmly believed in Mass, martinis, Scotch, cigars and football. Once Father Jacobson was entrenched in the day-to-day activities of St. Augustine High School it would become more and more difficult to see mom and Catherine. However, their relationship was as strong as ever. Where there was a will there was a way, and be damned with what anyone else thought.

Back home on Broderick Street what was left of my parents' marriage was dismal. My dad was now gone on business trips most of the time. His visits home were becoming infrequent. And the crazy thing was I still thought of our home and family as relatively normal. Maybe I was mentally blocking out a little too much. I always hoped things would get better, even though I saw my mother was cheerful around Father Jacobson and hostile around dad.

Mom was quickly becoming extremely uncomfortable in our neighborhood and St. Micaelis Parish in general. As a result of my dad's meeting with Father Kramminnion, she stopped attending church and doing her volunteer work there. When we did go to church, we'd drive way out to a different part of town and whole new parish. One Sunday it would be St. Luke's, way up north. The next Sunday it would be far-away St. Ann's or St. Benedict, which was one of mom's favorites. They had a 12:30 Sunday Mass and it was okay to walk up the stairs and sit in the choir area. We always slipped in quietly after services began, then slipped back out the door right after communion. The lower our profile, the better. Mom started doing more errands when it was dark. She now avoided going out in the daytime. Father Jacobson continued slipping in at night, taking Catherine out for the evening, and bringing her back late. But mom knew it couldn't go on much longer. She now felt everyone was watching her. She felt that our family should leave the area and get away from St. Micaelis Parish, never to return. She also felt betrayed by Father Kramminnion for going behind her back to the archbishop. Our house on Broderick Street would go up for sale.

In November 1965 we finally moved to a sleepy little side street called Leabor Road, dad's final effort to keep us together as a family. As the movers hauled away our stuff, I sat by myself listening to the radio play Len Barry's "1-2-3." It was the last song I heard in our house on Broderick Street. I could only pray this move would be a blessing for our family. Time would prove me very wrong.

The move to Leabor Road was a major transition in my life. I'd begun to be aware of girls and rock-n-roll music. I was starting to actually like girls instead of assuming most of them had cooties. I'd started to learn to cook, more out of necessity as opposed to liking it for a hobby. Later on, just like the Field, Leabor road would become a state of mind. In our later adult lives my brothers and I would describe a bizarre situation as "Leaborroadish." No one but us would know what that meant. The move there would be dad's last desperate effort to keep his family and marriage together. It would turn out to be a dismal failure.

We pulled into the large, semi-circular driveway of the Leabor Road house with the movers behind us. "Carl, wait in the car while your father and I talk to the moving men," mom said. I flipped on the radio station. The Beatles' "Nowhere Man." I sure could relate to that. Next up: "Baby The Rain Must Fall" by Glen Yarborough. That's weird. Two songs in a row I really liked. Then dad

157

came out on the front porch and motioned me inside. I proceeded with caution.

He asked, "What do you think so far?"

"It seems big. Is the inside as big as the outside?"

"For the most part, yes," he laughed.

Right away it didn't feel right. As I stepped past the front door into the living room I sensed a presence — something unnerving. More family chaos? Bad spirits? Did something bad happen in this house before? How much longer would dad be around? I felt a distinct premonition of sorrow. I was getting a lot of negative vibes.

But on to the grand tour. This large, one-story limestone house was built in the middle '50s. It had a slate roof, slate steps to the front door, a little breezeway-type patio area outside, a big outdoor porch, two fireplaces, and a full basement. It was huge; it felt as big as a football field. There were four bedrooms, a long, sunken living room with three large picture windows, a dining room, a kitchen, and a library-type room. This was the coolest room in the house. It had parquet floors, two sets of bookshelves, wooden walls, a fireplace, and its own half bath. We called the bedroom past the kitchen the "back bedroom." A door in the kitchen led to the basement.

Another thing I noticed was how relatively secluded the property was. In the neighborhood we moved from it was one house right next to the other, but not here. There was a thick woods in the back of the property and on its north side. On the south side and along the road in front of the house were extensive amounts of foliage and shrubbery. The foliage in front of the house surrounded a separate yard. That yard had a pine tree in the middle of it then two magnolia trees on both sides. The driveway had two entrances coming in on the south end of the house and exiting on the north. It was like a semi-circle in front and was lined with a continuous row of shrubbery. In the middle of the drive were slate steps to the front door of the house. In the back of the house was a two-car attached garage. Fifty or so feet from that garage was another double-car garage. That garage wasn't limestone like the rest of the house but had white aluminum siding.

The property was a whopping two-and-a-half acres. Well guess who's going to mowing this lawn? I thought. There were two fruit trees. One apple tree was in the south end of the property and one pear tree on the north side behind the detached garage. There were lots and lots of other large trees like oak and hickory. All this I observed in the first 20 minutes of the grand tour and yet I still didn't like it. Most other kids would have been in outdoor play heaven. Most adult people would have thought the property grand, but again, I didn't feel good about it at all. I would have settled for a three-bedroom apartment if I knew my parents were going to stay together. But who gave a damn what I thought anyway?

All of a sudden I decided to break away and wander back into the house alone before anyone else knew I had left the tour group. After living in the Broderick Street house I had a slight fear of basements. If there were demons and ghosts down there they wouldn't be out yet. I hoped Sakers and Keylock hadn't followed us over here. I carefully descended the stairs and slipped into the basement. It was dark, musty, and damp. There were cement floors and mortar-and-brick walls. Plain light bulbs hung in the ceiling fixtures. I stood frozen at the bottom of the stairway. My five senses registered everything. My sixth sense was on alert as well. The only real light came from the light bulb directly above me. Weak sunlight forced its way through the dirty basement windows.

In the eerie light I saw some old furniture in the room to my left. I turned right and my expedition continued. I found a small water pump room and then further on a furnace room. Two sump pumps were down there, too. At the very back of the basement was the largest room. I started toward it, looking all around me as I crept. There were two entrances with a mortar-and-brick wall separating them. I carefully approached the room, then heard a sound from the other side of that wall. It sounded like someone dropped something and it hit the floor. It wasn't glass or something breakable. It sounded like an empty plastic bottle or some sort of toy that bounced a couple of times. However, as far as I could see into the two entrances, the room was empty. I stopped dead in my tracks, my skin tingled and the hair on my arms stood up. But there was no way I was going to go into the room and look behind that wall. That was where the noise came from. I slowly backed up, then turned around and ran toward the stairs and up to the relative safety of the kitchen. I quickly shut the basement door behind me. Unfortunately, there was no lock on that door. I ran outside and found everyone back by the apple tree. I hoped that what had happened down there was my imagination.

"Carl, where were you?" asked dad.

"Oh, I just walked around the basement. But there wasn't anything down there."

"Well, the furnace, the sump pumps and the main water pump are down there. And the hook-ups for the washing machine. We can check all that out later. Let's all go back inside and start putting things away. Carl, your room is the last one on the left."

"Can't I have the neat one with the wood floor and the fireplace?"

Mike said, "No way. I already asked dad." A privilege of being older, I thought. Karen got the room next to me, and mom and Catherine had the very back bedroom on the other side of mine. Karen wouldn't be around much as she was away at college most of the time now.

"Dad, you won't be in the same bedroom with mom in this house, either, will you?" Dad didn't answer me, but walked away. I knew then this new house wouldn't change anything. In my bedroom, after moving my things in, I turned on my clock radio. A beautiful song I liked, "Lovers Concerto" by the Toys, put me in a better mood.

Two other things weren't quite right. The water tasted horrible. It was well water with too much iron. It seemed to turn the sinks and toilets orange. And then this. It had dawned on me that this new house was much closer to St. Augustine High School and Father Jacobson. I was surprised dad went along with a move to this location. And with all of the seclusion provided by the surrounding shrubbery it wasn't nearly as vulnerable to prying eyes.

✝

I would finish my fall 1965 semester of grade school at St. Micaelis. I'd then start the spring 1966 semester at the local Catholic school, St. Macarius. Mom would drive me to St. Micaelis until Christmas break in mid-December. I'd be formally enrolled in St. Macarius in January, 1966, and take their school bus to class. Catherine would start first grade at St. Macarius in the fall semester of 1966.

✝

As the weeks went by we settled into the Leabor Road house and all its spaciousness. I was slowly getting used to having to walk further through the house just to get somewhere. It was a longer walk to the bathroom and the kitchen. Another thing I didn't like was the large, sunken living room. One Friday night a couple of months later I was home alone and getting ready to watch my favorite TV shows. I'd put a box of frozen French fries in the oven to bake. But they wouldn't be done by the 7 pm start of my shows. So I turned the oven up to 550 degrees to hurry them along. That was as high as the oven would go. Come

161

on, come on, hurry! Please bake faster, I frantically said to myself.

I ran back to the other end of the house where my bedroom was. Oh good…a commercial is still on! I ran back to the opposite end of the house. The commercial wouldn't last much longer so I went on good faith that the fries were done, turned off the oven, and pulled the tray out with a dish towel. I hurriedly dumped the fries on a plate, salted them, and topped them off with a huge glob of ketchup. I scooped up the plate in both hands and raced to my bedroom at the opposite end of the house.

As I approached the first two steps down into the living room I leaped off them and onto the living room floor, keeping my stride. I kept running, balancing the hot French fries, and approached the second set of steps leading out of the living room and into the hallway. As I leaped up toward the top step, my back foot didn't go high enough and I tripped. I fell forward onto my stomach and lost control of the French fry platter. It flew out of my hand like a Frisbee and landed face down, several feet in front of me. As much ketchup splattered on my face as on the carpeting.

I wasn't yet at the routine swearing stage. If I had been, you would have heard some bad words. Luckily, no one was home and I managed to clean up the mess and bake another batch of fries. But I missed all but the last 15 minutes of *The Wild Wild West*. But I was ready for *Hogan's Heroes*, *Gomer Pyle, U.S.M.C.*, and *The Smothers Brothers Comedy Hour*. They were funny and sometimes they had a good rock band or folk singer like Joan Baez.

✝

Our dog Mickey never got used to the new house. When we took him out to pee he'd run off and we'd have to chase after him and drag him back. Mike was the only one who could halfway control him, but he wasn't around as much as he used to be. He took advantage of all the secret places to poop and pee inside the house. When we tried discipline him he'd try to bite us. He got away with it easy enough, for a while. I cleaned up every dried-up pile of poop I could but didn't mention it to mom. But when she had to start cleaning up more of the hidden shit piles herself she didn't like it one bit. Mickey would eventually pay dearly for that.

The first Christmas in the new house was the last time we were together in any semblance of family. Karen was back from college in Chicago and Lanny stopped by with his two little boys. Mom and dad made a marginal effort to pretend things were normal. I so wanted to believe it. But in the back of our heads we all knew the truth.

As 1966 got started I enrolled in the second semester of my fifth-grade year at St. Macarius. I had just recently finished my altar boy training at St. Micaelis and had served several months' worth of Sunday Masses, reciting the required ritual prayers in Latin. The changes of Vatican II were in the process of trickling down to street-level Mass practices. When I told everyone, including the school principal Sister Cornelia, I was "altar-boy ready," everyone was very pleased. This gave me a ready-made group of friends. It meant automatic membership in the exclusive Altar Boy Fraternity.

†

Over the next several months dad, Mike, and I worked on cleaning up the downstairs. We got a nice sofa and a couple of chairs and a second-hand TV. One Saturday afternoon dad asked, "Carl, do you and Mike want to come downstairs for a little bit?"

"Are we gonna have to do more work down there?" Mike asked.

"No, I think we're all done for now. We can tackle that back room later. Carl, don't you have a lot of that cleaned up already?" I nodded, but I had plans of making my own altar down there where I could say Mass. If I did that maybe it would scare away whatever was back there. That little project was still my secret.

"I just need you boys to help me move something." Dad started down stairs and we followed. "Wow!" cried Mike. I sped up and took a look. There stood a brand-spanking-new, full-size pool table.

"What do you think?" dad asked.

"I don't know how to play, but it'll be fun to try," Mike said.

"I don't know how to play at all," I said.

"Well it's almost time for *The Jackie Gleason Show,* and *Get Smart* is on later. I think your mother put a couple of pizzas in the oven. So let's watch and I'll give you some lessons. Sound good?"

"It does to me," said Mike. "Can I be first? Carl, you watch carefully."

Mike grabbed a pool cue and rubbed the chalk on it. I watched intently as he, under dad's inspection, handled the cue and took aim to break the racked pool balls. CRACK, they went and scattered all over the table! It was one of the most fascinating things I'd ever seen in my life. I wanted to learn this game. Two of the balls fired right into the holes.

"Wow! Dad, did you see that?" Even Mike was shocked. Dad shook his head and blinked in disbelief.

"Mike, that was a pretty decent shot."

"Can you do that again?" I asked.

"Since Mike got two balls in he gets to shoot again. That's how the game generally is played," dad explained. "He got two of the solid balls in so he has the solids. I have the stripes. Whoever hits their respective balls in wins the game. And Mike is already two ahead of me."

"What does respective mean?" I asked.

"It means something that pertains to you."

"What does pertains mean?"

"Hey, *Jackie Gleason* is starting. Can we watch while we're playing?" Mike asked. We all stared at the TV as Jackie Gleason walked out on stage. The crowd roared. When he sipped a cup of coffee and smugly said, "How sweet it is," dad did his own Gleason impression. Mike and I fell on the floor laughing.

"Okay, now, where were we? Is it Mike's shot again?" dad asked, barely able to contain his laughing.

Such were the good times in the early days of Leabor Road. Dad, Mike, and I had a good year and a half together there.

✝

The darker side of Leabor Road set in when summer hit in 1966. That meant the whole oversized yard would have to be mowed, more than once. A large, three-blade riding mower and a smaller push mower for trimming came with the house. I usually did the trimming with the push mower. Mike helped out a lot and sometimes let me use the large riding mower. I really liked that mower. Riding it gave me a huge sense of power and control. I envisioned myself as a policeman of sorts. I policed the never-ending violations the overgrown lawn imposed on me. Later on I did most of the lawn myself.

The better weather meant dad traveled more. He eventually spent even less time at Leabor Road than on Broderick Street. But one day in February he said, "Carl, Mike, I want you to clear off your busy calendars. How about spending four days in Oklahoma with me on the job site? There's a lake where we can fish and you can roam around a lot in the woods. We're working on a nice country club golf course there. If you want, we can play some

165

rounds, Mike. Carl, you can help caddy the clubs for us or we can get a golf cart." I stared straight ahead in utter shock. It would be fun to get away, stay in dad's construction trailer, eat out and go fishing every day.

"Yah!!" I cried. Mike said he'd like to go. But he wasn't sure — he and a friend were starting up a painting business and already had a couple of jobs lined up.

"You two have a week for Easter break in April. I have to get back there by Sunday night and be onsite Monday morning sometime. We'd have to leave early Sunday morning and be over there by evening, depending on what kind of time we'd make. If we had to we could spend Sunday night somewhere then head on in from there."

"Dad, have you talked about this with mom?" I asked.

"Not yet, but I will when she gets back."

"Mike, can you come with us?" Mike kind of rolled his eyes at me.

"Dad, not this time. I have to finish those last two painting jobs we're in the middle of. The customers have paid us half and we have to finish. And I have other things to do like keep the lawn mowed." Mike looked at me sorrowfully.

"I understand, Mike." I suspected the "other things to do" meant running around and drinking with his friends. He seemed to prefer that to spending time around the family these days. He was growing up. I missed him. I missed watching Friday night TV with him. But I couldn't blame him with the hostile tension in our new home. But I was certainly ready to go with dad on this trip.

✝

One Saturday in early March there was another blowup. When mom came home rather late in the day, dad's mood changed. "You've been gone for quite a while. Where were you?" he asked.

"As a matter of fact, it's none of your damn business. Can't you wait until I get Catherine put down for her nap?" That dreaded feeling again. Mike shut his bedroom door. As I headed out the door and ran to the brush field behind the house, I could hear the screaming escalate. I knew what they were fighting about. Mom was away more and more herself, and it didn't matter if dad was in town or not.

In a safe, hidden spot in the grass I lay down. I stared up at the drifting clouds and noticed their beauty. I stayed in the yard until I thought the fight had died down. I stared at the house like a soldier who'd witnessed an explosion on the battlefield. I circled the house from afar just to see whose car was there. Dad's truck was gone. Mike's junky old car was gone. So just mom and Catherine were alone in the house. I cautiously entered.

"Mom," I called out. No answer. I knew she must be in her bedroom at the other end of the house. I noticed her bedroom door was closed. I walked ever so softly toward it and put my ear up to the door. I could hear her crying. So I quietly walked away and back into my own bedroom. All of a sudden there was a knock at my door.

"Carl, are you in there?" mom asked. I always got nervous talking to mom or dad after a fight. The sadness, anger and hopelessness in their eyes were so plain.

"Yah, mom, come on in."

"I'm sorry you had to hear all that again. It was nothing against you. I hope you know that. Are you okay now?"

"I'm okay. Are you alright? Don't cry, mom, it'll be okay." It crushed me to look at her. She never told me exactly what the fights were about but I now knew.

"Your father says he wants you to come out to Oklahoma during Easter break. Is that something you want to do?" she asked.

"Yah, mom, I'd like to if it's okay."

"It's okay with me. You can drive out with him in the truck. But you'll have to fly back on your own. Are you okay with that? We'll be right there at the airport when you come back."

"Mom, yah, I am. Mike isn't going is he?"

"No, he has some things to do with his business before his school starts again. I'll get your clothes ready. You'll be leaving Sunday morning early and flying back Friday." Dad apparently wasn't going to be home for Easter, I thought.

"I have to run over to grandmother's now. Will you be okay here for a little bit? I'm not sure where your father or Mike went."

"I'll be alright, mom. Go on."

I followed her out of my bedroom and walked her and Catherine to the car. She was still extremely upset. Her facial expressions always gave her away. As I watched her pull out of the driveway, a strong feeling of depression came over me. Turning around and walking back into the house I could feel the negative vibrations of the fight that had happened just an hour earlier. It was always weird being in that house alone, and this just made it worse. I decided to walk back to dad's bedroom.

Looking around, I sensed that fewer of his things were there. I thought to myself, Is this all dad owns? I then walked clear to the other end of the house and into my mother's bedroom. On the way, I slipped into my room and turned on the radio to keep me company. Catherine slept with mom just as in the old house. I looked around at the contents. My mom's magazines were scattered around. I picked one up, *Redbook*, and briefly leafed through it. I looked at her sparse jewelry collection, clothing, and other personal things lying about. Then I heard a song coming from the clock radio in my bedroom. It was "Elusive Butterfly," by Bob Lind. Its timing was either meant to be or couldn't have happened at a worse time. I stared straight ahead and sadly listened. The song sent me into a pensive mood about my mother. As I stood there I was enveloped by an intense sense of sadness. I could feel her despair. Whether the marriage situation was her fault, Father Jacobson's fault, or my dad's fault, or all their faults, I felt sadness for her. I sensed the emotional difficulties she endured. I shuddered to think of her gone or out of my life in any way.

✝

A few days later we started to get ready for that drive to Oklahoma. I was really excited to get away from the tension of Leabor Road. The music alarm went off at 6 am with The Lovin' Spoonful's "Six O'Clock." I took that as good luck for my trip.

Mom rushed me along, as she didn't want to interact with dad any more than she had to.

"You be good, and I love you."

"You too, mom. Bye."

Dad said, "Okay Kingosabee, are you ready?"

"Yah, I can't wait."

"We have to run over and pick up Jerry. When he gets in you can sit in the middle," dad said.

I nodded. We drove halfway across town and picked him up. Jerry was one of dad's foremen and a really nice guy. He'd be working with him on the golf course project in Oklahoma. Then the long journey began. We drove for hours through southern Illinois and part of Missouri, stopping for lunch and then dinner in the evening. Dad didn't like fast food but preferred to eat at local restaurants or cafes. As long as they had hamburgers, fried chicken, Coneys or French fries, I didn't care. After we ate, we drove on for another hour or so and slept at a Howard Johnson's motel. We got up early and continued several more hours until we got to his job site outside of Tulsa.

Dad said, "You and I will be staying at my construction trailer."

"Oh, neat!" His trailer was right next to a large golf course.

"Am I going to golf with you at all?"

"I won't have much time for that. But I thought you might like to go up in an airplane with me." I thought, What!?

"I didn't know you could fly a plane."

"Well, I can't fly alone yet, but I take my test soon."

Dad drove me around, showing me where I could play and fish and set me up with a fishing pole and bait. I was in heaven. He spent the rest of the day on his job site. That night we all went out to eat again, then back to the trailer to watch TV and get a good night's sleep. The next morning, dad cooked breakfast in the trailer. Then we headed over to a small airport on the other side of town. His instructor was waiting for us.

"Hi, Alice. This is my son Carl. He'll be coming with us this morning."

"Well, Carl, it's good to meet you. Are you ready for a little adventure?" She gave my dad an odd glance, which I couldn't quite interpret.

"I think so. I've flown in larger planes before."

"This will be a little different. The plane we're going in is a lot smaller than a commercial aircraft. But you'll have fun, I think. I hope."

"Okay, Dean, are you ready? Do you have the last flight plan?"

"Ready as I'll ever be, and yes, I have it." Dad looked over at me and winked. The plane was a little single-prop Cessna. Dad hoisted me into the back seat. For some reason, I started to get nervous thinking about Alice's strange expression. Dad and Alice climbed into the front with dad at the controls. Alice looked back at me.

"Are you ready, Carl? Put that seatbelt on," she said. I cinched it as snug as I could. The very small cabin gave me an uneasy, boxed-in feeling. Should I be doing this? Dad and Alice started going through some sort of pre-flight checklist. Then Alice took on a very serious, almost dark tone.

"Now Dean, you need to listen. Do you remember what I said about the navigation and the compass?"

"Yes, yes, you don't have to remind me again." Their student/instructor relationship sounded a bit antagonistic. I wondered how much flying dad had done.

"Alice, this isn't my dad's first lesson, is it?"

"No, it's his fifth. Don't worry, we'll be fine." I wasn't sure I was going to like this. But now it was too late. We taxied out onto the runway and waited while he and Alice had an intense discussion about a few other pre-flight issues. I couldn't make out much of it over the roar of the engine. Finally, Alice said, "Okay now, go ahead, Dean." The engine got much louder and I felt the plane accelerate down the long runway. The speed was really picking up when suddenly the plane jerked up in the air, then came back down to the runway.

"Dean, lift up, lift up!!" The plane jerked up again. Now we were in the air and climbing fast.

"Didn't you listen back there?" I knew immediately the last thing I wanted to be when I grew up was a flight instructor. We quickly climbed thousands of feet. I felt very nervous and scared. I definitely was not ready for this. The plane climbed and climbed. Everything on the ground got much smaller at a very fast rate. We might as well have been on the edge of outer space. We flew for a while, then

Alice started telling dad to do turning and banking exercises.

"Okay, now I want to see a right-bank turn." The plane took a sharp right turn and suddenly I was looking thousands of feet straight down at the tiny specks of houses below me. I thought, OH GOD, HELP ME!!! OOHHH NOOO!!! We twisted like a slow roller coaster, like the one I hated and never rode at Waterside Park. Dad's right bank smoothed out. Alice then casually said to do a left-hand bank. I thought, GOD, NO! NOT AGAIN! It was so sharp! I was looking straight down once again!

"Now Dean, do both turns one more time, smooth it out, and let's take it back in." I simply closed my eyes and prayed. Dad finally leveled the plane and we slowly descended, thank God. I dreaded the landing but he did well. We weren't up in the air all that long but it seemed like an eternity.

The rest of the time I fished and explored the woods around the golf course. Dad and Jerry golfed once and I got to swing the club a few times (a disaster). Dad cooked in the construction trailer and we watched a lot of the western movies we liked. Dad also took me to see some of the really nice homes near the golf course. I decided right then and there I wanted to live on a golf course.

Those days in Oklahoma were some of the best of my life. They were the last good days I spent with my father as a child. It was also the last time I'd ever go away with him on one of his job sites.

I didn't want to go back to the dismal atmosphere of Leabor Road. I wanted to stay with my father. He would not be driving me back. We hugged long at the airport and I boarded the four-propeller TWA airliner. I usually liked to look out the window. This time I stared straight ahead. It just entered my head that dad never did say when he'd be home.

I arrived back home a couple of days before school started on Monday. It was too much back-to-back culture shock for me. Mom and Karen picked me up at the airport. Mom never asked me if I had a good time or what I did. And I never volunteered any information except a brief statement that I did have a good time. I moped around the house until I had to go back to school.

That Sunday night I had a dream about the past few days with my dad. I dreamed I was fishing with him on the shore of a beautiful lake. He was helping me with my pole in the water. It was too short a dream and I awoke remembering it vividly. In a depressed state, I got ready for school and sat by myself on the bus, saying goodbye to a beautiful world with him I somehow knew I would never experience again.

✝

One afternoon after school mom came into my room. "Carl, get ready. We're going over to Father Jacobson's for pizza." Pizza was a treat we didn't get very often. Mom and Catherine had gone to see Father many Friday evenings since we moved into the Leabor Road house. I had liked staying home on Friday nights watching my shows. I just shut and locked the bedroom door and escaped into the TV. I always made sure I had a hot plate of French fries or a platter of Stouffers macaroni & cheese. Now it was time that Father and mom eased me into the St. Augustine pizza & Cokes scene.

I was bewildered and nervous. I hadn't been around Father Jacobson that much. But with the St. Augustine Rectory now so close and dad so far, I knew more frequent times like this would be inevitable.

"Are we spending the night there?"

"No, we're not. Just clean up. We're leaving in a few minutes." I was amazed at how short the ride was.

Mom pulled in behind the building in the playground area, which was shielded from the main road. We got our things and knocked on the back door. A priest I'd never seen before answered.

"Hello, Madeline, how are you?" said Father Bill Harriett. He was a younger, friendly man with a nice smile.

"We're fine, Father." With surprising familiarity, mom led us down the long hallway toward Father Jacobson's room. This was my first time in a priest's rectory. Mom knocked on his door. A jolly man with a confident, million-dollar smile answered.

"Well hello there, honey!" he said to Catherine. I did notice he seemed to be looking at my mother and Catherine simultaneously. He picked Catherine up and led us into his apartment. It was rather spacious with a living room/dining area and a bedroom/bath in the back. I saw comfortable furniture and a console color TV set. Off to the side was a gun rack full of guns.

"Well, Carl, how are you tonight?" asked Father Jacobson.

"I'm fine, Father. Have you shot all the guns in that case over there?"

"Yep." His attention immediately turned back to Catherine. I looked at the guns, trying to figure out what type they were. Then I sat on the sofa and watched his interactions with mom and Catherine. They were all extremely familiar with each other and had a very positive synergy. Then came a knock on the door.

"Carl, see who that is," Father Jacobson said. There stood a man I'd never seen before.

"I'm not the pizza guy, but is it okay to come in?"

"Hello, Barry, come on in," Father Jacobson said.

"Hi, are you Carl?" he asked.

"Yes, Father."

"I'm Father Butterfinger, but you call me Father Barry. I'm one of Father Jacobson's assistants. I understand you're an altar boy at St. Macarius. Do you play any sports?" He was robust and muscular with a strong personality. Now wait a minute, I thought. Without the Father title, is this guy's name actually Barry Butterfinger?

"I'll play football when sixth grade starts up in the fall."

He and mom briefly exchanged greetings. She seemed a bit nervous, but relaxed when Father Butterfinger turned down the invitation to share our pizza.

"I can't stay tonight. Bill and I are going to that function at Holy Rosary. But I'll take a rain check." He looked right at me. I noticed he did not interact with my mom at all.

"Alright, well tell Ron I said hi," Father Jacobson responded. I thought it sounded weird, priests calling each other by first name, when we had to call them Father.

About 30 minutes later the front doorbell chimed. The pizzas had arrived.

"Well, it's about damn time," laughed Father Jacobson.

"I know, we're all starving," mom said.

"Carl, come help me bring everything back up," Father Jacobson said. I followed him to the front door.

"Well, man, you finally made it. My people are starving," he said.

"I'm sorry, Father. We're swamped tonight," the poor delivery kid said. Father Jacobson whipped out his wallet and peeled off a couple of 10-dollar bills.

"Keep the change."

"Oh, thank you very much, Father." He handed over a sack of garlic bread, two large pizzas, a six-pack of Cokes, and napkins.

"Carl, can you carry the garlic bread and Cokes and I'll get the rest?" Father Jacobson asked. I took a whiff of those delectable pizzas and about passed out. We didn't eat like this much at home.

"Okay, Father," I said. Making a beeline back to the room, I kicked on the door. Mom let me in.

"Carl, be careful! Put them right on the floor in front of the davenport," she said. Father Jacobson followed me in almost immediately.

"Let me go get some ice and paper cups. Madeline, do you want anything?" he asked attentively.

"No thanks, Father. This looks good enough. I think we're all really hungry. Was the pizza guy nice?" mom asked.

"He was better than that last knucklehead. You remember, the one who couldn't count the right change," Father Jacobson responded.

"Now, don't get started!"

"These kids today. In my day they didn't... "

"Okay now, let's enjoy our pizza." Mom cut off yet another one of Father Jacobson's rants on the depravity, stupidity and general undisciplined behavior of the younger generations. The few words he got out were the beginning of many dissertations on the failings of the younger kids. He didn't mention the fact that many of them were doing the fighting and dying in Viet Nam. He believed that once rock-n-roll music, long hair and marijuana hit the scene, kids weren't the same anymore. Every time a young person didn't live up to his standards his thought was, These kids today don't know what it was like to grow up the way I did. I was never sure how he grew up. But was it any worse than what I was going through?

"Okay, here's the pepperoni and the other has sausage and onions. Take your pick!" Father Jacobson said. I grabbed three pieces right off the bat and started chomping on them.

"Carl and Catherine, what do you say?" mom asked.

"Thank you, Father," we said in harmonic unison.

"Well enjoy," he said. I ate pizza and drank Coke until I was sick. We got to stay up late and watch Father's color TV until around midnight. Catherine fell asleep and I was almost asleep when mom announced we had to go. Back to *our* house? After eating and lying around here in paradise? Father Jacobson and mom had some words in private, then mom announced it was time to go.

On the way home I just stared out the window. I always dreaded coming back to that creepy house late at night. The property was so big and the woods around it made me feel something was always staring back at me or hiding in the overgrown shrubbery. Once inside the house I hurried to my bedroom and turned on as many lights as I could.

That was the first of many nights of pizzas, grilled steaks and Cokes at the St. Augustine Rectory. Father Barry and Father Bill joined us a couple of times, but later they were always "out" on Friday nights.

✝

Christmas of 1966 was dismal at best. Dad said he spent it at his mother's house, or so we were told. His trips back home became less frequent. He had been home only a few times since I went to Oklahoma with him over a year ago. Whenever he was home, the fighting between him and mom was terrible.

✝

Mike was graduating from St. Censurius High School in May '67 and would start freshman year at Xabat College in the fall. It looked like dad wouldn't be here for his graduation ceremony. He had apologized to Mike, but Mike wasn't too thrilled.

Mom's plans were that she, Aunt Margie, and I would go together, then have dinner at grandmother's. I had to wear a suit and tie. I hated suits and ties because I got yelled at whenever I got a smudge on them. And I had no idea how to tie a tie so, mom got me a fake clip-on. No one knew the difference and I didn't care. It would be easier to yank off later.

As the big night approached I felt sad because I knew Mike was leaving for college. Karen had already been gone and would soon graduate from Rose College. She had been seeing a mysterious someone and rumor had it marriage bells would ring at some point. I'm sure she couldn't wait to get away. I didn't know her boyfriend except they always parked out in the driveway late at night when he brought her home from a date.

The big night came, and mom, Catherine, Karen, and I piled into the car and headed over to pick up Aunt Margie. Everyone looked great but I felt like a dumbass in my suit and fake tie. Just a couple of hours earlier I had been trying to catch frogs with one of my friends in a nearby creek, so I was having a bit of mental wardrobe conflict. Margie came out in a tight pastel-colored dress.

"My god, it's hot as hell out," Margie said, getting into the back seat where mom made me sit. My eyes flew wide open and I glanced down. Then I glanced at mom to see her reaction to that bad word. Mom generally gave her family a pass on that kind of thing. I blew it off as being "adult privilege" and let it go. But I didn't dare talk like that.

"At least it's not outside like they had it last year," mom responded.

"Father Wilhelm said they decided at the last minute to have it inside, which is fine with me. There's no air conditioning but it will be a little cooler with those fans," Margie said.

"Well how are you, kiddo?" she asked me.

"I'm fine, Aunt Margie. What's that perfume you have on?"

"Chanel No. 5 like your mommy wears. Karen and Catherine, are you both doing alright?"

"I'm good," said Karen. "Only one more year left at Rose College and I'm all done." Catherine just smiled, overwhelmed at Margie's loud presence.

"How is Jerry doing? Now he has only one more year up at Chestwick, doesn't he?" Margie asked.

"Yah, he'll finish up in engineering. He'll be glad to get it over with." Karen tried to change the subject. Jerry was the boy she always parked with in the driveway late at night.

"Well, Madeline and I never went to college but we turned out okay, didn't we?" Margie laughed. Mom just smiled.

"Margie, why aren't you and mom wearing hats? Don't you wear a hat when you go to something like this?"

"Oh hell, I've never worn a hat. It would ruin my hair. Don't I look darling enough without one?"

"Uuhh, yah, of course."

By this time, women weren't wearing hats much outside of church and besides, the graduation ceremony was in the high school auditorium. Mom then informed us we wouldn't all be sitting together. She, Karen and Catherine would be in one section and Margie and I would be in another. It was the only way we could all go because so many people were expected. Margie and I found our seats, but there wasn't much wiggle room and it wasn't very comfortable. We weren't conveniently on the end of the row but squashed in the middle.

"My God, I didn't think it would be this damn cramped. If my girdle snaps, we'll all be crushed," Margie blurted. I broke out laughing and some girl my age in front of me did, too. We had to hold our hands over our mouths. Then Margie started laughing. Most of the adults around us weren't laughing, though. The ceremony droned on for about 90 minutes before I got to see Mike graduate.

179

After Mike's graduation life at home became even more chaotic. Dad wasn't around much at all now. I missed him but couldn't do anything about it or say anything about it. The only good thing was there wasn't any fighting in the house like there used to be.

After the summer of 1967 Mike and Karen would head off to college, leaving just me, mom, and Catherine alone at Leabor Road. Mom also was faintly alluding to the possibility that Father Jacobson might be transferred yet again. The major tragedy, though, would be the final time I would see my dad.

✝

One afternoon, in late summer of 1967, when I bicycled home from St Macarius pre-school football practice, I saw dad's familiar green pick-up truck in the back driveway. I hadn't seen or heard from him for months. By this time I was mentally blocking out a lot of things and my dad's increased absence was one of them. I had a very ominous feeling as I approached the house.

I went in through the back door and there was my beloved father. We hugged. I had missed that familiar, warm embrace. My mother, mercifully, wasn't home yet. I thanked God. This gave us a few last moments of peace.

"Carl, it's good to see you."

"It's good to see you, dad. Are you going to stay long this time?" I knew the answer. Tears welled up in my eyes.

"That's up to your mother, but…."

We heard a car pull into the driveway. It had to be my mother. She parked in the front driveway. I looked up, not believing this was happening.

Oh my God, there's going to be a fight. She's going to walk into a blind surprise and see him. I shuddered. She probably didn't see dad's truck in back of the house.

180

"Dad, mom's home! She just pulled into the front!"

"It's okay, Carl. I'll talk to her." I was starting to panic.

I ran to the front door to intercept mom. She seemed to be in a good mood, smiling and light-hearted.

"Mom, I have to tell you something."

"What is it?" I could see she knew something was wrong.

"It's dad. He's here in the back room. His truck is parked in the back." Mom's expression went to high-tension red alert.

"Where is he?" Her face now had that familiar stone-cold look—always a precursor to emotional trauma.

"I think he's still in the back room."

I backed slowly away from mom. Do I leave and go into my room now or do I stay? If I stay the fight might not be as bad.

Mom turned toward that back room, but then dad came out through the kitchen toward me and mom.

I wasn't going to say anything, but in desperation decided to try to break the ice. "Mom, dad's here now!" Mom turned and stared at dad. I looked on, helpless.

"Well, how long have you been back?" mom asked. I could hear anger, fear, and apathy all rolled into one.

"I'm just here for a couple of days. Don't worry. I won't stay long."

"Well that's just fine. It's just like you to come into town, get what you want, and then fly off again. Do you have any money for us to pay the bills here, Dean?"

"Madeline, yes, I can, but I haven't heard from you either in quite a while. I just assumed Father Jacobson was keeping the house up."

With this one comment the conversation instantaneously catapulted from Defcon 3 straight to Defcon 1. Tears welled in my eyes again. Their encounter would now dramatically escalate.

Then Mike came home. His timing couldn't have been worse. He took two steps into the living room and his mouth gaped wide open. He hadn't seen dad in a very long time.

"Don't bring his name into this, Dean! He's got nothing to do with any of it. Where is the money for everyone's school? Hell, they shut the electricity off two weeks ago and we barely had enough money to get it back on. You haven't paid any bills around here in months. Where in God's name has all the money gone?"

"I've been sending money back! You tell me!"

"That's a lot of crap!"

"Is Father Jacobson handling it now?"

Mike yelled, "Can the both of you just shut the hell up? I'm getting sick of this shit every damn time dad comes home."

This temporarily halted things, but then they started right up again.

"Did you set aside any money for Mike's college coming up next month?" asked mom.

"Well, yes I did. What did you do with it?"

"There's only enough for one semester." Mike looked like that was news to him.

"Well, Mike, do you believe him?" asked mom. Her eyes welled up. Mike stood there, staring at her.

"I don't know who to believe anymore. I can't wait to get the hell out of here, and the sooner the better."

"Do you know he's lying? Why don't you believe that?"

"I just told you I don't know who in the hell to believe any more!" Mike had a particularly nasty tone of voice when he yelled. He was fed up with yet another horrific argument and his mom and dad's inability to be civil. He stormed out of the house. The screaming back and forth continued. It touched on topics I didn't even know existed.

I ran to my bedroom and locked the door. But the shouting was so loud I heard everything the three of them said. This was not the first time I'd done this to escape the chaos and anger. I knew the argument would go around in circles and end badly with no winner, no loser, and no real conclusive peace. Their horrific encounter lasted only 15 minutes, yet the emotional devastation would have lasting implications. I sat in my room, frozen, for a few more minutes then reluctantly opened my bedroom door. The shouting had finally stopped. I deduced my dad had left the house.

Then I slowly and oh so carefully ventured out into the hallway and into the living room. No one was there, but I could hear loud crying coming from around the dining room table. I nervously ventured toward it with a sad and heavy heart. My mother was all alone at the table. As I walked slowly toward her, I hoped this was all just a very bad dream and I would wake up any second. I approached her from the back of her chair and lovingly started putting my arms around her. I didn't know what to say. She took my arms, slowly turning around to look at me.

"I'm so sorry you had to hear that, Carl."

It killed me to see her stressed and reddened eyes. This whole time Catherine, thankfully, was asleep in the car with a small bag of groceries. Thankfully, she never saw or heard any of this. Mom had told her to go back outside when she learned dad was here.

Mom asked, "Can you bring Catherine in and take her to the bedroom?"

"Yah, mom. Is there anything else?"

"No, Carl, not right now. Just go into your room for a while. There are some things I need to do out here." I went into my room and lay on the bed, staring up at the ceiling with tears in my eyes. Was this the last time I'd see my dad? I never even had a chance to tell him goodbye. Then I heard mom on the phone in her bedroom having a

very stressed conversation with someone. I had a very good
an idea who.

✝

By the late fall of 1967 I sensed dad was probably
never coming back. A clear sign of that was the fact that
Father Jacobson was boldly hanging around more and
more. We weren't going over to the St. Augustine Rectory
as much now. Talk was starting to surface there. I had a
good idea who, at the St. Augustine Rectory, was feeding
the archbishop inside information about my family and
Father Jacobson.

As I lay on my bed staring out the window, not even
aware of what I was looking at, a song came on the radio
that reflected my mood perfectly — BJ Thomas' "I'm So
Lonesome I Could Cry." I reached over to turn it off. But I
couldn't. As I listened I started to cry again. I cried for the
loss of my father. I cried for my mother for what she had to
endure. They were tears of sadness and confusion. My
father blamed my mother for everything and my mother
blamed my father for it all. And of course, I was blamed for
not understanding it in general.

There was more bad news. It now was official.
Father Jacobson indeed was being transferred out of St.
Augustine High School. He had not been there all that long.
He would administer a parish called St. Jerome's in
Monticello, on the Presser College campus. This transfer
would take place during the summer of 1967. Mom didn't
take this news well. And Father Jacobson wasn't ready for
the atmosphere of a liberal college campus at the height of
the Viet Nam war.

Christmas of 1967 would be a sad affair. I tried to
pretend it was all normal. But dad was officially gone.
Father Jacobson replaced my dad at this event and all future
events. Karen spent a lot of time with her boyfriend's

family. Mike and Catherine were there, but it didn't matter. Now I knew it was over. Mike was more bitter than usual as he couldn't continue to attend Xabat College anymore because funds had run dry. Instead, he had to go to Presser College down in Monticello. In January of 1968, he would live in the St. Jerome Parish rectory with Father Jacobson.

CHAPTER 10: ST. MACARIUS AND LEABOR ROAD

THE SECOND SEMESTER of my seventh-grade year at St. Macarius started off with a bang. In January of 1968 I was elected secretary of the Altar Boy Club. This was a very prestigious position in that it was exclusive to that closed group of boys. I was honored to have been chosen. I was so into it that I set up a makeshift altar in the basement and said Mass in front of Catherine, who took me seriously. And of course I had to pass the collection basket and took whatever money it held.

One morning stands out in the annals of Catholic Church history. I won an Oscar for this one as Best Actor in a Religious Comedy. The other altar boys who performed with me were nominated for Best Supporting Actors in the same category.

It started out like most mornings. My clock radio alarm went off at around 6 am with "I Say A Little Prayer" by Aretha Franklin. That song always calmed me, and of course was appropriate for the occasion, given the fact I had to serve Mass that morning. It was one of my "good luck songs" I liked to start my day with. But today before Mass the song title seemed more than a casual coincidence. I always placed prophetic connotations on whatever song woke me up in the morning. If I liked the song it would be a good day. If it was some sort of crappy song . . . well, then it wouldn't be so good. Today, however, it would prove that superstitions don't always hold true.

There were two morning Masses during the week. The 7 am Mass was poorly attended. It was easy to serve at if you could stand to get up at 5 am. It was staffed by two altar boys. The downside? What if your other partner didn't show up? If you were alone, you'd better know your prayer lines, because if you had a temporary loss of memory and you bumbled through even one of the prayers, the celebrating priest would know it. This was extremely embarrassing.

The 8 am Mass was staffed by four altar boys, and the entire school attended. Yes, that's right. All your classmates, the lay teachers, and of course the nuns. You were on stage. Just one little slip-up would haunt you for weeks or even forever if it wasn't covered up.

I was serving the 8 am Mass this particular week. Mom dropped me off at the church at 7:30. On the radio was The Tremeloes' "Here Comes My Baby." It was still dark out.

Two doors at the back of the church led into two separate sacristies. The priests used the door on the right and the altar boys used the left. We had our own private entrance, our own private little sacristy, and a small room with a large closet for our vestments. There was also a chair and a sink where we could wash up.

The stage was set. The characters were cast. Jim Mahoney was on bells position 1. The altar boy in this position, as the name implies, rang bells at all the pre-designated times during the Mass. Jim was a short, smart, and friendly sort of kid, a personable smart-ass. One minute he'd be complementing you. Then he'd turn right around and make a crack about your bad breath. He was one of the more popular kids, president of the Altar Boy Club, and quarterback on our football team. His girlfriend was Theresa Sadesky, one of the most popular girls in class.

Kevin Rolan was on communion position 2. This position primarily assisted with serving communion. Kevin was taller and somewhat quiet. He had dark, curly hair and didn't smile much. I could never tell exactly what he was thinking. He tended to stare at you when you tried to talk to him. He was always shaking his head from side to side like you'd said something stupid. He hung around with a different group than I did — kind of a rude group of boys that I avoided. I always blew hot and cold with him— sometimes friends, sometimes not.

Finally, there was Pete Lorenz on position 3. This role didn't serve any useful function except round out the altar boy servers to four, making a symmetrical, ceremonial look. This altar boy just knelt a lot and prayed a lot. If one of the other altar boys called in sick, this position could fill in. Pete was a short kid, quiet, with a very strange but funny sense of humor. He hung around the same group as Kevin Rolan. Pete would come up to you with a really straight face, look at you for a few seconds, and then go into some bugged-out impersonation of Tom Smothers of *The Smothers Brothers Comedy Hour* or President Lyndon Johnson. He did it well, too. And just as quickly he'd revert back to his quiet, unassuming self like nothing had happened. You'd be laughing and then wonder, did he really say that?

I was on communion 4. Outside of the priest, this was the most prestigious position on the altar and the envy of the other three. Communion 4 was like a coordinator. I would lead the altar boys and the priest out of the sacristy and onto the altar, signaling the beginning of Mass. Communion 4 was also responsible for pouring the water and wine into the priest's chalice. I led all the altar boy prayer responses and was the primary communion server for the celebrating priest. It was a high-pressure position and the easiest one to screw up. Communion 4 at the 8 am Mass was as stressful as it could get.

Jim would help the priest put his vestments on before Mass, while the rest of us got the altar set up.

As I got into our side of the sacristy, Jim pushed the door open. "Hey, I don't know about you but I'm ready to go back to bed," he greeted me.

189

"Well, you have a long time until that, unfortunately," I yawned. I looked at myself in the mirror in disgust. I was on deck in 30 minutes in front of the known universe and my face looked like it was covered in parchment paper. I washed my face again and massaged it a bit, trying to smooth out the roughness. You had to comb your hair twice. The first combing was when you got there and wanted to greet the priest. The second combing was after you had slipped on your vestments and messed up your hair. A good comb was an indispensable part of male attire at the time.

"Kevin and Pete aren't here yet," Jim said with a bit of trepidation. "They need to get here soon."

"Oh, they'll be here. You know how Kevin is, and Pete can get ready faster than anyone I've ever seen. He can walk in the door, throw on his vestments, comb his hair, and be ready to promenade in minutes," I replied, showing off a big word I just learned.

"What does promenade mean?" Jim asked, looking at me like I was trying to pull something over on him.

"It means to high step or march, I think." I had just heard my brother use that word a couple days before and thought it would be cool to use it at school.

"Oh. Why didn't you just say march?" Jim asked, smiling at me like I was some clownish professor.

"Well…I…uh…" And just then Kevin came stumbling into the sacristy.

"Sorry I'm late," he said, grinning. And before he could explain, in the door came Pete.

"Did I miss anything? You didn't start without me?" he mocked.

"No such luck, Pete," Jim smiled. "In fact, why don't you do communion 4 for the week? I'm sure Carl would be happy to hand it over to you. Yah, communion 4 with Father Rootz!"

"Oh, that's okay. I know how bad Carl wants it," he said, backing out of the offer.

So now there were four of us stumbling and bumping around the sacristy, hurrying to get ready and get over to Father Rootz to put his vestments on and make sure he was ready. By this time the two altar boys from the 7 am Mass came in, sporting a relaxed demeanor. Joe Adamsson and Lloyd Waimer were nice guys. Joe, like Jim, was a sort of jolly kid and friendly, with a good sense of humor. Lloyd, or "Bubba" as we sometimes called him, was somewhat eccentric but basically okay. His father was one of the football coaches I had in sixth grade and was well liked. And all six of us were in the same grade. It could be dangerous to serve with them though, as the least little thing could set us off on a laughing spree in church, or even on the altar itself. And that was something you never wanted to happen. It could be the kiss of death. Laughing in church was a Venial Sin or a Class A Misdemeanor in terms of our criminal justice system. But laughing on the altar was a full-blown felony, but only if you were caught.

As Joe and Bubba were changing out of their vestments, we could tell something had happened by the way they were snickering. During the 7 am service Bubba had lost his footing and come crashing down on his knees way too fast as they all started to recite the Confiteor prayer in the first part of the Mass. The priest recites it line by line first, and then the congregation and altar boys recite it back to the priest. This sort of uncoordinated screw-up was not all that uncommon and definitely not desired. Can you imagine reciting the long Confiteor prayer, while kneeling right next to the celebrating priest, and trying not to laugh, while everyone, including a nun or two, is watching your every move?

"I confess to almighty God
and to you, my brothers and sisters,

191

that I have greatly sinned,
in my thoughts and in my words,
in what I have done and in what I have failed to do,
through my fault, through my fault,
through my most grievous fault;
therefore I ask blessed Mary ever-Virgin,
all the Angels and Saints,
and you, my brothers and sisters,
to pray for me to the Lord our God."

They started telling us what happened, but we didn't have much time to enjoy their story. They spoke quickly. The school busses were rolling in and the church was filling up. Now Father Rootz wouldn't be in a good mood because of Joe's and Bubba's little comedy skit. Surely he had been aware of their foul-up. Father Rootz also had to serve two Masses in a row, which would put him a cranky mood.

"Did Rootz or anyone out in the pews see you guys laughing?" Kevin asked.

"I don't think so," Joe replied. "You know he can't hear well half the time."

"Well, did he see you?" Pete and I blurted out.

"I don't think so, but we don't know for sure. He didn't say anything," Joe said. Bubba shook his head in agreement. Thank God, I thought.

Jim, Kevin, Pete, and I looked at them as if to say, "Okay, we hope you're right." They left quickly, giggling, but then got serious and straightened up as they joined the congregation and the nuns out in the main church area. Yes, if you served the 7 am Mass, when you were done, you still had to sit it out for the main 8 am Mass. That was what we called Mass burnout.

There we were, the four of us, joking around in the sacristy and making light of what had gone on. We prayed Father Rootz didn't see or hear their laughing. There we were in our plaid dress shirts, wavy "cool combed" hair, penny loafers and our Roderick St. John's wallets sticking out just about an inch out of our back pockets. These were some of the signs of status back in seventh grade in 1968.

We finally finished putting on our cassocks and frocks and making sure they were straight, properly aligned, and wrinkle free. If we looked crooked or rumpled the snickering went on for a couple of minutes, then we would help one another straighten out. We took turns doing the "final combing." In a few minutes we would be on display in front of God, Father Rootz, all of our classmates, nuns, teachers and friends (including girlfriends), and of course, Sister Cornelia, the school principal. She was the strictest of all the nuns. It was better than a Hollywood movie with a cast of thousands.

I had to put on this performance several times a month or as required for special services. But I was getting good at it. I had all the long prayers memorized and hell, I was the secretary of the Altar Boys Club. It helped out with the girls, too. I went from cootie doctor to Altar Boys Club secretary in just a few short years.

But now we started to feel weird after hearing Joe's and Bubba's story. It left the four of us cautious and nervous, but it was almost show time. We made sure we had our pious faces on, then left the sacristy in a perfect linear formation, walking across the altar to Father Rootz's sacristy, genuflecting in choreographed unison halfway through.

Father Rootz was a man of few words. I studied his face for any trace of disgust about the 7 am Mass shenanigans, but didn't see any. I was relieved, but still cautious.

Jim helped Father put on his vestments while I filled the cruets with the water and wine. We also reset the altar and straightened everything. Pete and Kevin lit all the front-end candles. We didn't even have to speak to each other. Father Rootz always started Mass right on time so we had to move. The altar was now ready with cast and crew in place. Back inside the sacristy we lined up in perfect formation in front of Father Rootz. At 8 o'clock the opening hymn commenced while the congregation stood. It was time to rock-n-roll. It started as such a beautiful ballet. Much to my annoyance, I had to pee, but it was too late. I would pay dearly for that later.

Father gave the green light and we moved out like soldiers of Christ at the Macy's Thanksgiving Day Parade. Ceremoniously, somberly, and with pious faces we walked single-file onto the altar. Jim and I slowed down to let Father stand in the middle of us. We genuflected, then Pete and Kevin walked to their side of the altar. We arranged ourselves so that, facing the altar, you saw Pete and Kevin on the right, Father Rootz in the middle, and me and Jim on the left. Everything went smoothly from the opening prayer, through the Gloria, the reading of the Gospel, the Confiteor, the Eucharistic Prayer, and the Lord's Prayer. Even communion was uneventful. But after that things went terribly wrong.

As communion 4, I helped Father Rootz serve communion. Everyone was required to take part. Father Hermann came to assist and Kevin served with him. Serving communion means holding a gold serving platen under the chin of the person receiving communion. The communion wafer is a small, round, very crisp and flat piece of bread. It's like the material in a Chinese fortune cookie.

After communion was over, Kevin followed Father Hermann back up to the altar and gave him his serving platen. The priest wiped it off, then gave it back to Kevin, who bowed and walked back to place it on the table behind the altar. Then Kevin knelt at his place on the altar. I followed Father Rootz back to the altar with my communion platen and handed it to him for wipe-down. He handed it back to me. I bowed, and then walked to the rear table where the cruets of water and wine waited. I put the platen down and picked up the cruets, one in each hand. I walked slowly back to the altar, bowed, and waited. Jim, Kevin, and Pete were watching quietly.

Father Rootz finished his prayer, turned toward me, and held out the gold chalice. Into that beautiful, gold, long-handled cup I poured a stream of wine, then a wee bit of water until he nodded to stop. With cruets in hand I bowed reverently to Father. It was supposed to be a slow bow. But for whatever reason I came back up a little too fast on the upswing. Father Rootz, for some reason, too, was slow to pull back on the chalice and turn like a younger priest might have done. As I came up I there was a sharp bump. I felt something unnatural on my back and wet on my neck. Confused, I rose slowly and stood for a couple of seconds, gazing forward. Instantly a feeling of horror shot through me like Constantine's Sword. Staring back at me in equally open-eyed surprise and disgust was a hellish vision of Father Rootz, holding an empty chalice. The front of his bright-gold vestment was covered in water and wine! Oh, how that red wine coordinated nicely with the gold. In that split second I realized I had come up under the bottom of Father Rootz's chalice, hitting his arm and the still-full chalice of water and wine. It splashed on the back of my neck and head. I saw it dripping down Father's front like rain drops.

Oh no. Did that really happen? The priest's stern, angry glance confirmed it. My heart sank clear to the floor, then under my feet. Oh, please no! Sweet Mother of Mercy, did anyone else notice?

I had to think quickly and managed to temporarily compose myself. I slowly went back down the steps and put the cruets back on the rear table. My hands were starting to shake. I stayed there for a little longer than I should have, desperately trying to compose myself. The problem was I made the mistake of glancing down at Jim as I passed him. His hands folded in prayer were tight up against his mouth. Behind them he was straining to keep from laughing. Trying to help me, he looked away, but his face started to contort and pucker. Then I realized they'd all seen it from their vantage points. Things now began to move in slow motion. I wasn't in my body anymore. I felt like I was floating in some dreamlike, out-of-body experience. Moving on raw instinct, I needed every bit of self-discipline to save me from this terrible event.

I thought, Oh no. I have got to get through this! Oh my God, I didn't mean it! Why me? It was an accident! Where are the saints? God, I hope no one in the congregation noticed. I continued trying to compose myself and straighten up. After a few seconds of intense prayer and slow, deliberate breathing, I finally turned around and knelt next to Jim, frantically trying to pretend nothing had happened. I folded my hands in prayer against my chest and looked down. Thank God this happened toward the end of the Mass and not the beginning. When would Father Rootz mercifully start the concluding prayers? God, I hoped he'd hurry and end this debacle. I needed to get off the altar as soon as possible. We all did.

Once I was kneeling next to Jim, I knew if I looked across the altar to Pete and Kevin it would be impossible to keep a straight face. If Jim was smirking, so were they. This was an altar boy's worst nightmare. When you heard about this happening to someone else, all you could do was close your eyes and make the sign of cross. You dared not laugh at such a story because it would put a curse on you. Tripping around or even falling was one thing, but actually spilling wine on the celebrating priest was something else entirely.

But then – oh no, please – I heard a faint breathy snicker. It was Jim. I snuck a look and saw Kevin and Pete with the same hidden snicker expressions. I tried our secret coded sign language to get them to stop. No avail! Satan himself was now unleashed from hell. Yes, this was all the Devil's fault. I placed my folded hands over my mouth and tried to fight it off. I couldn't. My stomach started to convulse. I tightened my lips as hard as I could. Thank God we altar boys didn't exclusively have to recite any of the closing prayers. Somehow, all four of us would have to stealthily giggle our way through the conclusion of Mass.

Jim's snicker breathing got a bit louder. Kevin's and Pete's faces were red. Kevin's eyes were red. I leaned over and whispered at Jim to keep quiet. He either didn't hear me or wasn't able to react. And who was I to do that? I, too, was starting to giggle. I just couldn't fight it off anymore. We continued kneeling in our places, hands over our faces, trying to cover our distorted expressions. The immense physical intensity of holding in the laughing started to make my stomach cramp. Then it started to affect my bladder.

Oh, God, I wish I'd peed before leaving the priest's sacristy. Any more muscle spasms and I'd lose control. The passing seconds were now an eternity. PLEASE, Father Rootz, finish the closing prayers! St. Francis, my trusted friend, where are you? In that second, Father motioned everyone to stand and recite the closing prayers. Hallelujah! Maybe changing positions would stop the laughing and keep me from peeing my pants.

We all stood. OH NO!! Please, NO!! The nightmare now turned real. As I stood erect, I peed in my pants under the vestments! I tried to stop. My groin muscles were too weak from the intensity of trying to restrain myself for the past several minutes. I lost control. I stood there praying, while at the same time pissing in my pants right then and there on the altar. It wasn't funny anymore. My Sweet Lord, if only I'd had a few more minutes!

Father Rootz finally concluded the Mass and signaled us to lockstep with him to the front of the altar, genuflect, regroup, line up and lead him into his sacristy. It was too late, though. The urine ran warm, all down my legs and even into my socks. I peed as I walked right behind Father Rootz, off the altar, and toward the sacristy. My vestments and pants were getting soaked. I thanked God my shoes had caught the remaining stream and I wasn't tracking urine behind me. Now the five of us were in the sacristy, removing Father's vestments. I stood there, covered in piss, expecting a royal scolding. It thankfully never came. To this day I do not know why. He never said one damn word about it. We altar boys left Father's sacristy toward our own, smirking the whole time. The pews were emptying. No one was waiting to persecute me. Thank God, another landmine sidestepped!

We entered the altar boy sacristy, free at last to laugh. We were in hysterics. Now, though, I had a whole new set of problems. I had to go into damage control. I stood in front of the sink, took off my vestments, and turned on the water. Thank God I wore dark pants today — the pee down my front was obvious. Although the other three altar boys noticed I'd bumped Father's chalice and had seen the spill, they didn't know I pissed my pants.

"Oh man, did you see Carl?" Jim asked with a big laugh.

"Carl, were you upset with Father?" Pete asked, straight-faced at first, then laughing. "You should consider waiting tables in a fancy restaurant when you grow up."

"I can't believe you did that! God, man, I'm sure you got Rootz mad at you now. You should consider bartending as a career," barked Kevin.

"Ohhhh, I hope no one in church saw anything. I didn't see anyone laughing. But if Cornelia noticed it, you'll wind up in her office," said Jim.

"So, will the three of you keep quiet? PLEASE, guys, don't tell anyone. Okay? Let's hope no one in the pews saw us laughing. If anyone finds out it'll get to

Cornelia." Through their laughter they nodded yes as they ripped off their vestments. It was the altar boy's venerated code of silence in action.

My vestments were completely off. But if I turned around they might see the urine on my pants. No one but me knew I pissed my cassock and I intended to keep it that way. That *would* get around. I had to come up with something and fast. I acted like I was washing my hands, but "accidentally" splashed water on myself. The idea, of course, was to make it look like a water accident instead of a piss accident.

"Oh God, I don't believe this. Look what I did!" I said in faux shock. It appeared to work. Kevin rushed up with a towel.

"Hey, man, this isn't your day. You're already going to hell and now you'll be going there with wet pants! How exactly will you handle this in confession?" quipped Pete, while the others laughed. I dried off as best I could.

We finished straightening up the sacristy and ourselves. Our gut muscles were so sore we couldn't laugh anymore. We were just burned out by this point. I, of course, laughed the least. What if I got called into Principal Sister Cornelia's office for a good reprimand? We put on our straight faces and headed out of the sacristy into the first morning class. Miss Snyderdine, my teacher for that class, called my mom, saying I had had a little water accident at the sink after Mass. Mom came by with fresh underwear and pants. I was never so glad to see her. I gave her my freshly pissed-in clothing, including the stinky cassock.

We altar boys were stunned. Not one person in the congregation even mentioned the incident. Father Rootz didn't ever say anything either, for some mysterious reason. We apparently hid it all well. So this dark episode would be our secret, logged forever in the sealed vaults of altar boy history. One thing an altar boy can do is keep a good secret, when it suits him. And most of the time it suited him. Decades later, I told and re-told that story over countless cold beers.

✝

Back to Father Jacobson. Another clear indication that my dad was not coming back after that fateful August visit was Father Jacobson's ever-increasing presence at the Leabor Road house. He was now coming over with complete impunity and sometimes even unannounced. Father Jacobson had succeeded in running dad out. Dad had probably concluded it was a battle he could never win. The hurt inside me was unbearable.

I came home from school one day in September to find Father's car there once again, and a beautiful German Shepard tied up to the large oak tree by the garage. I rode my bike up to her and said, "Hey girl, what are you doing here?" She just gazed at me but I got good vibes from her and I think she from me.

"Are you okay?" I saw some marks on her but wasn't sure where they came from. I cautiously approached her.

"Hey, I'm not going to hurt you." I held out my hands. She sensed something friendly in me and started wagging her tail, so I began to pet her. We hit it off immediately.

"Carl, be careful!" mom said from the back door.

"It's okay, mom, we're already friends. What's her name?"

"Father brought her here for us. Her name is Duchay. I think she likes you." With Mike soon to be gone Father got her for protection from the vast darkness of Leabor Road and, of course, if dad happened to make an unannounced visit. Just then Father Jacobson came outside.

"Well, she's yours," he said.

"Where did you get her?"

"She came from the pound. Her other owners abused her. That's where those marks came from. She's beautiful, isn't she?"

"Yah, I like her. I can be the one to take care of her if that's okay." That began a beautiful relationship between Duchay and me. We had many fun days running in our big yard and in the fields in back of the house. She became my best friend and helped ease the pain of Leabor Road and the emotional loss of my dad. Father Jacobson then drove away with Catherine to destinations unknown.

✝

By the middle of 1967 Jacobson's days in Bridgeport were numbered. His transfer to Monticello and his new assignment as Pastor of St. Jerome's Parish was underway. He would stay in an old rectory/church complex while a brand-new St. Jerome's was being built. Mike would officially start his second freshman-year semester at Presser College, living at St. Jerome's with Father Jacobson. The money for his continued studies at Xabat College had officially disappeared. The stage was now set for frequent weekend trips down to see Father. My first one was in the fall of 1967.

"Carl, listen. With Father Jacobson now down in Monticello with his new assignment at St. Jerome's, it's more difficult for him to come up here as much as he has been. What do you think about us going down to Monticello on the weekends to the old St. Jerome's?" I knew this was just a formality, and I had no choice in the matter.

"Where would we stay?"

"Sometimes we'll stay right there at the church or at a motel."

"Well, I guess it would be okay. When are we leaving?"

"We're leaving this Saturday afternoon. Father's going to bake potatoes and grill steaks. Does that sound good? We can bring Duchay with us, too."

When the time came, true to mom's word, we jumped in the car once again. As we headed down state highway 37, I noticed some white crosses on the side of the road.

"Mom, what are those crosses there for?"

"That means there was a car accident there and someone was hurt." I knew hurt meant killed and dropped the conversation. Mom's silence confirmed that.

Down in Monticello, at Presser College, I noticed lots of college students walking around. I saw two couples dressed a little funny in old flowery clothes. The girls had long hair and wore beads or flowers or something. And the two guys had the longest hair I had ever seen on a man. I didn't know what to think.

"Mom, did you see those people?"

"Yes, Carl, and don't stare."

"I've never seen hair on a guy that long before. What kind of people are they?"

"Carl, they're called hippies. They're dirty and unpredictable and are always complaining about something. They take drugs, too. I don't want you talking to them or even looking at them." As we drove by, one hippie-type girl smiled and waved at me, but I was afraid to wave back and turned away.

The St. Jerome's Parish rectory was just off the downtown area in a large, old, two-storey house with several bedrooms, a living room and two dens. It was separated from the church by a parking lot. The church was also a big two-storey building from the 1800s. The actual church part was on the upper floor. There were classrooms, a large meeting hall, and a kitchen in the basement.

Father Jacobson was right there to greet us.

"Well, how was the drive?" he asked mom.

"Not too much traffic, but I don't like highway 37. People don't know how to drive anymore!"

"Well, hello, honey," he said to Catherine. "I'm glad you're here!"

"Hi. What are we going to eat tonight?" she asked.

"I picked up some barbequed ribs. We'll grill them out and I got some filet steaks too."

"Carl, do you want to help me get it all ready?" he asked.

"Sure, Father. What do you want me to do?"

"Just follow me into the kitchen. You all can put your things in two of the upstairs bedrooms. Then come back down and we'll get started." He poured himself a generous Scotch on the rocks.

He introduced us to his assistant Father Laughlin. "Ken, this is Madeline, Catherine, and Carl. This is Mike's family. You know, the student we'll have living here next semester."

"Well hi, how are you all?" There was some trivial chit-chat but Father Laughlin was clearly headed on his way out. He appeared a little uncomfortable, but was polite about it. Once he left, mom seemed more relaxed.

"Okay now, let's have some fun," Father Jacobson smiled.

"Carl, why don't you help me do the steaks. I'll show you how to make a great grilled steak." I was a relative newcomer to the world of steak grilling, so any instruction was welcome. From the fridge he pulled out the biggest T-bone and filet steaks I had ever seen. We put garlic powder and pepper on them. He grabbed a stick of butter.

"Your mom likes hers burnt. How do you want yours?" I had to think for a minute.

"Make mine rare, Father."

"Well, that's my man! We'll put ours on last."

"Father, a couple of blocks down the street it looks like there are a lot of neat shops. There are lots of weird people walking around," I said.

"That's Chelsea Avenue where the hippies hang out." He took a big puff on his cigar, blew the smoke out high and heavy, then spit some tobacco on the ground.

"Are we going to go down there after dinner? Mom said we might take a walk then."

"Yah, I'll take you down there and show you how they live. We'll take Duchay, too. You never know what they'll do," he growled.

"Are the hippies nice?"

"It's not so much if they're nice or not. They're dirty, long-haired brats that do drugs and don't know how to dress. They always want to argue about the government or the war. . . and that terrible loud music! That roll-n-rock or whatever the hell it's called! I can't understand it. And they're always smoking pot too."

He again took an angry puff of his cigar, but this time blew the smoke out more forcefully.

"What is that?"

"It's some kind of drug you smoke."

"Do any of them go to church here?"

"Oh yah, some do, but not the early Mass. They usually roll in for the 11:30 one," he chuckled.

"You'll see them when you serve with me Sunday. And you'll see them in Sean Meadow, too." He blew his smoke out again, but this time right in the direction of Chelsea Avenue. It sounded like I was going to be serving as an altar boy down here.

Father Jacobson threw our steaks on the grill and kept rubbing butter on them. "The butter adds a nice flavor and keeps them from getting too burnt." He showed me how to grill with the finesse of a master chef.

Once all the steaks were done, we went inside. Mom had the table all set and ready to go. The dinner was indeed delicious and there would be many, many more in the future.

"Father, that was really good," said Catherine.

"Yah, thanks, it was," I chimed in.

Mom and Catherine cleaned everything up. I wandered into the den and the living room. In the den stood Father's beautiful Voice of Music stereo system. I stared at it in awe then went over the layout. This system had its own bass and treble controls, which were easy to adjust. The sound quality was great. Father put on a Bing Crosby album while we were cleaning up. But all I could think was how damn good The Doors or The Byrds would sound on it instead.

Then mom said, "Carl get ready. You, Father Jacobson and Catherine are going to walk downtown."

"Are we going to take Duchay with us?" I asked.

"Father's getting her on the leash now."

"Now be careful down there. Sometimes you don't know what's going to happen with these people," she said. Father Jacobson smiled.

"Don't worry, Madeline. If they get past Duchay, this ought to take care of them." He pointed to a little pouch on his belt. I had an idea what it was.

"Father's got a gun! Can I see it?"

"No, Carl, you may not. Now stay close to Father and do what he tells you." Father Jacobson winked at me.

"Someday you can see the gun, but not now," he said in a very low whisper.

Then from his pocket he pulled out a fresh, big, black, bold cigar. In just a couple of seconds he peeled off the wrapper, bit off the end, spit it out, and lit it up. It fired up like a flame thrower. Father held Duchay's leash in one hand and Catherine in the other. The cigar stuck six inches out of his mouth. He was like a World War II B17 bomber pilot going through the pre-bombing-mission flight control checks. We lifted off. I walked alongside Duchay, who was her usual cool self, calmly taking it all in. We walked slowly and deliberately. After a couple of short blocks, we turned the corner and arrived on the famous Chelsea Avenue scene. It was a beautiful late spring evening on a large college campus in the fall of 1967 at the height of the Viet Nam war.

I looked around in wonder at the laid-back sights, sounds, people, shops and music. Exotic, strange scents filled the air. It was right out of a Federico Fellini movie or *Alice in Wonderland.* I was conflicted about what Father Jacobson and mom had told me and what I was seeing and hearing. What I was seeing and hearing appeared to be just a lot of happy people hanging out and having a wonderful time.

"Now Carl, you stay close to me. I'll take care of Catherine and Duchay."

We stood there while Father Jacobson decided the best route. We passed five people sitting in a circle singing, while one of them played the guitar. They had loose, kind of dingy, flowery clothes and long hair. One of the girls wore a colorful headband. That type of clothing seemed to be the general dress code. Music played from cars, transistor radios, and people just sitting around. Everyone stood or sat and talked in small groups. Many were smoking cigarettes and seemed to have bottles of wine or beer. Up and down the street it was a gay, friendly, freewheeling atmosphere, but with a strange air of beautiful intensity about it.

Just north of Chelsea Avenue was an open field with a stream that was located right on the campus. This area was called Sean Meadow. A lot of people were walking toward it and I could hear someone on some sort of loudspeaker. He seemed angry and the people in the field were clapping and cheering every time he said something.

"Father, what is going on in that field down there? Can we go for just a little bit?"

"I think I know what's going on, but we can walk past it for a minute." His face wore an expression of disgust. The crowd thickened as we got closer. The atmosphere felt more agitated and angry than on Chelsea. This particular scene clearly wasn't festive all.

"Father, what are they doing here? Who is the person on the loudspeaker?" Father Jacobson took another hard puff off his cigar. He then blew an immense amount of smoke out in the direction of the speaker. The puff of smoke appeared to take on the shape of St. Michael the Archangel flashing his mighty sword.

"These jackasses are protesting the war," he said with disdain.

"The war in Viet Nam? Why are they doing that?"

"Because these kids today don't know any damn better." I could see the hate in his eyes as he surveyed the scene. He quickly led us back to the relatively lighter atmosphere on Chelsea Avenue. We stopped at a clothing shop.

"Carl, will you hold Duchay while Catherine and I go inside?" he asked.

"Yah, I'll take her." Father Jacobson picked up Catherine and they went inside. I stood with Duchay and continued to survey the scene. A few feet from me and the store a couple sat talking on the sidewalk with their radio going. It played a song I'd heard before. It was called "San Francisco."

I slowly went up to them. "Hey, is that Scott McKenzie? I really like that song." The woman looked at me and smiled. She had the prettiest long cinnamon hair and the neatest perfume I had ever smelled.

"Yah, the song's called 'San Francisco.' Isn't it cool? One of The Mamas & the Papas wrote it. I really like it too," she said.

"Hey, little guy, that's a cool dog you have there. Is it friendly?" the girl asked.

"Yah, if she knows you."

"Can I pet her?"

"Yah, just be easy." The couple both petted Duchay, who thankfully remained calm. I think she liked the hippie scene as much as I was starting to.

"What is that perfume you're wearing?" I asked the girl.

"It's called Patchouli. Do you like it?" I smiled and shook my head yes. She smiled and started to ask me another question, but then I noticed something out of the corner of my eye.

Father Jacobson and Catherine were coming out of the shop. My God, he'd be looking for me and here I am talking to a couple of hippies!

"Uuhhh, I have to go. Thanks," I said, rushing off. The couple smiled and said goodbye. They had such a laid-back, cool way about them. I rushed back to the store entrance.

"Where did you go, Carl? I was looking right outside the store for you," Father asked.

"Duchay had to go. You know. . . go. So I walked her behind that building."

"Well, as far as I'm concerned, she can go pee on most of these knuckleheads here," he chuckled. We continued our walk and started to pass a record store. A sign in the window said 45 rpm singles were on sale for 69 cents. I really wanted to get that song "San Francisco." I thought long and hard. Then I got an idea.

"Father, if I clean up after Duchay downstairs would it be possible to earn a dollar?"

He thought for a minute then took a more gentle puff of his cigar. "If you keep her area down there clean all weekend I'll give you two dollars." Bingo!

"Can I have one of those dollars now and run into the record store real quick to get a song?"

I figured he bought Catherine something, so wouldn't he advance me a dollar? Much to my amazement, he pulled out his wallet and handed me a nice, crisp, one-dollar bill. I thanked him and ran into the record store. Five minutes later I came out with "San Francisco" and change! I was ecstatic. It was starting to get darker and the carnival-like atmosphere was getting too animated for Father Jacobson. He had had a taste of it and was now fed up. But deep down I think he enjoyed the shock value of it all. I believe he felt his priestly Catholic aura of moralistic imposition permeate the degenerate and sinful crowd. And for this it was well worth the walk. This cycle would repeat many more times over the next couple of years.

"Let's head down this way and back to the rectory. Your mom is probably wondering where we are." I wanted so much to stay there with all those cool people, but alas, I was just too young. We got back to St. Jerome's after an hour-and-a-half of walking.

"Well, how was it?" mom asked.

"Just a bunch of weirdos running around," Father said.

"Carl, what did you think?" Mom really seemed intrigued about my response. I couldn't sound too enthusiastic as Father Jacobson was still standing right there.

"Some of them were nice I guess, but I don't know if I'd ever wear my hair that long."

"You'd better not or I'll cut it off myself," Father said.

"Well, it's late and we need to get to bed. Carl, you know which room you're in, don't you? I'll be sleeping with Catherine in the last room," mom said.

209

"Yah, I know. See you in the morning." I still wondered about the neat people I saw on Chelsea Avenue. I wanted so much to stay with them in that carefree, friendly atmosphere.

The next day, Saturday, we watched a football game and then Father Jacobson took us all around the college campus, showing us all the different buildings and sites. We ordered pizzas that night. I asked if we could take another walk on Chelsea Avenue after we ate and the answer was a flat no. Father Jacobson didn't want to expose us to that awful scene too much. I was mesmerized by it all.

The next morning I served two Masses with Father Jacobson. While I was on the altar I couldn't help but notice a very cute Asian girl in the congregation. I had never seen one before. I was captivated. I stared at her more than an altar boy should have. I knew, though, it was impossible for us to meet and I was still very shy with girls at the time. I had to force her out of my mind. However, I was more than willing to serve Mass as much as needed whenever we were in Monticello. Maybe I would see her again some Sunday. I was slowly transitioning from thinking girls were gross little cootie-infested monsters to actually becoming attracted to them.

Later in the afternoon we went over to the construction site of the new St. Jerome's Parish complex. It would be bigger and grander than the old one. They were already starting to break ground on it.

"Father, when is the new church going to open?" I asked.

"January of 1969 is when it's scheduled to be done."

I could tell he wasn't thrilled about overseeing its construction. He drove us around Monticello again for a little while. That Sunday evening was another wonderful dinner of pizzas and Cokes. This time Father Laughlin joined us. After some polite chit-chat he retired to his bedroom. It was getting late and I knew we had to drive back home for school on Monday morning. By the time we got things together it was 10 pm. The highway was dark and windy. Mom let me play the radio as long as I kept it very low. Catherine slept in the back seat. As we drove through the abyss they played the Zombies' "Time of the Season." I listened, half asleep.

We pulled into Leabor Road just after 11 pm. The house was scary at night. I always felt like we were being watched from the woods. Karen, who was home from college for a few days, was still up and very upset. She'd been getting some strange phone calls for the past couple of hours. Mom calmed her down, then at last we all went to bed. Karen didn't like staying home alone in that house but didn't want to go down with us to Monticello either.

✝

Since dad left, the Leabor Road house was physically deteriorating and our lifestyle had become more chaotic. The well water taste was terrible, rusty, and sulphuric. The utilities sent shut-off notices, but somehow at the 11th hour the bills mysteriously got paid. I suspected who was paying them and it wasn't dad. Plumbing problems were continual and the roof leaked over the living room fire place. If the leak continued, there would be some real expensive damage to deal with. By the spring of 1968 it had become an ever-present problem and the only real solution was a new roof, which no one could really afford. The house apparently was not in the best of shape when mom and dad purchased it. Aunt Margie to the rescue.

She recommended a maintenance man who had worked on roofing problems for years. He'd repair ours for cheap as a favor to Aunt Margie. Mom had a brief conversation with him over the telephone, describing the damage. All I knew was his name was Glen and he was a maintenance man where she worked. He didn't own a car so we had to pick him up at his apartment. I was so relieved that this roof would finally be fixed. He told mom what materials to get even before he came. It seemed strange to me that he knew that before he even looked at the damage.

One Saturday mom said, "Carl get in the car. We're going to pick up Glen." We headed into a questionable area of town mom was uncomfortable with. Glen seemed polite enough but quiet. The next thing out of his mouth after "Hello" was, "Mrs. Sanders can you pull in here? I'll just be a minute. Also can I borrow five dollars and we can deduct it from the repair charge?" Much to my surprise mom gave him the money.

We pulled into a liquor store. I noticed an ugly, scary man coming out. He glared back at me. Chill ran down to my bones. Was this a premonition of things to come? Glen finally came out with a brown bag. Since mom seemed to be kind of going along with this I thought it was normal. After all, Glen was recommended by Aunt Margie.

"Glen, you're not going to drink anything until the work is done," mom said.

"No, Mrs. Sanders, this is for later." He spoke in a very polite Beaver Cleaver tone of voice.

"Okay, good. We'll be at the house in about 20 minutes. We got all those materials you needed."

"Good, we'll get 'er done." Out of the corner of my eye, though, I saw him slip a half-pint bottle of whiskey out of a brown paper bag. He casually took a swig. Mom didn't notice and I became too nervous to say anything. At home I saw Glen stick the bottle in his pocket, but there seemed to be something else in the brown bag. My God, did he have two bottles? Duchay was in the yard wagging her tail. She was glad I was back. In the house mom showed Glen the roof damage.

"Oh Mrs. Sanders, this won't be any big deal. I can have this all fixed up in a couple of hours."

"Well, that sounds good. I'll be in the back room for a while."

Glen then cut through the patio outside and climbed our ladder up to the damaged area. I now felt a little more reassured. Maybe whiskey doesn't affect him that much. I went outside to play with Duchay. After a while I checked to see how Glen was coming along. I snuck through the back yard and came up from the rear of the house to escape his detection. He was not on the roof at all and it didn't look like anything had been done. The roofing materials were in their original place, unopened. I knew darn well we'd been home now for well over an hour. Maybe he was working on the inside. But no, the damage in the living room was untouched. Glen was nowhere to be found. I got a bad feeling. Mom was on the phone in the back of the house. Based on her casual conversational tone, she must have been unaware of what was going on. I walked past the living room toward the kitchen, looking for him. All of a sudden, Glen strolled out of the kitchen toward me.

"Hey, Will, I need to show you something downstairs." He didn't seem quite right.

"Glen, remember my name is Carl."

"Oh yah, I forgot, sorry. Follow me downstairs. I need to show you something that needs fixing."

I was getting very nervous with mom on the phone clear at the other end of the house. But if I didn't comply, would Glen get violent? His tone of voice was already different and a little bit menacing. He seemed to have a bit more of a coarse air about him as well. Reluctantly I followed him downstairs and then noticed that whiskey bottle sticking out of his back pocket.

When we got to the bottom of the stairs he pulled it out, smiled, then took a rather big swig. About a third of the bottle was gone and he'd been here for over an hour now. So I guessed he must have been on a second bottle at the rate he was drinking. Once downstairs he led me back to the water pump room in an isolated area of the basement. I followed him in, but left the room door wide open. The only light came from one 60-watt bulb dangling from the ceiling.

"Will, have you looked at this lately?"

The whiskey smell on his breath was now overwhelming. His eyes had a red, glossed-over look and seemed to be vibrating. Frankly, I had no clue what he was talking about – I didn't know about fixing a water pump from *taking* a dump from a humpback whale. And I wasn't about to correct him on my name again, in case his already bizarre and drunken behavior got worse. What was he doing looking at the water pump? Isn't he supposed to be on the roof?

"No, Glen, I haven't. Is there something wrong with it?"

"Well, look at this meter on the wall. See where the needle's at there? The pump isn't putting out much power, which means it's starting to go out. It sounds funny, too."

He took another swig of whiskey, which he wasn't being bashful about anymore. I wondered how he knew all this when he was supposed to be on the roof.

"I'll go tell my mom and we'll have it looked at later." Then the conversation took a turn toward the bizarre.

"Do you know what a banana is?" he asked. I felt a bolt of electricity go right through me. Now I was really nervous and knew I had to be cautious.

"Well, it's something we eat, isn't it?"

"Yes, it is, and how big is yours?"

Mom, unbeknownst to me, was now on the stairway, listening to this conversation. To this day I still thank my mother for that. It's called being in the right place at the right time.

She said firmly and loudly, "Carl, get up here right now!!" I shot out of that pump room and up the stairs. She shut and locked the basement door.

"We're going to get that jackass out of here right now. He hasn't done a thing on the roof! I think he's been sneaking whiskey from the moment he got here. I noticed an empty bottle in the trash. Then I heard what he said to you downstairs! Did he touch you in a bad way?"

"No, mom, but I think he was getting ready to." I was almost in tears.

"We're taking him back to his apartment now." She abruptly opened the basement door.

"Glen, please come up here. We're taking you home now."

Glen came up the stairs like Mr. Innocent. Now he was visibly drunk and slurring his words, clutching his second now almost-empty bottle.

"You don't have to take me home now. I haven't finished the roof repair yet," he said in an insolent tone.

"*Finished* the roof? As far as I can tell, you haven't done *anything* on the roof. And you apparently started drinking when I told you not to until it *was* done. Let's get in the car right now. Now!"

Glen shook his shoulders like he was confused. Mom herded us to the car as quickly as she could. I jumped into the front seat and Glen got into the back seat directly behind me. He still had a couple more gulps of whiskey left. He wasn't even hiding it in front of mom now. He started mumbling something under his breath, which made us even more nervous.

"Glen, I'm taking you home immediately. Please just sit quietly. We'll have you home in about 45 minutes." Mom fired up the station wagon and we sped out of the driveway. This was the fastest I'd ever seen her drive. Glen sat quietly for the first 15 minutes or so. Then he started getting belligerent.

"I could have finished that damn roof leak if you'd let me. You're probably not going to pay me anything now," he mumbled.

"It's okay. We'll take care of it later. Right now we're taking you home." Mom was getting more nervous, yet assertive, as Glen got more arrogant.

"Will, you look very handsome," he said. I stared straight ahead in horror.

"That's enough, Glen," mom said. Glen reached over the back seat and started running his fingers over my hair. I pushed his hand back.

"Glen, that's enough! Now knock it off!" mom screamed at the top of her lungs. Glen then reached up further and put his arms around my neck and locked me in a chokehold.

"Did I ever teach you how to do this?" he slurred. I struggled to get his arms off of my neck. Mom was driving as fast as she could, disregarding the speed limits. I think she hoped a police officer would pull her over for speeding. Finally, I got Glen's hands off me.

"I just wanted to touch your hair. What the hell's wrong with that?" Glen fell back into the seat. His behavior was getting more and more delirious.

Mom tried to pull onto an alternate street to take a shortcut, but the lane was clogged with traffic. She then quickly jutted out into it, and we were now moving rapidly with the rest of the traffic. We approached a yellow light. It turned red. The cars in front of us went right through it. Mom followed, still hoping to get pulled over.

"My God, did you see that?" she said.

"Yah, they ran that red light, but so did we." The drive was getting dangerous.

We approached yet another yellow light. It turned red and again the cars in front of us ran it. Mom was right behind. "What is going on here? We're all running red lights and there aren't any police around!" I, too, was surprised. And the strange thing was that the cars behind us were not stopping at all. The same thing happened at a third light, when mom finally realized something.

"Oh, dammit, Carl! We're not going to get stopped! We're in a funeral procession!" A patrolman sped by on his motorcycle bearing funeral signage. Mom honked and honked, but he didn't seem to hear and sped to the front of the line.

"Carl, I'm pulling over at that gas station. I've had it! When I stop, get out as fast as you can." She pulled over and we both jumped out of the car. Glen, by this time, was half passed out and just rambling to himself.

"You drunken bastard!!" she screamed at Glen. Inside, she explained the situation to the attendant, who immediately called the police. Luckily, they showed up quickly and hauled Glen's butt far, far away. Mom was really upset.

"He didn't touch you down there, did he? I just want to be sure," she asked. Her voice was strangely calm now.

"No, mom, he really didn't but he might have been getting ready to. I don't want him back in the house or ever see him again."

"He's not coming back." I got back in the car and sat stunned. We drove home in silence. Once we arrived, mom immediately called Father Jacobson. I went outside and sat with Duchay in the back yard.

†

As spring of 1968 went through its motions the presidential primaries occupied mom and Father Jacobson. Robert Kennedy led the Democrats. It was April 4th, the night Martin Luther King was shot. Kennedy was campaigning in Bridgeport. My Aunt Margie, heavily involved in the Democratic Party, called mom.

"Come to Kennedy's hotel! Maybe we can catch a glimpse of him." Catherine stayed home with Karen, but mom and I jumped in the car, picked up Margie, then headed downtown. Kennedy finished his campaign speech, then spoke about Martin Luther King, calming down the angry crowd. We heard a rumor he was heading back to the hotel right afterward. Margie ran into a newspaper reporter she drank beer with.

"Well hi, Ron, how in the hell are ya?"

"Well hello, Margie. It's crazy down here. I'm surprised you got through the front doors at all."

"We're trying to find out if Kennedy's coming in here after his talk."

"Rumor has it he's already back. Anyway, gotta run. See you at the K of C tomorrow night," Ron said.

"You got a date." We walked around, then started talking to another group of people.

"Hi. Are you from around here? My name is Margie Kristol. This is my sister Madeline and her son Carl."

"We're Bob and Cindy Howard, and this is my brother Bill. We're Democratic precinct committeemen from Alton. We followed him down here this morning," Bob said.

"I would love to meet him if I could," said Margie.

"Well, rumor has it he's in suite 1276 up on the 12th floor. We got that from the bartender in the lounge. That was the most expensive tip I ever left for a beer," Bob said. There was a silence and we all looked at each other.

"Well hell, let's go up to the 12th floor and pay Senator Kennedy a visit," Margie laughed.

"That's what we're thinking, but were afraid to do it alone," said Bob.

"Damn, I forgot my camera. Madeline, do you have yours?" Margie asked.

"I didn't bring one either."

"Listen, I have one," said Bob, "and so does Cindy. If we see him one of us will get a picture and we'll send a copy to you. We'll get your addresses before we leave. Let's grab an elevator."

"I guess we're gonna do this. I'll bet he's not going to be there. Just our luck," Margie said. The six of us headed toward the elevators. Mom pressed the button and up we went.

"Hell," said Margie. "I can't believe we're doing this."

"It's a long shot. Even if he is up there we probably can't get near him. That bartender could have been feeding me a line of bullshit to get a good tip, too."

On the 12th floor, Margie asked, "Madeline, are we really going to do this?"

"We're already here. Let's find out." We crept down the hallway looking for 1276.

"I'm surprised no one else is up here," Cindy said.

"Probably means he's not really here," said Bill. We then stood directly in front of room 1276.

"Well, who's gonna knock?" asked Margie under her breath. "Sounds like somebody's in there."

"I will. Here goes nothing. Bob and Cindy, get your cameras ready," whispered Bill. "If he's here, you'll have to get a picture quick."

He knocked. A few moments went by. Then the door opened. Much to our utter, stupefied shock, out popped Robert Kennedy himself. At that split second Bill snapped his picture. We introduced ourselves and Mr. Kennedy greeted us. He was very gracious, considering all he had done that day. Margie and Bob got his autograph. After a couple of minutes some other men came to the door, ending our little meeting. They asked us to keep the room number under our hats. We left in total euphoria.

"Bob, here's my address," said Margie. "We'd love it if you could send us a couple of copies of that picture."

"Give us a few weeks to get them developed, but you got it." We said our goodbyes and he promised to have a beer with Margie the next time he was in town. Three weeks later Margie and mom were visiting my grandmother. The pictures indeed had arrived.

"Oh here, Madeline, here's your copy," said Margie. In the envelope was a shiny five-by-seven-inch photograph of Robert Kennedy standing in the open door of room 1276.

A couple of months later on the night of June 5, mom woke me up. It must have been 5 in the morning.

"Carl, come with me. It's all over the television. They shot Robert Kennedy. I think he's dead." I was numb. We had just met him! I liked him. Why did they shoot him? Why did they shoot his brother? Why did they shoot Martin Luther King? It was a very frightening period. I still wonder why to this day.

✝

One beautiful Saturday morning in mid-July our lawn mower wouldn't start, no matter how hard I pulled the string. The grass was getting high. I told mom. She didn't know what to do.

"Don't worry about it for now. It can probably go another couple of weeks." A couple of weeks came and went and the mower still wouldn't start. I even changed the spark plug. But what did I know? Beyond that, I wasn't a lawn mower mechanic. Another couple of weeks came and went. It was now mid-July. The lawn looked like the wild, open field behind the house. You couldn't tell the two apart.

"Mom, when are we going to get the lawn mower fixed? If it goes too much longer it won't be able to handle the high grass. It probably can't now."

"I don't know. Father Jacobson is supposed to be getting someone who works on lawn mowers."

"Do you know when they're supposed to be here?"

"He hasn't said anything. He's been very busy in Monticello. Can't you get it to work yet?" She was getting agitated.

"No. I keep hoping it will start but it's still broken."

"I'll mention it to him tonight. Let's don't talk about it anymore." Her tone of voice put a stop to more discussion. About a week later mom said someone was going to look at the mower. The repair person took it away and brought it back a couple of days later. True, I was excited, but apprehensive. The grass was over a foot high. I got on the mower and it started it up just fine. But the grass was so high. When I started cutting it, the long blades got tangled up. Then I heard something snap. The blades wouldn't move. Oh no, not again!

"Mom, the mower quit working again."

"We just got it fixed! Did you break it?"

"No. It started up okay, but when I went into the tall, thick grass something broke. I don't know what happened."

"I'm not going to ask Father for any help again. He's too busy. Can you use the other mower?" Huh? I'm going to mow two-and-a-half acres of high grass with a push mower?

"That one works just fine, but it'll take a long time."

"Try it. If it gets too hard I'll help you." Mom went back in the house.

Mowing a small section took forever. I showed her my work. "That was as fast as I could go with the grass this high."

"Let me try it for a while," she said. After about 30 minutes she stopped and looked around, frustrated. Her eyes welled up.

"I am going to call Father Jacobson. I just hate to bother him." I push-mowed for the next several hours, inches at a time. By the time it started to get dark, I'd mowed only a small patch.

"This is all you managed to get done?" mom asked.

"That's it, mom." Again, her frustration showed. As I lay in bed that night I heard Hensin Cargill's "Skip a Rope." It sure reflected our family situation over the past eight years. One more song that perfectly fit my mood and life.

Later mom said, "I talked to Father and that man is going to come look at it again." The news was not good. The part we needed this time was on a one-month backorder. We didn't have money for another new or used mower. This was just another desperate example of the deterioration at Leabor Road.

We then rented another push mower. Mom and I mowed together. The tedious, hot, sweaty task went on for the next several days. Two feet forward. One foot back. Two feet forward. One foot back. We were constantly attacked by mosquitoes and horseflies in the knee-high grass. The mowers stalled constantly. I wound up cutting a poor gopher in half in the tall grass. That trauma made things all the more bizarre. The weather turned rainy and the grass we had just cut was now growing faster than it had all summer, which meant we had to use the push mowers a second time. This time we had to haul the grass we cut earlier out to the back woods in a wheelbarrow. By the grace of God the weather stayed very dry after that. Divine intervention spared us a third mowing. God thought we'd had enough.

✝

I started to notice mom was getting seriously fed up with Mickey. His ever-present messes and nasty temperament on top of the weekend trips to Monticello, deteriorating house, and general chaos pushed mom to the edge. Mickey was finally banished to the basement. I knew this was coming but I didn't feel sorry for him. Mike was the only one who could handle that dog, but he was either away at school, working at his painting business or running around with his friends.

Mom was the only one now who took Mickey food and water. She left it on the very first step inside the door. It eventually got to the point where no one was allowed downstairs at all now. Mickey had essentially been "disappeared" into the dungeon-like environment. Out of sight, out of mind. After several months I forgot about him, assuming he was okay.

One rare Saturday evening when Father Jacobson was up from Monticello, we were talking in the living room. Well, Father Jacobson and mom were doing most of the talking about preparations for Karen's wedding, which would take place in the fall of 1968. Catherine was asleep in the back bedroom. Father Jacobson noticed Mickey wasn't running around like he usually was.

"Hey, I haven't seen that poodle. Did Duchay eat him?" he chuckled.

"It's been down in the basement for the past few months. I got sick and tired of him stinking up the upstairs and that nasty temperament of his," mom said. "That reminds me, I have to run downstairs to get those extra tablecloths for the wedding reception. I'll be right back up."

Father Jacobson and I watched TV. Suddenly we heard a blood-curdling scream. Mom came running up the stairs, wailing at the top of her lungs.

"Oh my God! They're all over me! Get those goddamn things off of me! Get them off! Get them off!" Father Jacobson and I looked on in total horror.

"Honey, get what off? What are you talking about?" Father Jacobson asked, in hysterics himself. All I could do was stare. I was shocked at mom's frightening behavior and equally shocked that Father Jacobson called her "honey."

"God dammit, I can't get them off of me!" Mom was acting like she was on fire. She ran from the dining room toward us in the living room.

"Come on honey, what do you need me to do? I can't help you unless you let me know!" Father cried.

"I'm sick and tired of all this shit!" she screamed.

Mom pulled her skirt right off to the panty hose and underwear. Outside she pulled her pantyhose off. She was outside, crying. Father Jacobson told me to stay inside and went out after her. I peeked out the window. He was hugging her, trying to calm her down. I couldn't make out what they were talking about and would never know. I didn't want to know. He finally came back inside.

"Carl, go in your mother's bedroom closet and grab her robe." Thankfully Catherine had slept through it. Mom came back in the house. Her face was puffed up and red.

"I'm sorry you had to see that Carl," she said.

"It's okay, mom. Are you alright?"

"Yes, I'm fine. I'm going to go take a shower. Do what Father Jacobson tells you until I come back." She went to her bedroom. I stood there in shock. Whatever had happened I felt terrible for her. When she disappeared I turned toward Father Jacobson.

"Father, what happened?"

"Hold on. I'll tell you in a minute. Right now I need to go downstairs. Just stay up here." He had a very serious look on his face. After a while he came back upstairs. In a slow, deliberate tone of voice, he asked, "How long has Mickey been downstairs?"

"I don't know, Father. I think around maybe four months. Mom got tired of him and put him downstairs. We weren't allowed to go down there. Mom was feeding him."

"I'm going downstairs again. Is there any bug spray in the house?" I got him a can. That was one product we had in plentiful supply. After he ventured downstairs with his flashlight, I heard the spray can go off for what seemed forever. Then Father Jacobson came back up with a somber expression on his face.

"He doesn't look very good. Has he been to the vet lately?"

"Father, I don't think he's ever been to the vet."

"Well, at any rate, he has new food and water."

Mom came out of her bedroom in a better frame of mind. "Carl, it's your bedtime. I'll stay up and talk to Father until he has to leave." Her eyes looked terrible. I lay in bed, numb, listening to the radio. The outside world sounded so normal. I could hear mom talking to Father Jacobson over the radio's soft noise. But I couldn't make out what they were talking about. Richard Harris' "MacArthur Park" sent me off to sleep.

✝

Preparations for cleaning up Leabor Road before Karen's wedding in September were underway. This cleanup was a massive, full-court press. For two weeks before the wedding, mom, Aunt Margie, my grandparents and all us kids combined forces. My older brother Lanny trimmed all the shrubbery. The lawn was cut nicely. My grandmother and I worked on the numerous large windows, including the little rectangular ones in the patio. Bathrooms, bedrooms and the kitchen were spotless. I cleaned out the garages. Grandmother even rented a steamer for cleaning the carpeting. It would be the cleanest I had ever seen the Leabor Road house since we bought it. We would never see it this clean again. Multitudes of friends and family would be visiting. Our house would host a post-reception get-together where the heavier partying and drinking would take place. Father Jacobson was conducting the ceremony. The only problem, though, was that no one touched the basement.

The ceremony was really nice and everyone was in a good mood and got along great. The reception dinner was at a nice restaurant called The French Skillet that was very close to our old Broderick Street house. Many of Karen's and John's college and childhood friends attended.

Lanny and Mike decided to do a last-minute check at the house on all the preparations before the hordes of people arrived for the evening party scene.

"Is there enough ice for the beer?" Mike asked.

"There should be. I have seven cases in the coolers iced down and there are five more bags in the freezer."

"All the wine, whiskey and vodka are on the table with plenty of plastic cups," Mike said.

"I'm ready for a beer right now," Lanny said. Mike nodded in agreement.

"By the way, do you know if anyone has been down in the basement lately? Do you want to check on Mickey's food?" Lanny asked.

"Mom has been shitty about anyone going down since she stuck him there," said Mike. "I tried to once and we almost got in a fight about it so I backed off."

"Well, I'm going down to check on him. If there's no food or water he'll start barking and it'll be a pain in the ass for the guests." Down into the basement he went. Mike followed closely behind. It had been several weeks since Father Jacobson had gone down there.

"Damn, the top light doesn't even work. Do you have a flashlight up there? And is there any bug spray? I think we're going to need it." Mike grabbed both from the garage. As they went down the steps, a stench hit them like a ton of bricks.

"God, it stinks! What in the hell is that?" Mike asked.

"It smells like something dead and I think I know what it is," Lanny said. At the bottom of the stairs they started to fight through thick clouds of flies. Lanny found Mickey's food and water bowl, both empty. A few steps away was the cause of the smell. Mickey was being eaten by maggots. He had been dead for God knows how long.

"Jeeesssuuusss Christ. Come look at this."

"Good God. Unbelievable! Oh shit, do I hear a car pulling in?"

"Shit! People are starting to arrive. Grab that snow shovel over there. Run upstairs and grab a roll of paper towels, trash bags and some bleach and throw it back down to me. I'm going to start fucking spraying as much as I can. Then go back up and handle the guests. Keep them away from here until I can get this taken care of. We have to get him out of here now!"

Lanny, in a suit and tie, scooped Mickey up, ran upstairs, out the back door, and into the woods where he dumped him. Then he ran back down to the basement. He quickly cleaned up the area where Mickey had lain, gagging the entire time. He shoved the dirty towels into a double-lined trash bag, spraying the flies constantly. He then washed his hands in the sink, adjusted his tie, and went back upstairs. While all this had gone on Mike, in a suit and tie, cheerfully greeted guests as they arrived at the front door. Mike had done a great job elegantly playing host and diverting the formally dressed people away from the kitchen area.

Later in the evening as the beer was flowing, Lanny and Mike had a few words off to the side. "Where did you put him?" Mike whispered.

"I had to take him out back past the apple tree and out in the woods. We can bury him tomorrow. Thank God he was still in one piece. Did anyone see me?"

"No, but thank God they all came in the front door. If they hadn't, you'd have run right past them with Mickey on that shovel. You know it's bizarre shit like this that turns people into alcoholics."

They both shook their heads in subdued, macabre laughter while sipping their beer. The rest of the evening went well and all guests had a great time. The music and the dancing went on into the wee hours of the morning. The guests would never know what had taken place just a few short moments before. The Mickey incident would, for decades, symbolize the overall chaos and insanity of our family life at Leabor Road.

✝

After Karen's wedding and the events of the past summer, things settled down a bit. I was back in the routine of school. I had a bit of time to breathe and tried not to think about things too much. Mornings were getting colder and darker when I went out to wait for the school bus. It was now November of 1968.

As I stood alone in the darkness at the end of the driveway by the street, I watched the moonlight cast long shadows over the fence posts across the street. They tended to take on distorted, yet human-like forms. It was a little scary at first, but those shadows eventually became my friends and kept watch over me until the bus arrived. I referred to them as "The Shadows" and would greet them when I came out. They in turn greeted me back in their own way. One morning as I gazed over at them, my dad popped into my mind. He'd been gone over a year now. For some reason, Sonny and Cher's "Bang Bang" always came to mind when I was with the shadows on those chilly mornings.

Chapter 11: St. Jerome's and Leabor Road

IN JANUARY 1969 the new and improved St. Jerome's church complex opened for business, both spiritual and financial. It was a much larger facility than the old one. Abandoned Catholic churches always stood as vacant reminders of the grand, old-world, gothic styles of the past. No longer in vogue were beautiful, detailed, and inspirational stained-glass pieces depicting Jesus, Mary and the saints.

Gone were the larger-than-life statues with their loving, protective faces. Gone were the solid oak and cherry wood pews. In Monticello, Iowa, the Catholic Church had entered the nuvo religious era. This church felt like more of an institution than an inspirational house of worship. I thought, who wants to worship God in an institution? Lackluster statuary looked like bored souls, posing without purpose for an audience. The furniture looked like it came from an office-supply warehouse. Random, shapeless colored-glass panes in weird geometric forms were intended to say something, but sat mute. Gone were the large, beautiful, marble holy-water fonts. They were now stainless steel, like in a hospital. The main altar table at the front looked like an oversized office desk.

Directly over the altar, high in the air for all to see, was the biggest, ugliest, abstract mosaic I had ever seen. It was supposed to depict the crucifixion of Christ. I stared for a good five minutes, tilting my head up and down, cocking it to the right and left, and closing my eyes and opening them again. After all that, I still thought it belonged in a landfill.

The pièce de résistance sat downstairs in the main hallway, highly visible from the west entrance. It was another oversized, abstract mosaic encased in a large, yellow, flimsy-looking wood-and-glass box. It looked like a cheap grade-school art project — another failed attempt to depict the crucifixion. The piece itself should have been crucified (and later was). It did, however, spark my interest in the work of Salvador Dali. Unfortunately, when St. Jerome's was being built and furnished, Father Jacobson had little say in much of the actual decor. He was a hardcore traditionalist and the entire new-wave church style grated on him. Two wealthy parishioners had created and donated both mosaics and he was essentially forced to accept them by the higher-ups. He had to bite his tongue when he talked with them about their religious works of art. I was privy to one of the conversations after Mass one morning. It concerned the work of art I just described.

"Father, I'm so glad you like it. It took us six months to design and construct," said Kevin Anderson with pride. His beaming wife Margie stood beside him.

"Well, Kevin and Margie, I have to say what a welcome addition this is to the St. Jerome's. And all the time and effort you put into it is impressive. I still can't believe it." He chomped down hard on his cigar. Father Jacobson always chewed on his cigar as much as he smoked it. I could always tell when he was bullshitting. And now he looked down at the ground with a big smile and his signature warm, hearty laugh.

"Father, will this lower-level be its final place?" Margie asked. Apparently she wanted it in a more prominent position, out of the basement.

"Well, Margie, for the time being let's keep it here until I can find some place more suitable. Father Jacobson then winked at me. This is a good area because people see it right when they walk in for classes and social events. This area is always high traffic."

"Father, we can't tell you what this means to us," Kevin said.

"Well, I can't tell you what it means to me, either." Father Jacobson again winked at me. After they left I turned to him.

"Father, where were you going to put this later?"

"In the janitor's storage closet."

A quaint chapel stood off to the side of the north entrance – a smaller version of the main church. In the upper balcony at the rear of the church was a grand organ, not the beautiful pipe organs of old, but still a beautiful, large, impressive organ. In the back of the facility over the four garages were three dorm-type rooms and a bath-shower room. Six Catholic college students, including my brother Mike, now lived here. In exchange for free room, they maintained St. Jerome's. It was a good deal for anyone who could get on the long waiting list.

At this new facility Father Jacobson had only a temporary secretary until a full-time one could be hired. In addition to Father Laughlin at the old St. Jerome's, Father Jacobson had three assistants working and living with him. I was too naive at the time to wonder what mom and the three of us looked like coming down almost every weekend. One of the justifications of our being there so often was that mom was doing more and more secretarial work for Father Jacobson. Sometimes we spent the night in a local motel or sometimes right at the new rectory, which had several guest rooms. Now though, when we cooked steaks, the other priests rarely joined us.

At this new facility I wouldn't be serving Mass. The altar boys from the two other Catholic parishes handled that. In other words, I was out. I was now in eighth grade anyway, and my altar boy days were fading. In high school I would not continue to serve Mass.

Father Jacobson did not like the Archdiocese continually instructing him to be more up with the times now that this expensive new parish complex was open on a large, somewhat liberal college campus. The Archdiocese needed to see the money start rolling in. The old traditionalist Catholic Church ways wouldn't cut it. One of the new directives that came down from on high called for including a folk Mass in the Sunday morning line-up. Father Jacobson hated folk music and rock-n-roll in general. One evening I overheard his reaction on the phone.

"That damn archbishop wants me to make the 11:30 a damn folk Mass! God, I knew this was coming. I can't stand to listen to that shit on the radio, let alone during my own church service! Well, I'll tell you, I'm passing that one off to Laughlin. He can deal with it. If they want that bullshit folk music in church I'll stick it in the 8 am slot. That'll teach those jackass hippies to drag their tails in early after running around all night," he laughed.

Ready or not, a folk band was scheduled for three weeks later and at the 11:30 Mass — the most heavily attended Sunday service. Father Laughlin was indeed scheduled to be the performing priest. I had never seen a band like that perform in a church. Music lover that I was, I really wanted to see what they were like.

"Mom, would it be okay if I went to the 11:30 folk Mass?" Her answer surprised me.

"Carl, that's fine. Catherine and I are going with you." I was surprised, but then I thought back over the past few years. Mom couldn't wait to see the television debut of The Mamas & the Papas on *The Ed Sullivan Show*. One of mom's favorite songs was The Beatles' "Hey Jude." She also loved Elvis Presley. She was a bit more open minded to music styles than most people of her generation.

Now the Saturday evening before, Father Laughlin had come down with a high temperature. Yes, he had caught the nasty flu that had been going around. Early that Sunday morning he informed Father Jacobson he wouldn't be able to perform the 11:30 folk Mass. He could barely get out of bed.

Father Jacobson was not the least bit thrilled about having to celebrate the first folk Mass at St. Jerome's. You would have thought a shit bomb went off. He wanted nothing to do with it, but given this last-minute crisis, he had no choice.

We arrived for church around 11, hoping for an up-front pew. The church was packed. I was so excited for Mass to start I stood on the kneeler — a big no-no.

At exactly 11:30 the band — two guys and two girls — positioned themselves to the side of the altar, complete with guitars, tambourine, bongos, flutes, bell-bottom jeans, flowery dresses and long hair. They looked like formally dressed-up hippies. The guys looked really cool with their long sideburns. Someday I would have long sideburns.

They opened the Mass with "Go Tell It on a Mountain." As soon as they started playing Father Jacobson himself paraded out of the sacristy with two altar boys and one of his assistants, Brother Samuel, in front. He wore one of the sourest expressions I had ever seen. He took his place on the altar and raised his hands, ready to read the opening prayers. But the band hadn't finished their song. In fact, they sang a second, then third verse, with Father Jacobson standing up there with his hands still up in the air.

Finally, he lowered his hands, stuffed them in his pockets, and with his head cocked, stared out over the heads of the congregation. Watching his "hell, aren't you finished yet?" expression and body language was as entertaining as the band. Father Jacobson was a master of facial expressions. But if you didn't know him, you'd assume he was intently and respectfully listening to this progressive yet spiritual music. I, of course, knew better.

One second after the song ended Father Jacobson started the opening prayer loud and clear. He was now

233

competing with this group of hippies who had invaded his sanctum. His homily espoused the value of the durable, time-tested Catholic traditions. Father performed beautifully during the rest of the service, reading the traditional prayers with an extra degree of inspirational enthusiasm. He would not be upstaged for one damn minute.

Between the various parts of the Mass the band played a few more songs. As the congregation lined up for communion they started in on the Youngbloods' "Come Together" — a big hit on the radio. My eyes opened wide and my antennas went up. My God! These are the Youngbloods! How did they get them to play here?

"Mom, I think that band is on the radio! That's one of their songs!" I whispered. At school on Monday I told everyone that I'd seen The Youngbloods "perform" at St. Jerome's in Monticello. What was bizarre was the fact they all believed me.

✝

1969 found the Leabor Road house malfunctioning on a regular basis. One morning before school I was washing my hair in the shower. Suddenly, the water flow just stopped dead. My hair was full of shampoo and my body covered in soapy lather. I cried out for mom, who came running into the bathroom.

"Mom, the water doesn't work anymore," I said, wiping the soap out of my eyes.

"It doesn't work at all?" She turned on the faucet in the sink. No water. I prayed the shower head was clogged. But her expression was gloomy.

"Carl, we don't have any water in the other bathroom either. I'll have to get you some water from the toilet to at least rinse off with." She came back with a pitcher. There were tears in her eyes.

"Don't worry, it's clean," she said. "I'm going to call Father and see what he suggests. I think the water pump is out. I'll get some distilled water for today. When we run out of that we can go to grandmother's and fill the jugs back up." I thought, here we go again. . . now something else is wrong with this stupid house.

That afternoon mom bought about 10 one gallon-containers of water. She said, "The water pump did go out. I called Father Jacobson and told him. Grandmother said to call the plumber and she'd pay for the repair." I'd wondered who would pay — grandmother or Father Jacobson. But when the plumber came out and looked at the pump, he said he had to order one and it wouldn't be in for a few days. Dirty dishes started to pile up in the sink and, of course, the toilets became inoperable. That evening while we were sitting around with no water in the house, I got the worst stomach cramps. It knew what it meant. I had to go to the bathroom and not to just pee.

"Mom, I have to go to the bathroom! My guts hurt."

"Carl, can you go in the woods?"

"Not this time I can't. I have to...well you know."

"My God, there's no water left for the toilets. It can't wait?"

"No," I moaned.

We then jumped in the car and sped to the nearest gas station, but their restrooms were out of order. Mom roared up the street to the next one, but someone was already in the men's room and I just couldn't wait. I think mom was afraid I was going to crap right there in the front seat. I didn't realize she could drive that fast.

"Hurry, mom, it hurts!"

She sped further up the road to the Burger Chef fast-food restaurant. I jumped out of the car and sprinted recklessly inside, trying to get to the john and almost knocking down some poor old lady. Finally, I attained salvation I walked back to the car with a look of full relief on my face.

"My God, you were in there a long time."

"I'm sorry. Now we can go back home?"

"Father's coming to watch Catherine. Then you and I are going to load the dishes into that tub in the garage and wash them at the quarter carwash on 38th Street."

Sure enough, Father Jacobson arrived with pizzas a couple of hours later. As mom and I headed out the door with the dishes, I saw him give mom some change. With our quarters we hosed down the dishes as best we could. Then mom told me to turn the nozzle onto her hair. I had to put in another quarter to rinse her hair and the dishes. It was one of the weirdest things I had ever done in my life. While everyone else there was washing their cars like normal people, we were showering and doing the dishes. We took home two plastic five-gallon jugs of water for showering.

The next morning we used up most of the distilled water but I made it to school looking and smelling relatively decent. After school we took all the empty jugs and filled them up at grandmother's. One more night of this before the plumber would be here. Back home mom announced, "Father is taking Catherine and me to Howard Johnson's motel to spend the night. If there is another person in the room they'll charge us extra. I think you'll be okay here. There's food in the refrigerator and Duchay will be with you." I raised my eyebrows but nodded okay.

"So you'll be gone all night and not back until morning?"

"Yes, but it's only for one night. They'll be here to fix the pump tomorrow."

"When are you leaving?"

"After I pack Catherine's things." I started mentally preparing myself for spending the night *alone* at Leabor Road. At least Duchay would be outside to guard the house. Mom left around 9 pm. I locked my bedroom door. If Duchay didn't bark, I'd be okay. After a while I turned off the radio and started drifting off to sleep. All of a sudden I heard what I didn't want to hear. Duchay started to bark. That meant something or someone was outside. I lay there frozen, hoping, praying whatever she was barking at wasn't a person. I turned the radio back on to help ease my fear. Right then Simon and Garfunkel's "The Boxer" came on. It calmed me down a lot. By the time the song ended Duchay had stopped barking. I finally drifted back to sleep, thank God.

The next day mom returned and the pump got fixed. I felt like the people in that TV show *The Pruitts of South Hampton*, with Phyllis Diller. Here we were, living in this impressive house on a big property, but we were paupers. A few days later I recalled the drunken weirdo, Glen, telling me in the pump room that the pump was ready to go out. Too bad I didn't listen, but he had lost his credibility with me after he started talking about bananas.

✝

A month later on a Monday evening we got a call from Father Rootz at St. Macarius. He said Rick Klemma, who was supposed to serve the 7 am Mass the next couple of mornings, had hurt his ankle and had to stay off it for a couple of days. The 7 am Mass required only two altar boys. Rick was the only experienced altar boy to help with that Mass. The other altar boy was brand new and wasn't ready to serve Mass alone. I was just getting over the flu, but agreed to fill in for two mornings. So the very next morning I got up at 5:30 so mom could get me in by 6:30 to help Father Rootz get set up. I entered the special altar boy entrance to find Father Rootz already there, getting things ready.

"Well, Carl, I'm so glad you could fill in for Rick. His ankle accident was so unfortunate," said Father Rootz. Normally he never spoke to me. This morning I was getting

237

his ass out of a sling so things were different. With just one green altar boy he'd have had to do everything himself.

"How did it happen, Father?"

"He just fell off of his bicycle and landed on his foot funny." I wondered, does Rick Klemma ride bicycles that much? He must weigh 500 pounds. I slipped into my cassock and did the pre-Mass checklist. I lit the front candles, but as I walked around I felt unusually hot. Maybe the heat in the church was set too high. At 7 am Father Rootz, the new altar boy, and I waltzed out onto the altar and exchanged the usual opening prayers without much fanfare. There were only six people in the congregation.

By the time the Offertory was over. I felt even hotter and time seemed to drag. I was barely able to serve communion. After I handed Father Rootz the water and wine cruets I knelt down and started to get dizzy. Come on, Carl, I said to myself. There's only a few more minutes left. I prayed to St. Cyprian of Antioch to give me physical strength. St. Cyprian and Jesus, please, help me not faint on the altar in front of Father Rootz and the strangers out in the pews.

But I felt weaker still, and thought the unthinkable: Sit down in Father Rootz's own seat on the altar. But it was too late. The last thing I remembered was falling backward with my hands still folded in prayer. I dreamed the angels came down out of the sky, picked me up in their arms, and whisked me away to heaven and far away from Leabor Road. What a beautiful way to enter heaven in my altar boy cassock.

I had blacked out right there during the closing prayers. After I fell and hit the floor I rolled right up against the table that held the cruets, communion platens, and wine. My head missed the metal legs but my shoulders didn't. This shook the table pretty good. I'd also forgotten to put the cap back on the wine cruet after communion. It tipped over. The cruet rolled on the edge of the table with the spout right over my head. Wine splashed onto my face. It woke me up. A couple people from the pews rushed onto the altar and to my side. Instead of angels picking me up, it was a couple of old women and Father Rootz. The new altar boy stood back in shock, thinking I was dead.

"Young man, are you okay?" someone asked.

"Yah, I think so ma'am. I guess so." I was in a fog, embarrassed, smelling like a skid-row wino. They all helped me into the sacristy and sat me down.

"Father, is the uuhh Mass over now?"

"Yes, Carl, services have been concluded. You had quite a fall." He thanked those who'd helped and quickly ushered them out the side door.

"I'm going to get Sister Cornelia. Please wait here."

Father Rootz pulled a handkerchief from his pocket and told me to wipe the wine off my face. All I could do was give a delirious nod. I looked like a drunk just pulled mumbling and moaning from the gutter. Father Rootz seemed a bit disgusted and was in a hurry to get me out of the way before setting up for the main Mass.

I wanted to get out of there and fast before anyone else saw me. My peers, teachers, and the altar boys setting up for the next Mass would be here very soon. If any of those guys got wind of this I'd never live it down. Two minutes later Sister Cornelia rushed into the sacristy.

"Carl, I've called your mother and she's on her way. Are you okay to walk?"

"I maybe think so, Sister. Yah." She sensed my embarrassment and knew the social ramifications if this were found out.

"I told your mother to come around to the back door to the sacristy. I'll wait here with you until she arrives." Father Rootz had mysteriously disappeared.

"Thank you ever so much, Sister. Oh, and can you give this to Father Rootz for me?" I held out the wine-drenched handkerchief, or snot rag, as we called them. I had seen him blow his nose in it many a time and had hoped it wasn't full of boogers this time. I don't think she knew this belonged to Father Rootz, and I didn't tell her.

I couldn't bring myself to wipe it on my face — just on my clothes. Instead I wiped off my face with the sleeve of the cassock. But I was still sticky with a sour wine odor. Mom finally showed up. As we pulled out of the parking lot I hid my head in shame so no one would see me. Mom was driving a little faster than usual. Once we were safely out of the parking lot I rolled the window down and stuck my head halfway out.

"Carl, are you okay now? I probably shouldn't have let you serve Mass. You were still under the weather. Sister Cornelia said you fell over on the altar." She kept looking over at me and smelling the air.

"Is that...alcohol I smell?" I had to explain this very carefully. I was finally getting a little more coherent.

"Mom, when I fell down I rolled into the wine table and the wine cruet spilled on me."

"Well as long as you weren't drinking any of it," she laughed. I just stared straight ahead.

"Let's get you home and into the shower. Then you'd better stay in bed. We'll see how you feel in the morning." Tomorrow was Friday, then the weekend. That gave me a four-day cushion before I'd have to face everyone. And hopefully Sister Cornelia and Father Rootz would keep their mouths shut.

On Monday morning no one seemed to know what had happened. But in later years as I got to drinking age it was a great bar story I loved to tell. It was the old "I passed out on the altar and red wine splashed on me after I hit the wine table and the taste made me sick" story. It's the reason I don't drink red wine to this day.

✝

We continued the weekly odyssey down to St. Jerome's. We'd leave Friday after school or Saturday morning and come back late Sunday night. It was an endless and tiring routine. But I liked the walks on Chelsea Avenue and being around the hippies. Even in grade school I identified with them. I liked the way they questioned everything, the way they dressed, and their dim view of society, the war, and the government. I didn't feel good about the Viet Nam war even then. Every adult I tried to talk to either said they didn't really know much about it or couldn't give a straight answer to any of my questions. All they would tell me is we were fighting communism. I always felt there was a little more to it than that. I mean, we defeated the major powers of Nazi Germany and Japan in four years during World War II. But after seven or so years we were still tangled up fighting little old North Viet Nam with no end in sight? It didn't quite add up for me.

As the spring of 1969 drifted by, my last semester at St. Macarius was coming to an end. I was in the twilight of my grade-school years with the end rapidly approaching in May. On my last day, all graduating eighth-graders were going home after lunch. Father Rootz gave us a talk on the virtues of leading a good Catholic life in high school. Then we all shuffled downstairs into the cafeteria. I sat with fellow altar boys Ted Stone, Jim Mahoney, Joe Adamsson, Kevin Rolan, and Pete Lorenz. Jim, Kevin and Pete were my fellow servers at the Mass where I pissed in my cassock.

"Man, I can't believe how fast this year's gone," Ted said.

"My mom says enjoy it while you can because you're not going to be young forever," Jim responded.

"Carl, what are you going to be when you grow up?" Kevin asked.

"I'm going to try to be an archeologist, but if that doesn't work I'm going to learn to play rock-n-roll music,"

I said with a straight face. Everyone seriously nodded in approval.

"Pete, what do you want to be?" I asked.

"I don't know. It would be kind of cool to be like Dick Smothers on *The Smothers Brothers Comedy Hour*," he said.

"What about you, Ted?" Kevin asked.

"Maybe own a ranch and raise cattle." The truth of the matter was none of us knew what the hell we wanted to do. We were consumed with trying to understand life from one day to the next. We were also numb with realizing that our grade-school years were finally over. The confused conversation continued.

"What was Father Rootz talking about being a good Catholic when we're in high school?" Jim asked with a snicker.

"I'm not sure, but I didn't like the way he looked at me during that lecture," Ted said.

"I guess we won't be altar boys in high school. Just the grade school people do that, don't they?" Jim asked. We nodded. We sat in silence as if at a memorial service. Joe Adamsson snapped us out of it.

"Well, guys, it was fun while it lasted. Maybe I'll see you all around this summer." I kept silent. We would be moving to Monticello for good in the next few months. We made the rounds together and said goodbye to our teachers and Sister Cornelia. Pete and I got on our bicycles and started riding away into the abyss.

"Well, Carl, take it easy. I'm sure I'll be seeing you."

"Yah, we will."

"See ya."

"See ya."

I sat on my bike and watched him ride off. I didn't know what to feel outside of a little sadness. I looked up at the sky, then back down. I rode slowly back to Leabor

242

Road. Duchay ran up to greet me. I wasn't sure if she was coming to Monticello with us or not. I ran into the back yard with her where we roughhoused a little. I brushed her coat for a while. She loved that. Then we both lay in the grass. I stared up at the absolutely beautiful clouds rolling by. Peter, Paul and Mary's song "Day Is Done" went through my head. It fit the mood. They wrote that song just for me.

✝

One July morning my clock radio went off like countless times before. The song I heard was "Love Will Make You Happy" by an obscure band called Mercy. I fell into a pensive state of mind. I stared at the ceiling and thought about the things I'd been hiding deep in my heart and mind. More changes were coming whether I wanted them or not. I was at a crossroad and my days at Leabor Road were numbered. I knew it.

In September of 1969 I'd start my freshman year of high school in Monticello, where Father Jacobson was. The constant round trips and the whole situation had taken a toll on us all, but mostly on mom. Her mood swings were more pronounced and she cried more, just out of the blue. I did what I could to console her but it was hard when she didn't want to talk about it most of the time. Bills were being paid late and things continued to fall apart. She socially hid a lot. Any and all talk of dad had officially ended. The only way I could deal with his absence was to block him out of my mind.

Now I selfishly thought about me and how I'd fit into the coming changes. Where would I go to school down there? There were no Catholic high schools in Monticello. What were the other kids like? Would I play football again? Would the studies be harder? My grades started falling after dad left. Mom was always hammering on me to study more and "get on the books." But I had no interest in it. How had everything gotten into such a mess? Had I done anything to contribute to it?

That September we moved into a rented home in Monticello in a professor-type neighborhood. Catherine was enrolled in a local Catholic grade school. Winford Junior High started for me before we were completely moved, so I had to live at St. Jerome's for about a week. Mike was already there along with another student, Pat Chesterton, who was really nice to me. The first night Mike and Pat were sitting around drinking Hamm's Beer. I'd never had a whole beer. I was mesmerized at the sight of them drinking beer, laughing at the Johnny Carson show and all the intensely wise conversation.

"Hey, Mike, can I try a beer?"

"You can have a couple, but that's it." I didn't think I could down two but I was going to show those guys just how strong I was. I downed the first two and as a bonus, they gave me two more just to see how I'd act.

"Mike, how am I supposed to feel when I'm drunk?"

"I don't know. It's a little different with everyone. Do you think you're drunk after four?" Pat whispered to Mike that I was only 14. Four was enough.

"Listen, we're going to cut you off. I don't want you bad off in the morning. We're going to order pizza. How does that sound?" Mike said. I liked the taste of beer, and felt a little woozy and started jabbering. I started to cry a little bit about dad. Mark shoved a few pieces of pizza down my throat and then escorted me to bed. As I drifted off to sleep I could hear them laughing. In later years I told Mike I'd learned to drink more intelligently, but I had fun those few days at St. Jerome's.

Mom was now the official secretary of St. Jerome's. She had a front office next to Father Jacobson. The building had an extensive intercom system. You could speak to someone clear at the other end of the building. But unfortunately it was a two-way system and sometimes you would also hear conversations. We'd been in Monticello barely two months. One Saturday in mid-October I was at St. Jerome's and went to the kitchen to get a drink of water. Mom was standing at the sink, looking out the window. I could tell she was crying.

"Mom, what's wrong?"

"I'm sorry Carl, but I'm just very upset right now." I thought, my God, what now?

"How upset are you? What happened?"

"Upset enough to leave Monticello."

"Can you tell me?"

"I can't say anything here. All I'll tell you is I overheard a conversation between two of the priests who are living here with Father. You know who they are. They said terrible things about us. I won't repeat them to you. That's all I'm going to say."

Mom went back to her office and tried to work. I went out to the practice football field in back of the building. It was a good time to think. I could only imagine what mom overheard and what those priests were talking about. Men of God? Those phonies, I thought. From then on I hated that intercom system and the Catholic Church. Ignorance can be bliss, as the old saying went. Despite what they thought about us and the situation, mom was doing a great job as secretary. I hated the way they talked behind our backs.

As the weeks went by, that incident died down. Mom and Father pretended with us they didn't know what the other priests there were thinking about us. It was one more tragic incident I hid away in my subconscious.

✝

November of 1969 started out like any other month. It was another how-did-we-get-through-October-and-what-is-next-month-going-to-bring? kind of month. I was beginning to settle in at my new middle school, anticipating Thanksgiving and getting a few days off.

Mom started planning the annual Thanksgiving dinner. It was a grand family affair with grandparents, aunts, uncles, and cousins, maybe 30 in all, including Father Jacobson. Everyone brought the dish they fixed the best. The beer, wine and liquor flowed freely. After all, an Irish Catholic gathering wouldn't be an Irish Catholic gathering without that. It would take place at the good old Leabor Road house, which my oldest brother Lanny was now renting from mom. People started showing up for the buffet-style feast around 2 or so.

As everyone milled about with plates full of food in one hand and drinks in the other, the decibel level rose. People were talking, cackling and laughing. As the dinner plates emptied and the alcohol consumption increased, the animation skyrocketed. My Uncle Tom, who was married to my real Aunt Freida, ran a furniture business he had taken over from his father. Tom was an easy-going and personable man with a great smile. He interacted with me like he'd known me for years. He approached me with a small plate of food in one hand and a Johnny Walker Red in the other.

"Carl, how have you been? I never get to talk to you." He swerved a bit.

"I'm fine, Tom. How are you?"

"Hell," he said. "I don't know from one day to the next." How depressing that sounded. But it was honest.

"How's your furniture business doing?" I wanted to be polite.

"Awww...it's okay. I don't know," he said in a sober tone and smiled.

"I heard it's doing good."

"Well Carl, it's nice of you to say that. Hey, aren't you drinking anything?"

"I can't. Mom won't let me."

"But you're an altar boy, aren't you? Right?" He winked at me.

"Well yah, but…"

"You want a sip of this?"

"What is it?"

"It's whiskey with ice. It's Scotch whiskey." And he held out his glass.

"Okay, Tom, I'll take a tiny sip just to taste it." I scanned the room. If mom caught me, life would be tough for the next week. And my Uncle Tom wouldn't be on speaking terms with her for longer than that. Luckily, we were semi-isolated. I took a small sip.

"Oh, that's strong!" I made a face.

"Okay, maybe in a few more years," Tom said with a smile.

"Tom, do you need anything? Want me to fill up your drink?"

"No, Carl…well yah, get me a refill. It's the whiskey in that bottle with the red label. And make sure there's plenty of ice. Thanks."

"I'll be right back, Tom. Stay here." I hurried off with his empty glass, filled it with ice, then glided over to the kitchen table where the liquor was. I filled his cup about three-quarters full. All of a sudden my cousin Marla snuck up behind me.

"Carl, is that for you?" I about passed out. What was she doing at that table?

"No, I'm getting it for Tom."

"He drinks Johnny Walker Red," she informed me.

"I know. That's what I put in here."

"You'd better get out of here before your mom sees you." I disappeared from the kitchen.

"Here you are, Uncle Tom. Hope you like it."

"Wow, Carl, thanks."

"I didn't want to be seen back at that table again, so I filled it up," I said. Tom laughed and dug into his pocket. Out came a twenty-dollar bill.

"Hey, I want you to have this."

"Tom, I can't. I really can't. I was glad to do it." I really wanted that $20. He held it toward me. Then, all of a sudden, my mother came around the corner and saw us.

"What's going here?"

"Hey, I hadn't seen Carl in a while and wanted him to have a little something for the holidays."

I jumped in. "I wasn't going to take it, mom."

"Tom, that's nice but just keep it. Carl doesn't really need it." WHAT? I thought.

"Well, I just want you to know Carl's a good boy," Tom said, refreshed drink in hand.

"Most of the time," mom replied, looking at me.

"Carl, I need you in here to help clean off the dining room table." I dutifully followed her, fantasizing about that $20 and how many rock-n-roll records it would buy.

The conversation, laughing, beer, wine, Scotch, football and parades went on, but in a revolving order. Then more of the same back in their original order. My Aunt Margie, with a Carling Black Label in hand, had her usual little group around her laughing at her latest beer-laced family or work story. As darkness took hold some people left for home or other parties. The food was diminishing, but not the drink.

My grandmother was getting ready to leave, wearing a very sour look. It seemed she was trying to get to the bathroom but was having difficulty.

"Grandmother, let me help you." I took her arm. We took only one step before she started throwing up green liquid. I gagged, faltered back, and let go of her. She tottered into the bathroom and more green stuff came out and splashed on her dress, which happened to be white. I

248

recoiled again. Bad as I felt, I couldn't bring myself to help her.

"Mom, grandmother is throwing up in the bathroom! It's really bad."

"Which one is she in?"

"I just got her into the hallway bathroom."

"Okay, I'll check on her. Get her things and put them in Aunt Margie's car." Lanny came up to me.

"What is going on?" he asked, half repulsed, half grinning.

"I don't know. Grandmother's in the bathroom throwing up. Mom's in there with her. She had this green stuff all over her."

"Green?"

"Yah." I didn't want to talk about it anymore.

"I think I know what happened. There was half a bottle of Crème de Menthe on the table. A little while ago most of it was gone. I thought, who the hell drank all of that? Now we know. We have the evidence. I believe she's the only one who likes it." He seemed proud of his little deduction. It was the police investigator in him coming out.

The bathroom door opened, and with mom's help, grandmother made a wobbly exit. Off she went with Margie and Uncle Tony. This little mishap started a general steady exodus of most everyone.

Ever since dad left, things were more tense between mom and my brother Mike. Thanksgiving day was no different. Their interactions all day sounded curt, and on Mike's part, almost rude. Mike's intense drinking that afternoon was making it worse. I kept a nervous eye on things. Maybe if I kept them away from each other, things wouldn't deteriorate. It worked up to a point. I was hoping people would stick around, at least until mom and I left.

But as more people left, I started getting very apprehensive. Mike was not leaving like I hoped he would. By 9 pm, the only people left in the house were mom,

Catherine, Aunt Freida, Uncle Tom, Mike, and me. And to make matters worse, for the past hour Tom and Mike had been sitting in the kitchen, pounding more beer and Scotch. Mike was looking more and more menacing. The weather outside was dark, cold, and rainy, just like the atmosphere inside.

"Mom, are we leaving soon?" I asked.

"I don't know yet." She didn't even look at me.

I persisted. "Do you want me to start loading the car?"

"You can if you want." My stomach was in knots. She was going to take her sweet time. I knew my mother, and she wasn't going to be rushed or bullied. The tension felt like the thick, cold rain. Catherine was too young to feel it. Tom was half popped and was too drunk to feel it. But Aunt Freida, who had a few drinks herself, felt it. She was trying to make light of things. She was continually trying to divert mom away from the kitchen.

"Madeline, what do you want me to do? I can help load the car. The leftover food is all put up. I put some on the table here for you by the door," she said.

"Nothing right now, Freida, thanks."

Mom didn't look at Freida. Her voice sounded lazy and drawn out. But ever so slowly she was starting to pack things up. If I knew my mother, nothing, especially not a hostile and drunken son, was going to force her out of her home. It was almost like she wanted a confrontation. Meanwhile, Freida was getting nervous. She strolled back and forth between the kitchen and living room, trying to distract Mike and Tom with trivial conversation.

Mom and I finally finished up the packing. As soon as she put the last box of leftovers and cookware next to the door, I ran it out to the car where I anxiously waited.

Aunt Freida now permanently lodged herself in the kitchen, trying to keep Uncle Tom and Mike occupied while, she hoped, mom and Catherine would head for the car where I was waiting. At long last all the crap was in the car, but mom was still in the house waiting for Catherine, who was in the bathroom. Mike now sensed we were leaving.

"Where is everyone? Are they leaving? No one has the decency to say good-bye?" Mike asked Freida. His face looked almost evil. He jumped up and headed out the back door and around toward our car.

"I think they're all in the car. I know your mother really wants to get on the road."

Watching from the car, at last I saw mom and Catherine head out the front door. I prayed she wouldn't head back into the kitchen with Catherine to tell everyone goodbye. Dear God, please make her hurry! Much to my horror, though, I now saw Mike come out of the back kitchen door toward our car. Just as he rounded the house toward the car, out the front door came mom and Catherine. Mike and mom were now face to face. Please God, let there be no confrontation. My heart sank and I got weak as I realized it wouldn't matter. As I watched in revulsion, the explosion began. One of the most hideous arguments I would ever hear in my life was about to take place.

"Mike, we're leaving. Please get out of the way." I heard trepidation in her voice.

"Why didn't anyone tell me you were going?" demanded Mike.

"How much have you been drinking?" mom asked angrily.

"What fucking business is it of yours?" Mike shouted.

"Don't use that language. Don't talk to me in that tone of voice!"

"I'll say fuck if I want to!" Catherine stood in a frozen state of horror.

"Catherine, honey, stand behind me." Mom's voice quivered. I could tell she was starting to cry. From the car all I could do was watch the carnage unfold.

Mom had been carefully trying to move toward the car while avoiding Mike, but he stood in her way. The exchange continued.

"My God, Mike, can't you at least be civil in front of the kids?"

"Why in the hell should I? They need to hear what I'm going to say too!"

"Mike, shut up. Just shut your mouth now. We're leaving!"

By this time, Catherine had started to cry. She looked up at Mike with the most wretched, helpless expression.

"Mike," she pleaded, "please leave mom alone! Can we just go now?"

This fell on deaf ears. Thankfully, Aunt Freida came out at that moment, grabbed Catherine by the hand, and led her toward me and the car. I took her into the back seat and covered her ears against the extremely loud shouting. I looked away, not being able to face the confrontation myself. Freida, no stranger to turmoil, went back inside and tried to call the police. Trouble was, the phone had been disconnected a couple of days earlier. Mike's screaming continued.

"What the fuck is Father Jacobson still doing around this family? He doesn't have any damn business here! I want him gone!" Mom tried to say something, but Mike cut her off. "You two should have gotten married years ago. Do you have any fucking idea what an embarrassment you are?"

"You have no right to say that," sobbed mom. "Can't you please just stop it now? You don't know how much he's helped our family."

"Or ruined it!" Mike shot back. I thought he might get physically violent.

I rushed out of the car and yelled, "Mike shut the fuck up!" It made no difference. I got back in the car and covered Catherine's ears again. Please make this scene end, I prayed. Please make it end.

"Have you two had sex? Have you? Are you going to bed together?" Mike shouted. "Is Catherine his daughter? Is she? I deserve an answer! At least he should have had the fucking decency to leave the priesthood and marry you!" Silence. With tears in my eyes, I looked over at Mike and mom, completely helpless to do anything.

"Oh my God, Mike, how can you say that? And in front of Catherine and Carl! How could you? Oh, God!"

Mom now wept uncontrollably, tears dripping off her face. At this moment she was broken. Mike watched her for a couple of seconds, then stormed back into the house. I got out of the car and helped mom toward the car. I opened the driver's-side door for her.

"Get in, mom. It will be okay." We were both crying. Two sacks of leftovers were still sitting on the lawn where she dropped them. Screw it. Let them stay there. I got in the front seat next to her. Catherine sat in the back seat with her eyes closed. On the drive back to Monticello, I tried to think of something to say. There was nothing to say, though. So I asked if I could turn on the radio to break the silence.

"Yes, but keep it low so you don't wake Catherine." Thankfully, her eyes were still closed. I turned around and checked her again a half hour later, but this time she was staring straight at me. Her expression was frightening. I wasn't sure just how much of that hellish conversation she had managed to process. I had covered her ears as best I could. I turned on the radio, then turned it right off, once I heard the song that was playing.

Mom asked, "Why did you turn it off?"

"I don't know. I guess I didn't like that song." The song was the Bee Gees' "How Can You Mend A Broken Heart?" I couldn't stand the eerie quiet. The only thing that broke the silence was mom's sporadic crying. It killed me to see her defend herself from her own son. Did Mike know something? Had he seen something? Had he heard something? I was still in the dark about the relationship between mom and Father Jacobson. I believed what I was told to believe, and mentally blocked out the rest. The one-hour drive home seemed like several hours.

At home, Father Jacobson's car sat in the driveway. I was relieved. He was the only one who could help her now. We started to unload the car in silence, and straggled into the house like war refugees from a faraway, war-torn land. Mom walked in without saying a word, and went right upstairs. He looked confused and concerned.

"Carl, is everything okay?"

"No, it's not. Mike had a lot to drink and got into a bad fight with mom." I hoped he wouldn't ask me what it was about.

"Over what?"

Oh my God, how do I answer this? I decided on a vague, generalized response. Mom would talk about it with him in private after she calmed down.

"Well, I was busy keeping Catherine calmed down, but it had something to do with you and her." He just looked up and took a puff of his cigar.

"Who else was there when it happened?"

"Just Freida and Tom, but Tom was really drunk in the kitchen. Everyone else had left."

"Is there anything left in the car? Do you need help?"

"No, Father, I'll get it. You can go back inside." Finally everything was out of the car. I put the leftovers away. Father Jacobson sat at the kitchen table, puffing his cigar. Then mom came downstairs.

"Is everything out of the car, Carl?"

"Yah, mom, I think I got it all. Are you a little better now?"

"No, Carl, I'm not. Why don't you go on up to bed. I need to talk to Father for a while."

As I lay in bed I could hear mom crying and talking to Father Jacobson downstairs. Their conversation was muffled, but intense. All of a sudden the conversation stopped. I heard footsteps coming up the stairway. It sounded like more than one person. Was Father Jacobson coming upstairs with her? Was he? The footsteps went into mom's bedroom. My door was open a crack and I could hear talking, but couldn't make out any words. Then the conversation stopped and I heard what sounded like kissing. A few minutes after that, I heard one person go downstairs. The front door closed.

Of all the terrible things that happened that evening, one thing kept going through my mind—Aunt Freida shepherding Catherine to the safety of the car. Thank God she was there that night. I will never forget her for that, and would love her always for that quick thinking.

Over the next few weeks, there were many discussions between mom, Mike, Father Jacobson and Lanny. I wasn't privy to any of it. The less I knew, the better. Apparently, some sort of truce was reached.

Time passed, and mom and Mike managed to be on speaking terms again. I was glad. Christmas and New Year's were not far away.

✝

It was New Year's Eve, 1969. Mom, Catherine, Father Jacobson and I watched Guy Lombardo's New Year's Eve special and ordered pizza. Mike and his girlfriend Jennifer came over. I was glad. Her presence kept the evening calm, although I didn't think Mike would ever

255

explode like that again. He got it out once, and that was it. It drained too many emotions on both sides.

Jennifer was an attractive blond with a great personality and a good sense of humor. I heard her telling Mike a story.

"A few days ago, Kelly went over to Wasson's and bought a new pair white tennis shoes."

"White? Good God! Why white?" asked Mike.

"I don't know. She's nuts. You know that. But that's what makes her fun to drink with."

"She's going to have to rub some dirt on them or they'll all laugh at her," said Mike.

"I know. That was uncool." That's where I first heard the word "uncool." I liked it because it seemed to have a cool ring to it. Mike and Jennifer stayed for a couple of hours then went out to party on their own. The atmosphere was a little lighter after Mike left.

As the 1960s came to an end, I watched Father Jacobson, Scotch in hand, lie down by the fire. He looked pensive, the flames reflected vividly in his pupils. He was thinking about the past year. So was I. Here was a man who had de facto replaced my real dad. Here was a man who knew no shame. Here was a man who always got what he wanted. Here was a man who represented, and was backed by, an ancient, powerful, monstrous organization. Because of that he knew no fear. Here was a man I still didn't know and never cared to know.

✝

I began the '60s as a good little Catholic boy, and served with pride on the altar of the Eucharist. I believed what the nuns and priests told me and for a while I even prayed at night to the saints to watch over us. I had discovered rock-n-roll, girls, Italian food, beer, horror movies and the basic concepts of good and evil. I also saw firsthand that seemingly strong people, whom I love, can be very vulnerable and hurt.

By the end of the '60s at age 14, I had an entirely different view of life and had lost a father. Dad simply did not have the mental, emotional or financial resources to fight it all. But he also shared some of the responsibility for our severely damaged family. I still wanted to believe in the angels, saints and all the ceremonial devoutness of the faithful. I struggled hard to believe. But I had seen the dark, human side of it and the struggles my mother endured because of the choices she had to make and the choices Father Jacobson made for her and the rest of us.

I questioned why an organization as rich, influential, and powerful as the Catholic Church allowed Father Jacobson to covertly support us while forbidding legitimate marriage. I questioned why Father Jacobson chose the Church over my mother and the reputation of our family. He, I was sure, would come out just fine. But the high and mighty of the local Catholic power structure would look down on my mom. It would refer to her behind closed doors as a concubine. I'll never know just how far the talk went. But they all knew. For that I will never forgive them. No woman should have to endure what she did for any reason. They could have their pompous, thinly-veiled bullshit of so-called Church celibacy. What purpose does it serve? Even after all the years of grief, sorrow and desperation in the '60s, mom remained a devout Catholic until the end. My faith, however, would not remain as strong. I simply got tired of questioning it.

The uncontrolled and unquestioned powers of the Church were at their apex during the medieval ages. Can one imagine what went on behind convent and monastery doors back *then*? Can one imagine?

CHAPTER 12: THE DARK ROAD FORWARD

"CARL, HEY, man, wake up! Are you okay? What's wrong?" asked Dave the bartender. Mike had just come back from the men's room and saw Dave's attempts to snap me out of it.

"Carl, we haven't had that many, man. Get your shit together. Are you okay?" Mike looked at my cigarette with its three-inch ash.

"Dave, what happened? Hell, I wasn't gone that long."

"I don't know. I was at the other end of the bar filling Amy's drink order. I did kind of yell down to Carl if you two needed another round. He never replied. He just kept staring into the mirror." Mike gave the international sign language for two more beers.

"Carl, HEY!" Mike said, shaking my shoulder. Only then did I come back.

"Oh. Hey. Shit. I'm okay. I'm okay. It's alright. Crap. What's wrong? Did you hit the head already?" I asked, a little dazed.

"You weren't fucking *here*. Dave said you were just staring into the mirror the whole time I was in the bathroom. He asked if we wanted another round and you acted like you didn't even hear him." Across the bar Dave nodded in agreement.

"Are you serious? I was right here."

"Well you apparently floated into la-la land. Look at your cigarette. Look at it. Looks like you lit up and then just held it." I looked down and about fell off my stool. I hadn't taken one damn puff. It had burned right down to the filter with the ash still completely intact.

"Uh...whoa...I'm not sure what the hell happened. I must've checked out. Long day and then the fucked-up news you told me, I guess. Do you both think I'm nuts?"

"No more than any of the other crazies in here," Dave laughed.

"How long were you in the john?" I asked.

"Well, several minutes, but not that long. There was a line. Now I know how the girls feel." Mike rolled his eyes and gulped another sip. "Here, have a drink. You'll be okay. We'll need a few more to adjust to all this shit. We have a lot to think about."

"We most certainly do. Hey, can I get a light?"
We had several more beers, trying to get into damage control. We drifted in and out of conversation about dad. I told him about a talk I had with our uncle Robert, mom's brother, when I was a senior in college years before. He was a World War II vet and someone I greatly admired. Robert and I were having a few beers, when, out of nowhere, he brought up my dad. The conversation went something like this:

"Carl I want you to remember one thing."

"Okay, Uncle Robert, what is that?"

"Your father was a good man."

"I know. I loved him." I hesitated, as I knew the general topic he was referring to. But I wanted more. "Uncle Robert, can you tell me what exactly happened?"

"Just remember, your father wasn't perfect, but overall he was a good man."

Then there was silence, and I knew from his demeanor that the conversation was over. I know he knew more, but wouldn't say anything to hurt his sister. I knew my father had his faults. After that, Mike and I were burned out. The subject was too intense and we had a lot more thinking to do. We'd have another go at our next beer meeting. The women tonight weren't worth the bother, either. I wasn't in the mood for a Tuesday-night special.

We weren't in the mood for much of anything now. Outside of Dave, we didn't see anyone else we knew that night. We downed a few more beers and decided to call it a night. We weren't going to solve anything this evening. In fact, we weren't ever going to solve anything.

"We'll figure this out later," said Mike. Later, I thought. That's a good one.

"Are you doing anything Friday?" I asked. "Let's meet at the Cambridge Club at 6. It's a little quieter and we can think. We need a game plan to minimize the fallout."

"Sounds good. See you then. And don't say a thing to Lanny about tonight."

"We can bring this up to him later." Mike just smiled and rolled his eyes once again. We both had to do a lot of thinking, planning and damage control. As we shuffled out of Darby's, I glanced back toward the mirror, but quickly turned away.

Out in the parking lot I thought, You know exactly what in the hell happened tonight. You traveled back to a frightening place buried deep in your subconscious past. I stared into the windshield for a few minutes after I started the car. I tried to play it cool. I started thinking about the past...again... How could I have sat at the bar stool and gone through 27 years in a few minutes? But I had, indeed, gone somewhere. It made me a little uneasy. As if I wasn't uneasy enough.

I pulled out of the parking lot and onto Veridian Street. On the radio played one of my favorite songs from '67— Sonny and Cher's "The Beat Goes On." I turned it up and thought, Ah yes, the beat goes on. How fitting for tonight. How fitting for the whole God-awful disaster. Maybe one day I'll write a book about this big damn mess. It would be for no other reason than to alert the world out there that the Catholic Church itself should go to confession someday.

And the beat goes on.

Made in the USA
Middletown, DE
30 July 2017